OLD SILK ROAD

A NOVEL

BRANDON CARO

A POST HILL PRESS BOOK
ISBN (hardcover): 978-1-61868-870-5
ISBN (eBook): 978-1-61868-871-2

OLD SILK ROAD
© 2015 by Brandon Caro
All Rights Reserved

Cover Design by Ryan Truso
Cover photo by Derek Meitzer
Jacket photos by Boyan Penkov and Steven Owens

Post Hill Press
275 Madison Avenue, 14th Floor
New York, NY 10016
http://posthillpress.com

This book is dedicated to
Kevin P. Connors
07/26/46—09/11/01

Special Thanks To:

JL Stermer, Mark Subias, Anthony Ziccardi,
Lauren Cerand, Steven Owens,
Mike Green, Billy Ferrel, Cody Morton, Phil Klay,
Elliot Ackerman, Katherine Caro,
Mike Caro, Marshall Caro,
David Winn, Michael Thomas,
Stephen Wright, Tim O'Brien,
Michael L. Wilson, Boyan Penkov and Jeremy
Warneke

PART I

CHAPTER 1
EULOGY

The sun shone hard and the wind billowed in from the west the day I first killed a man. He was more of a boy, really. He'd been spotted leaping up from a ditch near the site of an IED that had ripped through the belly of an Eleven-Fourteen up-armored Humvee, killing one soldier instantly and imprisoning four others in the truck's bombed-out cab.

The strength of the blast had curled my body like a whip, rapping the back of my head and neck against the hard vinyl of the seat before slamming my forehead into the dash. My seat belt gave way but didn't tear. I gasped violently for the breath that I needed to scream out loud, "Holy shit! Holy shit, what the fuck was that? What the fuck was . . ." I breathed deeply, trying to calm myself. "Did we just get hit? Did we just . . ."

I ran my hands up and down the length of my body, limbs and all, and gave special attention to the areas of strategic importance. There was blood flowing from my nose, but not from anywhere else. The impact of the dashboard against my helmet had dislodged my headset, cutting me off from communication through our internal radio system with Lieutenant Grey in the turret, our interpreter Raz Mohammed in the back, and the Sergeant Major in the driver's seat.

I felt a firm hand grab ahold of my blouse near the shoulder and pull me toward the center console.

"We didn't get hit!" the Sergeant Major shouted. "It wasn't us."

The windshields that came standard in the Eleven-Fourteens were divided into two pieces separated by a small steel girder. The glass panes in our trucks, four-inch-thick plexiglass designed to stop rounds from small arms and even shrapnel and debris from explosive ordinance, had just barely sustained the blast. They were white with splintering circular fractures, like two miniature frozen-over lakes, cracking and giving way.

"Are you alright?"

I nodded.

"What about Lieutenant Grey?" I hollered.

"He's fine. We're all fine."

I looked back over my shoulder and saw the laced boots and uniformed legs of Lieutenant Grey, his arms, head, and torso poking out through the gunner's hatch in the roof of the truck. He sank down behind the 240 Bravo automatic heavy machine gun that was mounted to the turret of our Humvee, rotating back and forth, firing at will. The gunners of the other Humvees started firing as well, and the air became flooded with percussive vibrations.

The Sergeant Major again grabbed my shirtsleeve; this time he pulled my ear all the way to his lips. "You okay for real, Doc?"

"Yeah, I'm fine," I said without pause, in a voice that felt somehow foreign to me.

His eyes scrolled up and down my face, scanning for fatigue or diminished capacity.

"Go help them." He pointed to the Humvee to our front, the one that had the one that had taken a direct hit.

"Cover me, Lieutenant."

"You're clear, go!"

I reached in the back of the cab for my medbag, located one of its straps with my fingers, and pulled it onto my lap. The battle locking mechanisms that came standard with the newer Eleven-Fourteens were designed to keep doors from being blown clean off their hinges by the force of IEDs and rocket-propelled grenades. They worked well, sometimes too well. Unhinging the battle lock and pushing open the two-hundred-pound steel-reinforced door required gorilla strength.

I slipped out of the truck and low-crawled a few meters to the hazard area, outgoing rounds from the convoy's mounted crew-served weapons whizzing and popping overhead. There was no incoming as far as I could tell, but I kept low, advancing up the beige, sandy road like a spider.

After a short while, the firing stopped and I began to hear the cries and the wailing/far-off dying animals sounds at first, then slowly more human as I approached.

Initially, I could not make out any intelligible language, but soon after I was able to register the distress call.

"Medic! Medic!"

"It's okay, I'm here, I'm here! It's okay, I'm coming to you!" I shouted in the direction of the voices. I tried to get a good look at them to see what I was working with, but it was useless. Thick clouds of grey and black smoke hemorrhaged from the site of the explosion, shrouding the vehicle.

The near-vertical wall of a cliff face bordered the left side of the dirt road. I lay on my belly in the prone position, unable to put eyes on the casualties; unable to stand up for fear of being hit with an errant round. As I lay there on the warm surface, a chance wind blew down across the rock face and momentarily chased away the opaque swirls of smoke and ash.

The smoke cloud broke apart and opened like the curtains of a stage play, and immediately I understood two things: the men in the Humvee were still alive, at least two of them, and there was no way of getting them out in time.

The power of the blast had flipped the truck onto its left side, with the roof pressed flush up against the wall of the cliff, eliminating the prospect of escape through the turret hatch. Their left driver- and passenger-side doors were pinned down beneath the mammoth weight of the vehicle. The gunner had either been blown clean out of the turret by the force of the blast, or had been ground into the side of the cliff as the truck was flipped onto its side.

No one on the convoy had tools capable of cutting through the steel to create an opening. The only practical escape route was through the rear door on the vehicle's right side. Even if they could have negotiated the battle lock and released the main latch, they would still have had to military-press the two-hundred-pound door, hold it open, and climb through the narrow space one at a time.

A few soldiers from the convoy dismounted and approached the wreck, only to be repelled by the unbearable heat of the fire. I could feel it gently peeling the skin off my nose from a distance of three or four meters, and I cringed at the thought of the men trapped inside.

Their screams grew louder and more childlike, and were torture to hear. They cried for their mothers and cried out to God, and they cursed us for doing nothing and we cursed ourselves.

I never knew their names. I believe they were part of the 82nd Airborne, the Army's maneuver element for the eastern part of the country. They were here to execute missions on behalf of the Afghans while we, the advisors of 4th Kandak, 1st Brigade (known colloquially as the Horsemen), were here to train the Afghans to stand up for themselves.

Everyone in the convoy climbed out of their Humvees and watched as the fire consumed the damaged vehicle. The roar of the flames helped to drown out the final dying whimpers.

"Doc, they need you up front."

I was still laid out next to the now smoldering steel tomb; still in the prone, unable to move. Temporarily paralyzed.

The dense moisture had a foul, smothering effect. Public plumbing and sewage treatment were concepts that had not quite taken hold in rural Afghanistan. Flies abounded. The area surrounding FOB Mehtar Lam was alive with the smell of human excrement.

"One of the guys from the 82nd dropped a hadji. He's all fucked up. He might be able to give us some intel. Doc?"

Soldiers in different vehicles, mostly from the 82nd, had dismounted and secured a perimeter around the blast site. Drivers and gunners remained in the trucks, the latter fixing their crew-served weapons outboard. The high ground lay just above our convoy, to the left, atop the cliff face against which the blown-out Humvee had been pressed. It was a vulnerable position, but we had to do what we could before returning to post.

"Doc, you fucking hear me?"

The Sergeant Major was standing over me. I pushed myself up, rifle, flak, medbag, and all, and rose to my feet. My uniform, saturated with sweat from the time I'd spent laid out on the ground, was now caked with thick Afghan clay.

"Moving," I obliged.

The Sergeant Major and I followed the dirt road lined with parked Humvees until we came to a fire team–sized element of Army soldiers in a loose formation, huddled together, kneeling over an obscured figure. Everyone else from the convoy had either pulled security or gathered around the IED site. Only the four PFCs attended the injured boy.

"That's what you get, you hadji fuck!"

"You like that, bitch?!"

"How's that feel, motherfucker?!"

The soldiers were not physically harming the boy as they hovered over him, chiding and chastising. However, they made no attempt to treat his injuries, which included a gunshot wound to the left arm and an abdominal evisceration.

"What the fuck are you doing?" The soldiers went quiet. "I know you weren't just abusing this prisoner, were you?"

"Sergeant Major, this fucking hadji just—"

"I don't give a fuck! Do you see a weapon on him anywhere?" The Sergeant Major pointed at the ground surrounding the boy. "'Cause I don't. That makes him a *patient*!" The men again went quiet. "Open up that hatchback," the Sergeant Major said to one of them, pointing to the convoy's lead vehicle, behind which we had all gathered.

"Roger that, Sergeant Major."

"The rest of you, move him into the trunk."

The truck's gunner turned around and tried to give us some lip about how their Humvee wasn't an ambulance, but a stern look from the Sergeant Major reminded him that his job was to shoot people and not to meddle in the affairs of those who'd been shot. That was my job. The gunner turned back around and faced forward, his .50-cal pointed in the direction of the road ahead.

The four soldiers obliged, transporting the wounded hadji from the dusty ground where he lay to the trunk of the Humvee as though he were a piece of fragile equipment. Their cargo delivered, they headed back to their vehicles.

"You'd better go grab Raz, Sergeant Major. If this guy has anything to say"—I gave a head nod in the direction of the hadji—"he's gonna have to say it real soon."

"Fuck it, just ride with him and meet us back at the FOB. Make sure he's still breathing when you get there."

"Okay."

The Sergeant Major stepped off in the direction of our vehicle. I turned my attention to the writhing patient. His face was beaded with sweat, his eyelashes fluttering like butterfly wings. He had clearly gone into shock.

It was time for me to go to work. Everything I needed was right there in my medbag. I had Israeli bandages, pressure dressings, tourniquets, blood clotting agents, IVs, blood volumizing solutions, Silvadene lotion and wet dressings for burns, and, of course, field anesthetics. I also carried 1mL glass vials of Narcan that were shaped like little green hourglasses to counteract a potentially lethal dose of morphine.

I reached into my bag of tricks and pulled out a 10mg auto-injector syringe of morphine sulfate. I said to the patient in my gentlest voice, "It's okay, buddy, you're gonna be just fine." He continued to tremor and sweat heavily. Unintelligible obscenities poured out of his mouth.

The auto-injector syringes were spring-loaded so that, in a pinch, the needle would punch right through the uniform and break the skin, no problem. The downside to that, as any fiend will tell you, is that the drug enters the system through the interstitial space just under the skin, which dilutes the hit so it does not come on as strong as an intravenous dose. My own personal research on the topic superseded any training I'd undergone in the service of my Military Occupational Specialty. When it came to narcotics, I was a subject matter expert.

I tied a tourniquet four inches above the wound on the kid's left arm and readjusted his abdominal dressing so that his intestines—both large and small, but mostly small—were no longer dangling out into the trunk space. The phrase "spilling his guts" appeared in my thoughts, and I smiled to myself and thought, going forward, this phrase will have an entirely different connotation.

Grabbing hold of his left leg, I slammed the syringe into his thigh. He let out a cool sigh of relief, which sounded like a slow gas leak, calm and perfect. His face softened. It was obvious the morphine was doing its job. I then pulled a second syringe. This one was not an auto-inject.

"What's going on back there?" I heard the gunner shout.

"Watch the fucking road!" I hollered back.

The hadji lay curled up in the fetal position, taking up most of the trunk space that was otherwise roomy enough to fit two people comfortably. "Move over, dude," I whispered as I shoved him aside to make room. He hissed a little, making that leaky gas valve sound again.

I lay down beside the dying boy. At this point, he was evidently circling the drain. He probably had only minutes left to live. I thought about hitting him with Narcan but decided he was too far-gone anyway; it wouldn't have made much difference.

The tourniquet I'd tied around his arm had worked effectively. The bleeding had subsided, so I applied a pressure dressing to the wound and removed the tourniquet.

"You won't be needing this," I muttered. I then tore open my vest, pulled my arm out of the grey digi-patterned blouse, and tied the tourniquet around my own arm. It was my turn.

The newer Combat Application Tourniquets were a brilliant design. A simple wraparound Velcro strap with a small winch for tightening enabled the user to clamp down on a raw appendage using only one hand.

Perhaps out of habit, I wiped the antecubital space on the inside of my elbow with an alcohol swab. The stick was sharp and painful, but the pain was short-lived. I watched the flash of red explode into the syringe. I felt like an Eskimo who'd just harpooned a walrus through a tiny hole in the ice. I had hit my mark. I grinned.

Still grinning, I gently pushed down on the plunger, driving the ten cubic centimeters of morphine sulfate into my vein.

I was thrown back into the trunk space by the force of the hit, and the warm gravy washed over me from head to toe. Now it was me making the leaky gas valve sound. The boy had all of a sudden gone quiet. I looked over at him and said, "Hey, you!"

Shaking him by his collar, I shouted, "Wake up, fucker! You still need to give us some intel!"

The child managed to half open one eye and meet my gaze head-on before nodding off one last time for good. I felt the truck rumble forward and begin to turn around before I nodded off myself.

I came to with a jerk of my limbs, as though waking from a frightened dream. Taking in my surroundings, I calculated that I was still in the trunk of the Humvee, though it was now parked in the motor pool, well inside the FOB. It was set in a long row, sandwiched between two other trucks. The row seemed to stretch out on either side indefinitely.

As I lurched forward from the supine position, I began to feel sick and realized I was alone. Everyone had vanished, even the boy I'd shot up with morphine. *Is he dead?* I wondered. *Was he even responsible for that fucking IED? Had he planted it himself? Did he even have the skills to pull off a hit like that?*

All these questions began to take form in my thoughts. They repeated as though part of some looping playlist. I felt cold and began to shiver.

"What the fuck are we even doing out here?" I heard myself blurt out, my speech slurred and unfriendly. "What the fuck am *I* doing here?"

The Humvees in the motor pool were organized into neat rows, with room between so the trucks could get in or out. The spaces between the rows looked like passages bordered on either side by the trucks themselves.

It was all so structured. So squared away. But I doubted seriously if even half of the vehicles were operational. Some had flat tires, while others had transmission problems or dead batteries.

The war was often like that, it seemed. Copacetic in appearance, but in a de facto state of disorder. And though clean-shaven, trained, and even battle-tested, our ranks were staffed mostly with dropouts and fuckups—the ones who'd nearly slipped through the cracks—redeemed for our delineation of the straight path to success by our taking up the cause of war. And I was the greatest fuckup of them all.

I'm not sure exactly how long I lay there, but I know it must have been a little while. The sun seemed to stretch out in every direction until all I could see was a sweeping, bright, pulsating light originating in the east.

The morphine had made the violence bearable, but at a great cost. I looked at my arm. It was oozing little droplets of blood from where the needle had torn a hole. The wound was not fatal, but I patched it up just the same.

I sometimes wonder if things really happened the way I remember them, or if I've got it all wrong in my head. And I'm still taken with a swell of pity at the thought of that child wiggling around in the dirt like a chewed-up earthworm. I tried so hard to be strong, but in the end, as I watched the last signs of consciousness trail away from his soft face, that boy murdered the best part of me.

CHAPTER 2
MONGOLIAN BARBECUE

The road that stretches from the cascading rice paddies and red hills and mountains of Jalalabad in Nangarhar Province, all the way down through the maroon desert of Kandahar and Helmand, was, at one time, part of the Old Silk Road. Centuries earlier, Genghis Khan and his great army had ridden west through the countryside murdering men, women, and children in expansion of the empire. He was a Mongol, a savage.

The advisors of Embedded Training Team, 4th Kandak, 1st Brigade, also traveled west. We traveled west on a Thursday, because Thursday was Mongolian barbecue day at the Camp Cobra chow hall in Darul Aman, outside Kabul. Unlike our downrange digs, FOB Mehtar Lam, the Forward Operating Base at Cobra had a chow hall staffed by the defense contractor KBR, a subsidiary of Halliburton.

Weeks had passed since the incident, and all that was left from the wreck was a burnt-out chassis that lay hidden underneath a blue tarp near the latrines. It had been dragged back to post, cleared of remains, and covered. I never found out what happened to that kid.

The Sergeant Major had tasked me with submitting this morning's Convoy Operation request to the Tactical Operations Center. I was low man on the totem pole, so errands like this one often fell to me.

"Doc, you filled out the Con-Op, right?"

The Sergeant Major had a strong Minnesotan accent, and when he spoke, the man on the other end of the conversation always got the impression he'd fucked up in some way.

He sat facing me in a beige foldout chair in the office of our hooch. Lieutenant Grey was in there futzing around with the radio. Major Peeve was looking over documents at one of the three desks. Neither of them put eyes on me.

It was a small room, just to the right of the entrance as you came in. The overhead fluorescent light bulb beamed a fierce, blinding glow into the room. The foyer behind me was dark. I stood in the doorway to the office, arms extended up and slightly out at forty-five-degree angles, fingers anchored into the unfinished wood trim of the frame. The light was bright, causing me to compress my eyelids.

"Yeah, I turned it in last night. We should be good to go." I looked up and slightly to the left as I responded, a subtle movement not lost on the old man who, at forty-six, could have likely broken me over his shin.

"Oh yah?" he replied, getting up from his chair and closing in on me. His eyes narrowed.

"What did you say we were headed out to Cobra for?"

I hadn't been right since the incident; since I'd smelled those men burning. It had reminded me of the moths that used to fly into our halogen lamps and get stuck back when I was a kid growing up in New York City; a real burned hair and rubber smell.

And ever since that afternoon, when I'd come to in the back of a Humvee in the motor pool, things had felt strange. My understanding of time had become obtuse. I didn't sleep at all some nights, while others I slept like the dead. Deep, bottomless slumber dispelled suddenly and unmistakably by the sound of the Sergeant Major's boot against the door to my quarters.

"What did you write in the mission's objective field?" the Sergeant Major asked in a curious tone.

"Re-up for medical supplies for the ANA."

"Oh yah?" he said again, though this time his tone was slightly more aggressive; a tone usually reserved for fools and unruly children.

He pulled a crumpled piece of paper from his right front trouser pocket and shoved it square into my chest. I stumbled backward a half step, unbalanced by the final loitering effects of the previous night's dose. It took me a second to unravel the crumpled wad.

"'Cause I'm pretty sure you wrote fucking Mongolian barbecue!"

"Oh," I muttered, not entirely surprised by my transgression, but with absolutely no recollection of it taking place.

"But isn't that why we *are* pushing out to Cobra?"

I knew right away that this was not the ideal response, but I let it ride anyway.

"You think this is all a fucking joke, don't you?" He took a blank Convoy Operations request form and pressed it once again into my chest. "Fill it out again. This time try to be a bit more creative. You're goddamned lucky the Colonel or anyone else didn't get a look at that other one. What if we get hit on our way out there and Brigade has to write up a report? They're gonna look at that Con-Op and see we got killed 'cause our crew had a hankering for some goddamned Mongolian barbecue! Fix it, and put the fucking gun up; we're already running late!"

"Okay."

I corrected the Con-Op and then grabbed the key to the weapons locker.

"Hey LT, can you give me a hand with the fifty?"

Lieutenant Grey was a bald, stout man of about thirty-five or so. He was twice divorced, but was still in close contact with both of his ex-wives.

"Sure."

Our .50-caliber machine gun was a devastating weapon. Its munitions were routinely soaked in depleted uranium so that they would burn hotter and penetrate the armor or cement of potential targets. It was meant to be used specifically on vehicles and fortified positions, not on personnel.

I did my best to shake off my morphine hangover as the LT and I mounted the gun onto the turret of the Eleven-Fourteen up-armored Humvee, pulled the chain-linked rounds across the carriage, and locked them down with the latch.

"Did you really put down Mongolian barbecue on the Con-Op?" Lieutenant Grey asked, bemused.

"What the fuck was I supposed to write? You know that's why we're going."

Lieutenant Grey chuckled to himself for a moment before disappearing back into the hooch. He would ride in the rear vehicle with Raz Mohammed, our interpreter, and Captain Harold, an emissary of the Old South. The captain and I did not see eye to eye on all things political or philosophical in nature, but I very much valued his friendship.

It must have been just before 4:00 A.M. local time, I thought, because the morning call to prayer that had jarred me awake so many times before had not yet sounded. When we'd first arrived in May at FOB Mehtar Lam, affectionately dubbed the Meth Lab by its occupants, and taken up residence in the abandoned Soviet Army barracks on the western side of the base, we learned very quickly that our proximity to the local mosque guaranteed us a 4:00 A.M. wake-up call every morning, without fail.

Every one of us feared and loathed the call to prayer, with the exception of Raz Mohammed, who left the hooch entranced at the first resounding invocation each morning, only to return fifteen minutes later in a state of unnerving tranquility.

The imam's voice was harrowing. It sounded like death from above, like a rolling thunder tearing through the air, or a low-flying jet, roaring and rumbling. Indecipherable language, which we imagined presaged our deaths and beckoned for a commencement to the End of Days. It felt always like the harbinger to our inevitable damnation.

We never could figure out if the broadcast was live or prerecorded and queued up to go off at the designated prayer times. The PA system was poorly maintained and seriously outdated. Sand-colored speakers held in place by a crude mounting mechanism pointed out in all four directions. The former Soviet barracks, now our hooch, was within hand grenade distance of the mosque itself, which meant that when the call went out, we were sure to hear it.

We'd joked openly about sneaking into the mosque just before the morning prayer and syncing up the PA to one of our iPods. AC/DC's "Highway to Hell" would have been top of the playlist.

I sat with my back against the windshield of the Humvee— my legs draped over the vehicle's hood—waiting for the morning call to prayer, that ominous warning. But it never came. Instead, the Sergeant Major emerged from the hooch in full battle rattle.

"Get your shit, we're rolling now."

I hurried to my room, grabbed my belt with my M9 pistol, my flak jacket, my Kevlar helmet, my M4 rifle and medbag and ran back to the truck. All together, I was hauling an additional sixty pounds of weapons, ammunition, body armor, and medical supplies. The sun had not yet risen, and my uniform was already drenched with sweat.

Grunting and straining, I managed to pull open the two-hundred-pound door of the Humvee and throw my bag in the back. I then climbed up over the hood of the truck, onto the roof, dropped down through the opened hatch, and settled into the turret. The hole in the roof was about three feet across. My feet were able to touch down on the steel of the interior even if I was seated on the thick leather strap that hung from either side of the hatch. I rotated the .50-cal forty-five degrees to the right.

The gunners of the convoy were supposed to stagger their weapons to protect the trucks from all angles. The rear vehicle was responsible for the bottom half of the clock, from three to nine. However, we often rode with Afghan National Army soldiers interspersed within our convoy, and with them, it was impossible to know which way they would point their weapons.

By the time I landed in the turret, the Sergeant Major had already started the engine. He handed me a set of headphones with a small adjustable microphone shaped like a garter snake attached to the left earpiece. It was always difficult to adjust the headset with my helmet on.

"You up?" the Sergeant Major asked.

"Yeah, I read you."

"Good, let's go get some fucking Mongolian barbecue!"

"Fuckin' A!"

The Sergeant Major flicked a toggle switch on the dark tan box above the center console in the vehicle. A fierce, electric wave of radio signals ripped through my headset.

"Ahhhhh!!!!! Goddamn it!" I hollered. The Sergeant Major laughed out loud. "I hate that fucking thing!"

"Guess the Duke is working."

"That thing is gonna scramble my fucking brains!"

"That thing is gonna keep us from get blown the fuck up, hopefully."

The Duke was our defensive measure against remote-detonated IEDs, our evolution of tactics. It was an invisible shield that broadcast a constant signal meant to jam the transmission of any radio frequency within a two-hundred-meter radius.

The hadjis used cell phones or garage door openers to trigger IEDs buried in the road. The Duke was designed to intercept these transmissions. Unfortunately, whenever our signal made contact with any other signal, a jolt of white noise would tear through our headphones, which were connected to our internal comms.

We never really knew if they worked or not, but it was a standing order that all Humvees that left the wire did so with their Dukes engaged. And if I removed my headphones, I would not (for better or worse) be able to communicate with the Sergeant Major.

"Are we taking any of them with us?"

A squad-sized element of ANA soldiers shuffled past our halted Humvee, grinning idly, dangling their AK-47s over their shoulders the way teenagers tote backpacks. Bearded men in their early twenties mostly, clothed in the hand-me-down tiger stripe–patterned uniforms of the war in Vietnam.

"Yeah, we're waiting on them."

"Big surprise."

The small contingent of ANA soldiers mounted their LTV, a beige pickup truck with a double-sided bench that ran lengthwise down the center of the bed. They sat four on each side of the bench, with another two in the cab.

"You know, if we get hit, we're sitting on six tons of steel-reinforced siding. There's a chance we might walk away. But those guys"—I paused for a moment, contemplating the vulnerability of our Afghan counterparts—"they're straight-up fucked."

"Fuck it, Doc. While we're waiting here, why don't you run over to the ANA clinic, see if Ghazzi really does need any resupply."

"Roger that."

I climbed out of the turret, onto the roof, then dropped down to the hood and then the gravel of the driveway and made for the ANA clinic where I figured my protégé, Ghazzi, would either be passed out or jacking off. I made plenty of noise on the way in to alert him of my presence before entering his office.

"*Salaam*, Ghazzi."

"*Salaam*, Doc."

I was fortunate enough to have been assigned one of the few Afghan soldiers from the Kandak who spoke English reasonably well, so that when I gave counsel I did not require the use of an interpreter. I preferred it when Raz came with me, though, as it greatly reduced the risk of any miscommunication.

Ghazzi was very light for an Afghan, medium height, medium build. He was from the Panjshir Valley up north, same as Raz.

"I have something for you," I said as I pulled a thumb drive full of downloaded porn from my cargo pocket and placed it on his desk.

"*Tashakur*, Doc!"

"No problem," I said, crouching down to open the narc locker. "Do you have the one I gave you last week?"

"Yes, I have here. I like this one much!"

"Yeah, me too."

I grabbed a 10mL bottle of morphine with a concentration of 10mg/mL that I knew would be good for between five and ten hits, depending on how hard I wanted to go.

"We'll be back later on tonight, Ghazzi. Tomorrow at the latest, and I'll have another one of these for you," I said, grabbing the thumb drive I'd given him a few days earlier.

"*Tashakur*, Doc."

I got settled back into the turret and put my headset back on.

"How'd that go?" the Sergeant Major asked.

"Fine, I guess."

"He ask for anything?"

"No, actually."

"Really?"

"Yeah, but he gave me back this thumb drive." I handed the device to the Sergeant Major.

"What's on it?"

"A lot of butt lickin'."

"Oh."

After another ten minutes or so, the ANA soldiers mounted their trucks and the Sergeant Major hailed the TOC, notifying them of our departure.

"Mehtar Lam TOC, this is Horseman One, SP time now, over."

"Roger that, Horseman One. Happy trails. Mehtar Lam TOC, out."

We rode out in a slow procession, four ANA trucks out front, followed by our Humvee, then the LT and Captain Harold and Raz pulling up the rear.

"You think they know we put them up front so if anyone gets hit, it's them, not us?"

"Yeah."

"Me too."

Our convoy exited through the back gate at Mehtar Lam, swung a left, and cruised through the village that bordered our FOB. As we passed the mosque, now on our left, we could faintly hear the far-off hum of the morning prayer, nearly out of earshot; no longer a threat.

We drove at a controlled pace, because there was always a lot of foot traffic and the last thing we wanted was to run over a villager's kid. The ride was bumpy. The road that served FOB Mehtar Lam was really just a small tributary of the much larger road that spanned the country, east to west.

The townsfolk, young and old, waved and smiled at us as we rode by. They wore light-colored pajama-style garments, except for the women, who of course wore black burkas with mesh veils that shrouded their heads and faces. They were forbidden to wave at us.

After a few short miles, we crossed a small bridge that passed over a green river and made the hard right-hand turn that put us on the main road. A few civilian cars tried to zipper in with the Humvees and LTVs in our convoy as we turned right, but a few of our gunners repositioned their weapons and the cars halted and formed a line.

The first hour or so on the road was always hypnotic, especially in the turret. Even the heat was tolerable, as long as we were moving, and that forty mile an hour breeze kept the sun from melting my uniform to my skin. The long, green river opened up to our right, and I saw, at a distance, a man floating in an inner tube.

Our official name for the road was Route 1, which reminded me of the Boston Post Road that ran from Greenwich, Connecticut, all the way up to Boston. But we always just referred to it as the Road. It was the first time we had travelled west since our big push out to Mehtar Lam in May.

With my weapon at the ready, I sank down into the strap and allowed my lower back to curl slightly. I was somewhat relaxed, though I would not allow myself to nod off. Not with the Sergeant Major behind the wheel.

Holding the gun was a great thrill. I was mesmerized by its power, but frightened by it as well. I was fired up and anxious. Desperate to draw blood for the first time, though terrified at the thought of being shot at, blown up, or burned alive. Terrified also of damnation.

According to the Geneva Conventions, so we'd been told, medical personnel were forbidden from operating crew-served weapons. Per the agreement, we were allowed only to carry personal weapons like sidearms. We weren't even supposed to have rifles. But we did. We all did. And we drove, rode shotgun, and sat up in the turret as well, just like everyone else.

The densely green landscapes of the countryside moved serenely by as we followed the twisting ascent of the road. At around what I imagined to be 7:00 A.M. local time, we passed a black banner tethered to a tree limb that had been driven into a pile of rocks on the right side of the road.

"Look alive, Doc. We're in Injun country."

The flag was an indicator that we'd entered Taliban-controlled territory, whatever that meant. The truth was, the Taliban were all around us. The local nationals who worked inside the FOB and did pace counts to measure distances for mortar strikes, they were Taliban. The merchants that peddled shitty bootleg DVDs in the shops off base, they were Taliban, too.

And those cocksuckers out front, leading the convoy, the Afghan fucking National Army. The ones we were here to train so they could take on the Taliban once we've left (assuming we'll ever have left); at least half of them were Taliban sleepers just going through the motions. Hanging back on missions, waiting for the right time to fuck us. In fact, I was certain they were involved, somehow, with the IED outside the FOB some weeks earlier. At least a few of them. But I couldn't prove it. I wondered what the Sergeant Major thought about it.

"It's all a scam," I muttered aloud.

"What is?" the Sergeant Major inquired.

"This whole setup. Whatever it is we're doing out here," I continued. Our radio connection maintained a low rumble between transmissions. "You see those motherfuckers," I said, gesturing toward the Light Tactical Vehicle filled with ANA soldiers just ahead of us in our formation. "They're never gonna stand up. Never! We don't even fucking know whose side they're on."

"Relax. Lieutenant Grey grabbed their cell phones before we pushed out."

"That's bullshit! We're putting our fucking lives on the line for these dirtbags, and we can't even fucking trust them not to inform on us!"

I realized I was shouting at the Sergeant Major. He was ranked a full five pay grades higher than me, and I was shouting at him.

"What the fuck do you wanna do about it, huh?"

I rotated the turret forty-five degrees to the left so that the .50-cal was trained dead on the vehicle to our front.

"I wanna shoot these motherfuckers, every goddamned one of them!" I meant every word. My thumbs rested gently on the butterfly trigger. There was no safety. A little push is all it would take. I could get them all in one shot, or in one burst at least.

"Calm the fuck down! Keep your eyes peeled. This is where Tulinsen's convoy got hit last week. Pay attention, stop fucking around!"

A long silence followed, and I thought about what the Khan would have done with this ridiculous insurrection or the possibility of traitors within his ranks. The Khan was a great leader. I would have been proud to have served under the Khan.

"They say this land is cursed, you know."

The ride was smooth enough in the turret, but it was not uncommon to be tossed around every now and again like a shoe in the dryer.

"What's that, Sergeant Major?"

"The land." In order to hail each other we had to press up on a steel toggle switch that sat erect in the middle of a black square box about the size of a coaster. The boxes were wired to our headsets and to the radio. "They say it's cursed."

To communicate with the other vehicles, Major Peeve back at Mehtar Lam, and whoever else was listening on our frequency, the toggle had to be pushed the other way. "Something about the bones of soldiers in the dirt."

"Oh."

I worried the Sergeant Major might have been on to me. Worried that he knew what I was up to; what I'd been up to this whole time.

"Listen, Doc, I know you're fucked up over what happened."

"What are you talking about?"

"You know what I'm talking about."

He paused a moment and sighed into the headset.

"I don't know how else to say it. Shit like that happens out here."

"I'm aware of that, Sergeant Major"

"I know you blame yourself, I know you feel responsible for what happened, even though you know it's not your fault. Shit, we all feel that way. And another thing"—he cleared his throat—"I know you feel like some part of you got burned up with those other guys."

I noticed my breathing pattern shift to long, deep breaths, and I felt a tightening in my chest and lump in my throat that made it difficult to swallow.

"This Con-Op thing," he went on, "might not be that big a deal, but where's your head at? You're our fucking medic. We need to know that you got your shit together."

I didn't want to cry in front of the Sergeant Major. I was in the turret, and he was driving. He would not have been able to see me, but he would have felt the frailty in my voice.

"Whatever happened to fighting the Taliban or al-Qaeda, or finding Osama bin fucking Laden? Everybody's focused on Iraq. I mean what the fuck are we even doing over there anyway? They've got a hundred and sixty thousand troops on the ground! How many do *we* have? Twenty? If that. It's all bullshit," I seethed.

"Look, there's nothing you can do about any of that. We've still got a job to do. Let's get it done. I don't want to have this conversation ever again, got it?"

"Yeah, I got it."

Looking up into the liquid orange sky, thick with the perspiration of the earth, I saw two Chinooks beat a path through the moisture, followed at a mile's distance by the sweet hum of an Apache gunship escort. It was a comfort to know that if we needed them, they were there.

"Doc, you got more of a reason to be out here than any of us," the Sergeant Major said, finally.

"I mean, if it had been my father up there . . ." He paused a moment, perhaps rethinking his words.

"Burning alive? Were you gonna say burning alive, Sergeant Major?"

He returned to his more familiar, exasperated tone.

"No, Doc. That's not what I was gonna say."

"Funny thing, Sergeant Major. I don't think my dad had it in him to jump."

Some benign chatter came over the radio. I think it was from a Marine convoy way out in Helmand or some other faraway place.

"No, I think he either died of smoke inhalation or he fucking burned alive. Or he was crushed when the North Tower collapsed."

Being a drug addict is a bit like being a secret agent. This is especially true when the addict in question is an active duty soldier and is forward deployed to an area deemed hostile. On my best day, I was an average, run-of-the-mill medic. But as a below-the-radar dope fiend, I was Medal of Honor caliber. Even so, I lacked the nerve to shove off with the Sergeant Major in the driver seat. After lunch, I'd be free to draw up a few syringes from the bottle of morphine sulfate I'd procured from Ghazzi's med chest. In the meantime, I'd have to settle for a few hydrocodone tablets to stay settled. I again noticed the sweeping, pulsating light with its eastern point of origin, but didn't dare mention it to the Sergeant Major.

"How long you been in-country now, Doc?"

The question caught me by surprise.

"I don't know."

"What the fuck do you mean you don't know?" His words grew fiercer. "Well, when are you headed home?"

The day thus far had been a montage of loaded questions and wrong answers.

"I don't fucking know! I have no fucking idea!"

The Sergeant Major remained silent. I understood that I'd best remain silent as well. My mind wandered carelessly as our convoy moved unobstructed and unthreatened through enemy territory.

It served me well whenever I was in the turret, I always felt, to try and put myself somewhere else in my mind while remaining in the moment somewhat in case we were ever attacked and I had to respond either with the .50-cal or with my medbag or with both.

I daydreamed about chicken and noodles, onions and peppers, and that special sauce unique to the cooks' palate all stir-fried up on that flatbed grill inside the KBR chow hall at Camp Cobra. I pictured one of the Kosovar or Nigerian workers smiling genuinely, appreciatively, at me and the crew as we lined up by the grill and called out our orders. In the wild, reduced to our primal selves, any semblance of modernity became novelty. And in the grasp of this new understanding of things, I lived for Mongolian barbecue Thursdays. We'd spent six months at Cobra before pushing east to Mehtar Lam in May. I was looking forward to seeing the old stomping ground, catching up with Santiago and Gomez, the two Navy corpsmen who ran the aid station. But we still had a ways to go.

To pass the time, I listened to my iPod through a mini headphone inserted into my left ear, a deviation from policy; a policy, however, from which many others also deviated. If the Sergeant Major noticed, he never made mention of it, which would have been uncharacteristic of his nature.

He had grown up in the Marine Corps during Reagan's first term; followed the streamlined evolutionary vortex from Eagle Scout to high school football captain to Marine Corps sergeant, building up strength in leadership, brick by brick, at each new station, until all that remained was a fortress of will and determination. The Sergeant Major was a born pack leader.

In the early eighties, his unit at the time was due to rotate into Beirut. But after the suicide attack on the Marines' barracks, the US halted all future deployments to the region, which burned him up inside.

He made up for his absence in Beirut by joining an Army Reserve unit after his enlistment with the Corps had ended. His unit had a direct combat role in Operation Desert Storm. Among other deployments, he could also claim Bosnia, Kosovo, and Iraq a second time for the invasion, Operation Iraqi Freedom in '03. He tried extending for a second year in Iraq but the Army, for whatever reason, wouldn't allow it, so he joined an Embedded Training Team unit at Camp Shelby three months before they were due to deploy to Afghanistan—the unit to which both he and I were now assigned. He loved being a soldier.

We drove on through the heat, no cloud cover from the Sun. The gathering of civilian cars that had accumulated at the hard right turn just over the bridge some eighty miles back was now a convoy in its own right. Traveling at a slightly slower pace than ours, every once in a while, their lead vehicle would break ranks and pull out ahead, approach our rear Humvee, only to be thwarted by the raising of Lieutenant Grey's 240 Bravo.

After some time, great cliffs began to rise up on our left side and we started the slow climb to the high altitude of Kabul Province, which was separated from Laghman by an enormous switchback. There were nine levels that we had to traverse in order to get clear of the low elevation. Our mini train of LTVs and Humvees slithered up the great mountain pass, rounding each corner to each new ledge, side to side, like a giant king snake.

By now, all of the drivers had adapted to one another's pace, and the convoy advanced like a single mobile organism. As we came up, I could feel the air temperature drop dramatically and the moisture disappear. It was like moving from a steam room to a sauna.

Kabul was, on average, ten degrees cooler than Laghman which, in the summer months, was usually the difference between 110 and 100 degrees Fahrenheit.

The switchback was a particularly vulnerable area for any convoy to move through. Generations earlier, it had been the site of a colossal military defeat for the British, the greatest in their violent history with the exception of Singapore. A large column numbering in the thousands had been slaughtered by the tribesmen of the pass and the surrounding areas. All but one man were killed or captured. This lone survivor hobbled on horseback to Jalalabad, as the fable went, though many of the locals believed his spirit haunted the region. Reports of a man on a broken horse staggering eastward on the Road had compiled over time. Many of the villagers from Mehtar Lam District had professed sightings.

Lieutenant Grey, in the turret of the rear vehicle, fended off the locals from encroaching into our convoy by extending his left arm, palm out flat, while maintaining positive control of his mounted 240 Bravo heavy machine gun. His posture managed to effortlessly transcend the language barrier.

I myself had always found it rather awkward to point a weapon at a car and stare down the driver for hours at a time. But, rules were rules. We had standing orders to fire on anyone that came within one car length's distance of the rear vehicle.

In a few short hours, we had reached the outskirts of the capital city. Climbing in elevation, we moved gradually through a corridor bordered on either side by two cliffs to break free of the switchback and enter Kabul.

We passed FOB Policharki on our right, a clear indication that downtown lay just ahead.

Kabul bears the scars of nearly thirty years of uninterrupted warfare. Once an important trade capital connecting Persia with the Far East, modern times had not been kind to the ancient city.

We approached from the eastern edge, and I couldn't help but imagine what it must have looked like after the Mongols had finished plundering it. I doubted seriously it could have been in much worse shape than it was presently.

Bullet holes adorned the decaying Soviet Bloc-style buildings that had not been completely destroyed by artillery or bombardment. Remnants of other less fortunate structures lingered on like ancient Roman ruins. Cracks in the cement and potholes were ubiquitous along the streets and sidewalks. The traffic was horrific. Late model European cars and buses congested the city squares and circles. Butchers and vendors of every variety lined the streets, up and down. Cattle-drawn carriages rode alongside cars and bicyclists.

Our convoy was disrupted by stragglers and nomads. We ground to a halt. I wanted to fire my weapon into the chaos. It wouldn't have made anything any better, but it could not have hurt much either.

"I'm fucking starving," the Sergeant Major groaned, ending the tense silence that had lasted several hours.

"Yeah, me too."

The Queen's Castle lay on a hill in the town of Darul Aman, just west of Kabul. A crumbling monument to the decadence of generations past. Whole sections had been blown out and all the windows had long ago been shattered. All this occurred prior to our invasion. The castle clung to life by sheer force of will and was known to take the odd mortar round fired from the city at

Camp Cobra, as it shielded the base somewhat from any direct attack.

The castle was a beacon. It was our way of knowing that we'd arrived safely at Cobra. Taupe-colored earth-filled containers called HESCO barriers sprawled out in a serpentine formation, creating a snakelike path to the checkpoint. They were laid out in this way to prevent suicide bombers from driving explosive-laden Toyota Camrys full speed into the point of entry. Cobra was set on top of a large hill, in plain sight of the decaying Queen's Castle. The grade was steep heading up.

"Cobra TOC, this is Horseman One. RP time now, over."

The Sergeant Major hailed Cobra, notifying them of our arrival.

"Horseman One, Cobra TOC. That's a good copy, out."

We passed first through the ANA checkpoint at the outer perimeter of the base before we approached the Entry Control Point to Cobra proper. Our Afghan counterparts continued on the main drag to their side of the FOB. We made a hard left and came to the second checkpoint, which was staffed by US Army soldiers who guarded the ECP in twelve-hour shifts and never left the FOB. We called them fobbits.

"How's it goin'?" the Sergeant Major asked one of the fobbits in his heavy midwestern accent.

"Good, Sergeant Major." The guard snapped to attention and nearly saluted.

We moved through the checkpoint, hung a right-hand turn, parked our truck in the motor pool, took down the .50-cal, and locked our gear in the cab. Lieutenant Grey and Captain Harold with our interpreter, Raz Mohammed, pulled up beside us. The lieutenant's demeanor never changed. He was always chipper. I wondered what he had done to make those women in his life ever want to leave him. He leaped off the roof of his Humvee onto the hood, then finally onto the fresh gravel of the motor pool.

"What do you think, Doc? How was the ride?"

At first I thought he was mocking me. I wondered if he'd somehow heard my conversation with the Sergeant Major. I pulled a hard face and stood up tall.

"What the fuck is that supposed to mean?"

Lieutenant Grey burst into laughter. "Whoa! Relax, Doc!"

The lieutenant stumbled away from the motor pool, still in shambles, toward the chow hall with the other two men following behind him.

Two familiar figures strolled out of the aid station and over toward our vehicle.

"Rogers, what are you doing here?" Gomez shouted across the open air.

"Oh, we had to pick up some supplies and kind of touch base with the rear," I replied.

"Bullshit," Santiago chimed in. "You just came for Mongolian barbecue day!"

I grinned freely.

"Oh shit, you don't know?" Gomez's smirk spread across her face. Someone else's bad news was, to her, the highest form of currency.

"They changed Mongolian barbecue day to Wednesday. Y'all just missed it." She perhaps couldn't help herself. "It was unbelievable."

"I heard about Tulinsen, Santiago." I brought my tone down a notch. "I'm sorry. I know you two were close."

It was clear I had hit a nerve, which was not my intention.

"It's whatever." Santiago smirked, rolled her eyes, and shrugged off my condolence. I turned my attention back to Gomez. She was far from a ten under normal, nondeployed circumstances, but out here it was slim pickins, and she was top of the heap. Large, firm breasts sat anxiously atop a smooth, round potbelly that was held in place by a skintight grey undershirt. She and Santiago both sported desert-drab tiger stripe trousers.

Her face was chubby and cute, and her smile was exciting. In light of her inflated sense of value, she was prone to fits of megalomania and often invited the scorn of the only other two females on the FOB, Santiago and a Navy commander. I wanted her.

"I'll come by the aid station later on," I said at low volume.

She looked at me and flashed the hint of a smile, but said nothing.

The Sergeant Major's unmistakable voice carried like a foghorn from the line at the chow hall all the way to the motor pool.

"Hey Doc, don't sweat it. They'll have burgers and hot dogs or some shit like that. Lunch is almost over; you coming?"

We could count on nothing out here, not even Mongolian barbecue. I wondered if it was worth it that we'd come all this way to begin with, committed ourselves to this boondoggle for which we would, one way or another, be held to account. Was it not all just a waste of time and effort? It occurred to me the way forward would be long and filled with unanticipated challenges.

"Yeah, I'm coming."

CHAPTER 3
ALL HANG TOGETHER

The B-huts that lined the FOB at Camp Cobra were simple log cabin style structures that housed anywhere from four to twelve soldiers, airmen, Marines, even Navy sailors. In an effort to stay relevant in the new millennium, the Air Force and Navy began sending their technicians over to Iraq and Afghanistan to free up the Army and Marines for combat patrols and operations. This resulted in unforeseen consequences; submariners leading convoys of up-armored Humvees through enemy-controlled territory because all the grunts had been pushed downrange. There was, perhaps, a sense of longing in all of us for the Cold War days, where, if nothing else, at least everyone knew his place.

Our mission had been a bust. We had showed up a day late for Mongolian barbecue. So, with our heads sunk and our spirits low, the advisors of 4th Kandak, 1st Brigade spread out across the camp in search of new, less obvious methods of passing the time.

There was the Morale, Welfare, and Recreation hut with books, magazines, and HP desktops wired in via Ethernet to a LAN connection.

There was a second MWR hut adjacent to the first that had Xbox and PlayStation consoles connected to big-screen TVs. There were DVDs—the real kind, too; not the pirated hadji copies that were sold in the auxiliary motor pool every Saturday when the bazaar came into camp.

There were pool and air hockey tables, board games, boxes of letters from pen pals and Soldiers' Angels. There were more books and magazines, movie posters, cookies, cupcakes, and candy of every variety. In a storage closet off to the side of the main playroom, there were boxes of even more letters from strangers, and care packages containing personal hygiene items like shampoo, mouthwash, toothpaste, deodorant, and teeth-whitening strips.

There were Holy Bibles, New Testament mostly, inscribed with loving admiration and prayer by good carriers of the Word.

There was Gomez, who would or would not be waiting for me at the aid station, depending on her level of interest which came and went without warning or indication, and which seldom endured beyond a single night. It's no great wonder why fat girls love deploying so much.

However, despite all these welcomed distractions, or perhaps because of them, the evening bled quickly and rather seamlessly into the following morning, wherein we advisors, including Raz Mohammed, our interpreter, found ourselves out by the motor pool, in the curious position of mapping out the details of our return to the Meth Lab. An opaque moon hung in the sky; the sun had not yet risen.

So as not to call attention to our flagrant dereliction of duty, we needed to come up with some type of plausible explanation for our sojourn out west that was both credible and not altogether extraordinary. The object was to not return back downrange empty handed.

"I say we go to that whorehouse the fucking Frenchies are always goin' on about," Lieutenant Grey interjected.

"How does that solve anything?" the Sergeant Major countered.

"It doesn't. The LT just said what we all were thinking," I said.

"That's not what *I* was thinking," Captain Harold clarified.

Raz kept quiet. His job was to translate, not to bullshit. He was from the Panjshir Valley in the north, same as Ghazzi, my protégé. Afghanistan's reputation of indomitability owed itself in large part to the bravery of their tribesmen. Their leader, Massoud, had been killed by al-Qaeda operatives days before the September 11 attacks on the World Trade Center and Pentagon. After the US-led invasion of Afghanistan, the people of the Panjshir Valley and surrounding boroughs banded together to form the Northern Alliance, a sort of precursor to the Afghan National Army.

"That idiot Mortin back from R&R yet?" The Sergeant Major directed this question to me personally. He knew that Mortin and I were friends, somewhat.

"I think so," I muttered. I was crouching down fastening my right trouser leg to my boot band. Without looking up, I felt the Sergeant Major's gaze fixed on my person.

I lifted my head to face him, my troubled complexion barely hidden in the fading darkness. "Yes, yes he is, Sergeant Major. Got back from Kuwait a few days ago. He Myspaced me," I replied.

Kuwait was the staging ground for all units and personnel moving in and out of Iraq and Afghanistan. There was even a US naval base in the Persian Gulf that had been built up during Operation Desert Storm.

"Good, that settles it," the Sergeant Major snarled. "We'll swing by Bagram on our way back to the Meth Lab, grab that cocksucker Mortin, and head back east before dark. Any dissenters?"

This was, of course, a rhetorical question. Even the officers knew better than to second-guess the Sergeant Major's orders.

"Doc, you're with the captain. Raz, with me and Lieutenant Grey."

The cool morning air was a pleasant contrast to the swelter of the east. Captain Harold and I bantered back and forth as we opened up the rear doors to the truck and began to grab and assemble the 240 Bravo machine gun weapon system.

"You like this gun, Doc?"

"It's alright."

Unlike the .50-cal, the 240 Bravo fired a 7.62 millimeter round, the same bullet as the AK-47. It was smaller, more maneuverable when mounted, and caused far less in the way of collateral damage than did the Ma Deuce, but it did not pack nearly the kind of punch.

I balanced the gun on my right shoulder, right arm outstretched, gripping the bipod near the bore of the barrel, and climbed on top of the truck's hood, then onto the roof. I then placed the gun down on the roof and plunged into the gunner's hatch.

Once I'd finished mounting the weapon, the captain passed me a headset. I held the set in my right hand as Captain Harold engaged the Duke, then did comms checks with the Sergeant Major and Lieutenant Grey in the other vehicle.

"We're up. Doc, you read me?"

"Roger that, sir."

"It's just us boys out here, Doc. None of that '*sir*' shit, got it?"

"Fine by me. Where's the fucking ANA?"

"Sergeant Major told them to meet us down here by five, so they'll probably show up around six or six thirty. Hey Doc, didn't you say something about a re-up for medical supplies for the ANA?"

I looked at my medbag, made a crude calculation, then answered Captain Harold.

"No, we should be good to go for a little while."

The darkness had given up steady ground to the approaching daylight. The change in elevation did make it ten degrees cooler. But 110 degrees less ten is still a hundred degrees.

"Enough of this horseshit," Captain Harold declared. "Hey, Sergeant Major?"

"Go ahead," the Sergeant Major obliged.

"Are we really gonna wait on these sodomites again?" There was a long pause, and some static came over the wire.

"Fuck 'em," the Sergeant Major eventually replied. "They know the way to Bagram. Take the lead, Captain Harold; we'll bring up the rear."

"Music to my friggin' ears! You ready to roll, Doc?"

"Let's do it."

"Cobra TOC, this is Horseman One. SP time now, over."

"Roger that, Horseman One. Stay safe. Cobra TOC, out."

Despite his many years, which must have numbered somewhere in the middle forties, the captain was easily excitable. He meant well, there was no denying.

We took the lead and pushed forward through the primary checkpoint, down through the serpentine roadway, and past the secondary checkpoint. A thick wall of HESCO barriers and razor wire rose up on our right as we descended, until the wall opened up into a final gate, and we were free of Camp Cobra and its boxes of unopened letters and care packages filled with shampoo bottles and tubes of toothpaste and inscribed Holy Bibles.

I loved being up in the turret. I felt like an unhinged, freewheeling cinematographer who, in the grips of a horizontal free fall, had traded in his motion-picture camera for a 240 Bravo.

I panned from right to left the entire 180 degrees that was my field of fire, observing for snipers or anything in particular that seemed out of place. But mostly I just took it all in. There were no traffic lights in Kabul, or anywhere else in-country for that matter, and even if there had been we wouldn't have stopped for them. It was a standing order that all convoys pressed on, no matter what.

We took care never to drive the exact same route twice while circumventing the city. Units that got lazy and made it easy for the enemy to strike, paid the price. Often times, alternate routes would mean more congestion on the roads. However, we made do. If there was traffic, we honked our horns, shouted, and pointed our weapons, or threw water bottles at the vehicles that obstructed our movement. Oftentimes, the operators of these vehicles would get out of their cars and try to grab up the bottles we'd thrown at them, making the whole exercise counterproductive. But who could blame them, really? Potable water was always in short supply.

"What's the Sergeant Major on you about?"

"Wish I knew."

"You know what the problem is with you Yankees?" It was clear from his tone that the captain was only half kidding. He carried around resentment against Northerners that dated back to the Battle of Gettysburg. And since it was bound to be a long haul up to Bagram, I made the informed decision to get the Civil War reenactment segment of our dialogue out of the way as quickly as possible.

"Why don't you enlighten me?"

Captain Harold had, prior to this exchange, taken it upon himself to gently inform me of the great disparity between the large number of US troops who hailed from the southern states and the relatively smaller number of those who came from the north. This disproportionate representation of American resolve was, in his mind, confounded by the fact that it was indeed the Union's own crown jewel, New York City, which bore the brunt of the injury that had caused our war.

"Problem with you Yankees is y'all don't really, truly love 'Murica."

Our convoy moved through the urban zoo at a moderate pace. I spotted an eight- or nine-year-old Afghan boy lifting his man-dress to shit on a bank of the Kabul River, a once viable water source that had been thoroughly contaminated, most likely after the Russians pulled out.

"That a fact?" There was a sort of give and take between myself and the captain. We had developed, over time, the rhythm and cadence of a vaudevillian duo.

"Son, that's the gospel."

Captain Harold's rant was part sermon, part performance art. He played heavily on my preconceived notions about good ole boys, but there was an underlying sincerity to his act.

"Preach on, brother!" I goaded him.

We pushed through the squares and traffic circles and passed the many giant murals of Massoud, the great martyr of the north, until we passed Camp Phoenix on the left and took the following left-hand turn onto the old country road that led directly to Bagram. This road had also been paved by US and Coalition forces because of the heavy traffic it supported between Bagram and Kabul.

"Now Doc, me, myself . . ." He paused for dramatic effect. "I love 'Murica."

It was a wonder where Captain Harold had acquired his skill for presentation. He must have absorbed the power of all those fire and brimstone lectures he'd sat through during his youth in Kentucky.

The road was wide open and had a smooth surface, so our convoy made up for lost time by accelerating. We were now separate cars of a bullet train, crew-served weapons staggered right and left, ready and willing to fire at a moment's notice.

"If 'Murica was a woman, I'd take her out for a steak dinner on a Friday night, hold the door for her, take her coat, and pull the chair out. We'd head to the movies, something classy of course. Maybe a John Wayne double feature. Then we'd end the evening in the backseat of my Chevy Malibu, makin' sweet love under the stars. No sense in waiting till we're married. We're destined to be together anyway. It's fate, really."

I mused at the captain's rhapsody. It was classic and timeless in a way. But it lacked a spontaneous element.

"What if America turned out to be a dude?"

The truck nearly lurched forward. I surmised that the captain had almost slammed on the brakes but had changed course at the last second.

"What the fuck did you just say, Doc?"

"No, really ... what if you and America were in the backseat, about to get it on, and you reached up her skirt and came up with a handful of cock 'n' balls? What then?"

"You're talking to a captain in the United States Army, son!" Captain Harold's tone was now no-nonsense. "I don't know what kinda queer business you New York boys are into, but goddamn it, I don't want to hear that shit ever again!"

The captain had made his position clear enough, but I simply could not resist the temptation.

"Well, sir ... if you *really,* truly loved America, it shouldn't matter all that much if she had a cock. I mean, if you really loved her."

"Your generation is fucked in the head!" The captain was alive with anger. It was the first and only time I'd ever heard him so fired up.

"You think that shit is normal? You don't think there's anything wrong with men fucking other men?"

"Sir, what passes between consenting adults is not for me to judge—"

Captain Harold cut me off midstream.

"Don't give me that PC bullshit! I'm not your fucking girlfriend, or your schoolteacher!"

He was in a full-on rage now.

"This is a man's world out here, Doc! We do a *man's* job! We're light years away from whatever kind of environment you're used to, and in the Army, in my *fucking* Army, thank God, it's still no queers allowed! And I'll be goddamned if they ever take that one off the books!"

I was beginning to think that I'd taken it a bit too far, but there was simply no turning back.

"I gather, sir, that you're referring to the law that forbids homosexuals from serving openly in our military? Don't ask, don't tell?"

"You're goddamned right, don't ask don't fuckin' tell! This is the United States Army, son! We don't abide queers!"

The rest of the ride was silent, save for the occasional chatter that squawked over the radio. I again observed the gentle strobe of that great white light emanating from the east, and was once more puzzled as to its origin. I thought perhaps it was a new weapon undergoing field-testing far away to the east, in the direction of FOB Mehtar Lam, our adopted home that we'd forsaken for what? Because we'd grown tired of the Army chow hall? It didn't make any sense. And what about the ANA? Where the fuck were they hiding?

It was difficult to wonder about such unknowable mysteries with the morphine flooding my circulatory tract. I had no recent memory of pushing off. Dosing had become a default function. I used every bit of strength I had left to delay the closing of my eyelids.

I valued the break in discourse between myself and the captain. It allowed me to ease back into the turret and focus on my high. I did my best not to nod off behind the 240, but I wasn't always successful. It was already midmorning, and I doubted seriously that we had time to grab Mortin and make it back east before dark.

CHAPTER 4
PAT TILLMAN

It must have been between ten and eleven in the morning by the time we finally rolled through the two checkpoints at Bagram Airfield and began our slow cruise down the main drag. The street ran south to north and was called George Bush Avenue. Captain Harold had made a point to keep quiet nearly the entire length of our ride following our brief discord over how America should and should not be loved, and I gladly welcomed the radio silence.

Bagram was alive with the movement of military men and women and contractors of every sort. On either side of the street, sidewalks bustled with the comings and goings of military types; bits and pieces of the greater machine. Aside from our own structures there were Polish, Korean, British, New Zealand, and Australian military installations located at different positions on the base, but many believed their presence to be purely symbolic.

Because the US military had an obvious interest in keeping its servicewomen as far away from any direct combat as was humanly possible, practically ninety percent of the females that were forward deployed to Afghanistan served their entire tours at huge bases like Bagram or KAF, never once leaving the wire.

The Air Force girls were routinely the best in show, but there were Army and Navy and even Marine Corps dark horse candidates that would surface now and again at the various MWR hotspots, the enlisted nightclub, the many coffee shops, the two gyms, and of course, the KBR chow halls. Bagram was our meat market.

The girls out here, many of them at least, would have been considered real prospects even back home in the world. Being deployed amplified their value tenfold. Gomez could not compete. It's no wonder she hated leaving Cobra, sacrificing her acquired sexual power.

There was no great love between us, but we had our moments, as indeed Santiago and Tulinsen had had theirs. There were encounters in the aid station late at night, as the rest of the camp slumbered, on the gurney or over a desk or even out back during the warmer months. And though I enjoyed my time with her, and counted myself lucky to be getting any at all out here, I kept myself open to the possibility of further conquests.

This particular morning, however, was all business. We rode to the fuel point, per the Sergeant Major's orders, and refueled both vehicles and topped up the extra gas cans that we strapped to the backs of our trucks.

Our mission was to collect Mortin, who had just returned from two weeks R&R in Dallas, and bring him back east with us. His presence would best explain exactly why we had ridden west in the first place, as we most certainly could not cite Mongolian barbecue as the impetus for our journey. The Colonel would understand, I hoped. Perhaps he was an understanding person.

I had never actually laid eyes on him; never rendered him a salute. There was no indication that he existed at all in the physical sense. For all I'd known he may well have been a phantom, haunting our convoys through the occasional radio transmission. Usually these occurred as we were leaving or returning to post. It was difficult to understand him over the radio, as his voice carried no inflection or intonation.

With the entire brigade downrange, he had been strategically placed at FOB Huey in neighboring Jalalabad, so named for a fellow Army medic who had fallen while caring under fire for an ANA soldier. The boy, Huey, had been lionized. Part of me admired him to the core. The rest thought him a damned fool.

He had lunged out into no man's land to aid an injured soldier, in accordance with our professional mandate. Only in this instance, the man he had treated was Afghan.

There was no concrete guidance, no historical precedent that established procedure for such situations. We were left to make those decisions on a case-by-case basis, as we saw fit.

However, failure to treat an American soldier under fire was regarded as dereliction of duty at best, treason at worst, and was grounds for capital punishment under the Uniform Code of Military Justice. Whether or not we were willing to make the ultimate sacrifice for an Afghan soldier or civilian was entirely our own decision.

And that was the razor-sharp line that we walked each day. How much of ourselves were we willing to give for these people when it was so clear, so glaringly, frightfully clear, how little they were prepared to do for us in return.

There was a second road called Dick Cheney Way that ran east to west and was perpendicular to George Bush Avenue. The two roads intersected at a junction called the Four Corners. The Pat Tillman USO and the R&R transient tent lay off to the right of our convoy, on the north and south sides, respectively, of Dick Cheney Way, east of George Bush Avenue.

Parking at the Four Corners was always a nightmare, so the Sergeant Major hailed our vehicle and instructed us to pull into the main shopping center just up the street and park alongside his vehicle.

The shopping center was laid out in an L shape. There was a Chinese restaurant, a sew shop, a gear and holsters specialty store, a jeweler, and a barbershop that employed massage "therapists" of Eurasian descent.

Behind the L-shaped structure was a food court with a pizza place, a fried chicken restaurant, and a few food trailers. Tables and chairs were lined up in two columns under an outdoor ceiling, creating a walkable space in between for busy patrons. Their origins and associations ran the gamut from US troops to allied military personnel, KBR employees and other defense contractors of a different breed entirely.

The latter were sometimes confused with high-level Special Forces guys or Navy SEALs, as they all uniformly wore the same type of unidentifiable, plain garments: khaki slacks, generic light brown or grey combat boots, simple plaid button-up shirts, green or grey baseball caps, black ballistic sunglasses.

Black ops guys, SEALs and Green Berets and such, grow their beards and their hair out longer than what is considered acceptable by basic military standards. They do this so they are able to more easily blend in with civilian populations, but also as an expression of pride because they can; because their elite status allows them to. However, a man donning the aforementioned attire, but who is clean-shaven with a high and tight, nine times out of ten, will likely exist in the negative space where the military ends and intelligence agencies and private security firms begin. We saw a few milling around near one of the shops.

It was clear as day to us that men like this were part of a different war, one we knew little about and had nothing to do with.

I removed my headset, took down the gun, dropped my vest, rifle, and Kevlar in the cab, closed up the hatch, and climbed down from the roof of the Humvee, onto the hood, then jumped down the three feet or so to the parking lot surface.

We formed an impromptu huddle between the two parked vehicles, as the Sergeant Major began calling the shots.

"Let's make sure all sensitive items"—he paused—"that's weapons, radios, Kevlars, and IBAs—are locked up in the vehicles."

This was not a new protocol. There were no keys for the ignition starters in the Humvees. Instead, there were tiny switches that turned the motors on or off. However, we padlocked the steel-reinforced blast doors to keep other soldiers from getting into our shit.

Most of our sensitive items could fetch a price, even out here. The individual body armor and Kevlar helmets were expensive per se, but were much more valuable in terms of a soldier's pride. Losing or having a weapon or personal gear stolen was a serious blow to the ego.

Low retention and recruiting numbers had forced the DOD to lift restrictions banning convicted felons from serving. This drastic measure was taken because, at the time, nobody wanted to join the military. As a result of the relaxed standards, we came to be surrounded by criminals.

And then there were the rank and file; the second- and third-string football squad, high school heroes who didn't quite have the prowess for college ball but were unable to part with their learned identities. Cocksure knuckle chucks, mostly from the flyover states, who got their kicks by fucking with other units, stealing, vandalizing.

The active and deployed military did not constitute a fair showing of America's best and brightest. Rather, we were the ones who were willing to incur the risk of bodily harm in exchange for the invaluable currency of meritorious wartime service.

"We're all good, Sergeant Major," I declared with some reticence.

He eyeballed me thoroughly and countered with, "Is that right?"

I had removed my sunglasses, exposing my bloodshot eyes and pinhead pupils to the morning sunlight and to the all-observing gaze of the Sergeant Major.

"We're gonna hump it a quarter mile to the R&R tent. Think you can handle that?"

His disgust was apparent. Moreover, it was starting to influence the team as a whole. Even Raz was beginning to look at me differently.

"Well, there's a litter in the back of our truck if you fuckers want to carry me."

The crew laughed. I was grateful. We were still a team. The extent to which I had crossed over into the land of the dead and dreaming, tumbled backward in time to the place without words, where warmth and love shrouded me in a womb of my own design, was for the most part a mystery to the crew. I still had the confidence of the other advisors of 4th Kandak, and I guarded it with extreme vigilance.

We route step marched, two abreast, down to the Four Corners then hung a right and made for the R&R tent. Lieutenant Grey and I brought up the rear, while Captain Harold and the Sergeant Major led the formation. Raz walked solo in the middle. Though he had gained our trust, it was standard operating procedure that we maintain constant supervision of him while inside the wire.

The unidentified light source that lay some hundred miles away to the east radiated with brilliant incandescence. I smiled.

"Everything alright, Doc?" Lieutenant Grey sounded a bit concerned.

The swell of the light had begun to encapsulate me entirely. I could not feel my feet touch down on the concrete of the sidewalk, though I was certain my legs were moving as I was able to keep stride with Lieutenant Grey and not lag behind the formation.

"Allergies," I replied. "This fucking place is awful. I have to take an antihistamine just to get me out of bed in the morning."

"Oh," Lieutenant Grey muttered with feigned interest.

I took a moment to exercise my duties as 4th Kandak medical advisor.

"How are your allergies, LT?"

He turned to me and smiled and said, "They're fine, Doc. I'm fine, thanks."

Lieutenant Grey was a good man.

We reached the tent after a short walk. It must have been the size of a football field. Held up by giant ribs, the beige skin was pulled taut all around. A sign outside the door boasted a two-hundred-man capacity. The Sergeant Major went inside to wrangle Mortin while the rest of us hung back and took to bullshitting once more.

"Man would you look at all the pussy that's running around free in this fucking place?" Lieutenant Grey addressed his inquiry to the group as a whole, out of respect and, perhaps, decorum. But he was more truly speaking directly to me.

"Can you imagine being stationed out here?" I responded.

The purpose of these discussions was not to arrive at some underlying truth, or to resolve any great systemic malpractice. They were instead meant to prolong the periods in which we were not in imminent danger, and could do our best to let our guards down just a little. It was our way of combating the permanent fear that had been instilled in us through the violence of action.

I was tempted on more than one occasion to bring up in conversation the sweeping bright light that had been dogging me since those soldiers had burned up in the Humvee back east, but I said nothing.

"He's not fucking here!" The Sergeant Major burst out of the tent through the glass partition door and approached our group at marching speed. "he's somewhere on base, but he's not in his fucking rack!"

The group paused for a moment. Chatter went silent, eyes fixed on the Sergeant Major. Perhaps this brevity was a gift? No one seemed in a rush to get back to the Meth Lab. In fact, I'd say that our trip thus far had been our own mini R&R, and none of us, with the exception of the Sergeant Major, was in any hurry to break up the party and get back to work. And even he didn't want that. He needed time to unwind, probably even more so than the rest of us. But he was compelled by an almost divine sense of duty to stay the course.

"Alright, fuck it." The Sergeant Major rubbed his brow intensely. "It's eleven thirty now. We'll meet back here at three."

A near silent expression of joy went out over the crew. The possibilities of exploration at Bagram were endless.

"Doc, you wait here in case he comes back," the Sergeant Major added just as the excitement over having some free time at Bagram had registered.

"Are you fucking kidding me, Sergeant Major?" I protested.

He stepped into my space, so close that his forehead nearly knocked up against mine. We were eye to eye. He was slightly taller than me, looking down just a touch.

"Really, Doc?" Frustration spread across his face. "You got a fucking problem with that?"

Having grown up a child of privilege in the bosom of Old New York, then later in the cradle of Greenwich, Connecticut, a town where people of relative means encountered people of real means, I had cultured a deep resentment of those who would attempt to hold dominion over me.

However, in the end, I was a soldier, and I knew my place. So I stood down and did as the Sergeant Major had ordered.

"Keep your fucking phone on. Call me if he shows up."

We communicated with each other via cell phone, using the Roshan network. They had a total monopoly over the Afghan cell phone market. Even Raz had one. The phones were prepaid. At a ridiculous rate, the network was able to reach the US.

I stood with my back to the great tent and watched my crew stroll off in the direction of George Bush Avenue.

I decided that the present would be an ideal time to fix. The bulk of my wares were in my medbag, locked up in the cab of our Humvee, but I took care to always carry several syringes and a few auto-injectors of morphine sulfate and Dilaudid for times like this, or in case anyone was ever actually shot or fragged.

I walked over to the Pat Tillman USO, pushed past the four or five Army douchebags all clustered together by the coffee dispenser, and made for the latrine that was single occupancy and had a lock on the door. I overheard them as I brushed by. They were going on about "body counts" and "night missions with NVGs;" the standard garbage that pours out of the mouths of newbies freshly arrived in-country with zero combat experience.

I was not exactly sure how many days it had been since I myself was making those absurd comments, nor how long it would be before I would again see home. And I had no concept of home, aside from the understanding that when I got there, it would somehow feel different from this place.

I noticed a saline lock secured to my left arm, on the inside of the elbow, granting me easy access to the vein. The saline lock was designed for use in unstable environments. Its purpose was to keep a vein open even when there was no IV solution being infused, without causing the patient to bleed out. This made a hasty evacuation of casualties much more manageable under the conditions of combat. It also made it profoundly convenient for me to dose on the sly.

The lock itself, basically an IV catheter with a rubber stopper through which the needle entered, had a prescribed shelf life of seventy-two hours once inserted. The rubber stopper effectively replaced the skin atop the vein sparing the patient (in this case, myself) unnecessary pinpricks.

Failure to remove or replace the saline lock resulted in phlebitis, cellulitis, and other harmful infections. Though I vaguely recalled putting it in back at Cobra, I had no idea exactly how long this one had been in my arm.

The blood inside the catheter was known to coagulate in as little as a few minutes, so it was recommended to flush the tube with ten cc of normal saline before an infusion of solution to avoid the potential for stroke. As painstaking as I was in making sure I always had drugs on me, I almost never remembered the normal saline, so I ran the risk of forcing a blood clot into my vein, which would have resulted in a stroke nearly every time I dosed through the saline lock.

I ejaculated in my pants from the force of the hit, and bumped my head on the sink after my knees buckled. Endorphins flooded my carcass, head to toe. I lay in a near fetal position, wedged between the toilet and sink. My head got stuck between the toilet and the wall, cradling me momentarily in a suspended animation.

★   ★   ★

I came to at the sound of the Sergeant Major's boot against my door. Only it wasn't my door, it was the door to the small latrine in the Pat Tillman USO at Bagram Airfield.

But when I pulled myself up out of the cramped space between the toilet and the sink, rose to my feet, and opened the door, there was no one there. Yet, the sound continued. A deep, even tempo, reverberated thumping, like the bass drum of a thousand Army drummers all marking time in collective unison. Like footsteps, almost.

As I exited the latrine, the pounding suddenly halted. I found myself in limbo, still quite fucked up, but not altogether laid out. The newbies had dispersed, gone off to fight the good war, no doubt, so I peddled myself through the carpeted greeting area, over to the coffee corner.

A healthy mixture of military personnel and private contractors took full advantage of the accoutrements that abounded in the USO. On my way to the coffee corner, I came upon a statue encased in glass, with several plaques surrounding it. The plaques and the statue depicted a man, brutally large in stature, with long flowing hair like the mane of a great lion. An image on one of the plaques featured the man suited up in football armor, helmet dangling at the facemask by his giant fingers. Another showed him clean-cut in a tan desert tiger stripe–patterned battle dress uniform, sporting a green beret. The latter read:

Pat Tillman
Army Ranger
Football Hero
Loving Husband, Son, Brother
Killed in Action, 22 APRIL 2004

I had heard of this man, this athlete who gave up everything—
fame, money, cars, women, a career in the NFL at the highest level
of competitive play; all the things we in this great country have
come to value above all else—to serve as an elite forces Army
Ranger in America's War on Terror. He had invaded Iraq with
the 2nd Ranger Battalion and had already completed multiple
tours of duty by the time he was "killed in action."

Everyone knew what really happened. In all fairness to the
brass, they certainly had their eyes on the prize when they broke
the story of how he'd been killed in a firefight with the enemy.

Recruiting numbers were down. The economy was robust,
booming even. Why would anybody want to join the military, a
military at war on two fronts, and run the risk of getting blown
up, shot up, or burned alive? For what?

The initial rage that had spirited forward so many brave
young patriots into wartime service had subsided. The brass
needed Pat. His capacity as a recruiting tool was an untapped
resource. If *he* was willing to walk away from it all and die for his
country, then what excuse could *anyone* have for not joining up
or reenlisting?

I glanced at my own wraith-like reflection in the glass that
housed the statue and plaques honoring Pat Tillman. I was
barely visible in the dull light of the hallway.

The loud thumping noise that resembled the Sergeant
Major's boot against my door resumed, only this time the
volume was going up in grades like a crescendo. I turned around
and sloshed forward to the exit door, still in my half-nod. Head
slumped forward, I pushed on the door with the crown of my
skull, then stumbled through the opening as it gave way to my
body weight.

Alone in the thoroughfare between the transient tent and
the Pat Tillman USO, I pushed east down Dick Cheney Way in

the direction of that ominous pounding that had begun to beat in sync with the flash of the pulsating light. I moved quickly, engulfed in the great light and in step with the heavy drum sound. Even my heartbeat coalesced with the rhythm of the thumping.

I was swallowed up in the sweet light. My vision disappeared. Moisture and heat hugged me from all sides and I began to sweat heavily. I kept moving, kept placing one foot in front of the next, as I'd been conditioned to in basic at Fort Jackson in South Carolina, then later in Army Combat Medic School at Fort Sam Houston. I kept pushing headlong into the unknown, the pounding of the heavy bass drum sound growing louder and the heat and light growing more intense with each forward step until I'd lost myself entirely.

In between blasts of white light and the heavy thumping, my vision began to slowly return. I could make out that the outer perimeter HESCO barrier which fortified the base was to my back.

I'd somehow wandered off post. This, in and of itself, was cause for alarm. I had left my rifle, flak, and Kevlar in the truck, and had only my 9mm pistol in a side holster to defend myself.

But of a more immediate concern was the figure moving toward me at Mach speed. Its giant feet or hooves striking the earth as it barreled forward in my direction seemed to be the source of that deep, heavy bass drum sound. It covered uncanny distances between strides. And when its feet made contact, bright bursts of white light swept across the whole sky from east to west.

As it closed in on me, I walked my fingers down the side of my abdomen, like a scorpion, and wrapped them around the grip of my pistol. I tugged and tugged on the weapon, but it would not loosen from its holster. I opened my mouth to cry out, but it was too late. The creature was upon me.

It dropped down low as it came in to make contact. I was able to see between the powerful bursts of white light that it wore a red football jersey stretched out by a six-foot shoulder span, and a white helmet with what looked like two red birds on either side below the temples.

As it slammed its right shoulder into my chest, I felt all the air in my lungs explode outward like a jet stream into the atmosphere. The giant lay on top of me, preventing my escape with the enormous strength of its arms. I felt as though I'd been run down by a seven-ton armored truck. Terror gripped ahold of me. I knew the end was near.

"Do you know who I am, boy?!"

The force of its breath as it shouted in my face blew my eyelids back, exposing the whites of my eyes and the tiny black specks that were my pupils.

I opened my mouth to speak, but all I could do was swallow and blink and appear dumbfounded.

"I'm Pat, Fucking, Tillman! You hear me?" The giant pulled my head closer to his face mask. "Pat! Fucking! Tillman!"

Just as I was about to pass out or die of fright, I saw his face soften behind the grid of his face mask. A smile appeared ear to ear. He let out the most terrific burst of laughter and slowly began to stand up, freeing me from my temporary captivity.

"I'm sorry, Doc." Pat Tillman managed to force the words from his lips between fits of furious laughter.

"I swear, you shoulda seen the look on your face!" he continued. "Priceless."

With great pain and tremendous effort, I managed to drag myself to a standing position; stumbling and wobbling like a newborn fawn. I feared I had suffered a minor traumatic brain injury, but I didn't want Pat Tillman to think I was a pussy, so I shrugged it off, gathered my bearings, and stood up tall.

"Pat Tillman?" I asked in as rugged and masculine a voice as I could muster. "But I thought you were—"

"It's complicated," he interrupted. "I'm mixed up in some pretty high-level shit right now. Can't really go into detail . . . "

As he spoke, I realized that a regulation-size football had materialized in his right hand. He was holding it laces out. Before I could make sense of what was happening, he was cocking his giant right arm back to throw a pass.

"Incoming!" he shouted.

The pigskin hit me square in the solar plexus; in exactly the same spot as I had been body-checked only moments earlier. My body collapsed around the immense power of the projectile, and I felt my legs come up from underneath me as I was thrown a good ten feet in the direction of the base. This game was getting old, fast.

I rose to my feet without any hesitation and rifled the football as fast and hard as I could toward the red numbers on Tillman's white jersey, allowing myself a modest grin as my shot hit its mark flawlessly.

"Not bad," he said.

For the next hour or so we went back and forth with the football, talking about the war, about home and about our families.

"So, who's your team?" Pat asked me.

"New England Patriots."

A confused grimace came over his face.

"I thought you said you were from New York?"

"Well, I was born in the city, but when I was ten, my parents moved us to Greenwich, which is technically New England . . . "

"Oh, what the fuck ever, dude."

He passed the ball to me, shaking his head in disgust.

"I'll tell you what, Doc," he went on. "That Tom Brady. What a little biatch." He chuckled loudly as he spoke. "Frady Brady. You rattle his cage just a little bit, forget about it," now in a full-on belly laugh. "He's done!"

The white light had receded back east and was no longer sweeping across the sky. Instead it blinked in a steady rhythm, lighting up the hills that looked to be hundreds of miles away in the distance, like a display of heat lightning.

"What is that?" I asked, extending my pointed finger out toward the now gentle strobe beating in the hills.

"Oh, that." He smiled and looked at the dirt. "You ask a lot of fucking questions, you know that, Doc?"

He spun the ball on his right index finger so quickly, all I could see was a blur of brown and white.

"You know, they say this land is cursed." He paused a moment, gauging my response.

"Yeah, I've heard that."

"Well, do you believe it?"

"I'm not sure what I believe."

He nodded his head approvingly, as though I'd solved his riddle.

"Your captain," he continued. "Captain Harold." He locked eyes with me. "Watch out for him. He's no good."

"What do you mean?" I queried.

My question went ignored, as a long pause ensued.

"Go long," he insisted finally, pointing his left index finger toward Bagram.

I ran headlong toward the base, which must have been ten football fields away. Pat let loose a torpedo that tore through the sky like an F18 fighter. A scraping noise followed the ball as it approached the sound barrier. My legs pushed forward at maximum speed, propelling me toward the base. My lungs filled with air, then purged and filled again like an accordion, oxygenating the blood as my heart pushed it back down to my legs. The light began to once again overtake me, flooding my field of vision. I kept moving, kept running full speed. I looked up, but could not locate the spinning football in the great pool of white light that had engulfed the whole sky. I could not see the base. I could not see two inches in front of me. And I could not stop running.

I came to in the bathroom of the Pat Tillman USO. My head had gotten stuck, wedged between the toilet and the wall. I pulled myself up from the cramped space, ran the cold water, and splashed my face. I was barely visible in the mirror's frail reflection.

I exited the bathroom, still quite fucked up, and moseyed through the lobby area toward the exit. As I passed the glass case with the statue of Pat Tillman, and the plaques surrounding it, I noticed a football beside one of them, suspended in a kicker's tee, laces out.

"Rogers!" I heard a familiar voice. There was a wealthy quality to it, as though it had been molded in an atmosphere of means and comfort.

"Mortin, man! What the fuck?" I nearly stammered.

He strolled up to me bright eyed and full of new life. The time away had done him good. Not that he'd been exposed to any real danger working in the commo shops at Camp Cobra or FOB Huey. But he'd left the wire on convoys a few times, so he could not, by rights, be called a true fobbit.

"Where the fuck have you been? Everyone's been looking for you. We're headed back east. You're coming with us. Let's go, we have to at least reach the switchback before it gets dark."

His bright smile morphed into an expression of amused bewilderment.

"Dude, what the fuck are you talking about?" he countered. "I ran into Lieutenant Grey at the massage parlor hours ago. We've been trying to fucking find you this whole time! We've been blowing up your phone all day and night!"

I pulled the black cell phone out of my right cargo pocket and flipped it open. I had missed nineteen calls from the Sergeant Major. There were five voice messages and fifteen texts.

"Oh and newsflash," Mortin went on, "it's fucking one A.M.! I don't think we'll be able to make the switchback before dusk!"

My heart rate exploded at the news. Nervous, I began to swivel my head right to left, searching in every direction for the other advisors. Mortin, aware of my predicament, tried to calm me down.

"Chill out, dude. They're asleep in the transient tent. They saved a rack for you too." Slowly at first, then all at once, my heart rate got back to normal. "Apparently, they weren't all too surprised you'd left your post either."

I thought about telling Mortin about Pat Tillman. Maybe then he and the rest of the team would appreciate my value. But I remembered what Pat had said about being into some pretty high-level shit, and I didn't want to be the one to blow his cover or jeopardize his mission, whatever that might entail.

"So how was your R&R?" I asked.

"How do you think, brother?" The smile returned to his face. "I love me some Texas women. You know what they all have in common?" He pulled a quizzical look as he posed this question.

"What?" I asked.

"They all have three holes." He burst into laughter after delivering the punch line. My expression did not change.

"Hey man, speaking of holes, did you hear about Santiago and Tulinsen? Apparently he paid one of the fobbits a hundred bucks to walk away from the guard tower so he could smash on Santiago up in there." He was in stiches. "There's more. He wound up knocking her up. She's fucking pregnant, dude! She got knocked the fuck up in fucking Afghanistan! How hilarious is that?"

I didn't laugh.

"What the fuck, dude? You don't think that's funny"

He looked as though his feelings had been hurt.

"I do. I think it's hilarious."

I paused for a minute, not entirely sure how to broach the subject.

"It's just that Tulinsen's dead, bro. He got hit on the way back to Cobra from Huey." Mortin's jaw plummeted to the carpet. "The commo shop needed some equipment, and you weren't around, so he had no choice but to roll out."

Mortin was just a kid, really. He'd turned twenty one while on R&R, and out here, among the advisors, he was a baby. He walked off in the direction of the transient tent without saying a word. I made sure to give him the space he needed, and after not too long, I followed. In the dark, I located the rest of the crew, all passed out in their racks, far away and dreaming. I found the empty rack they'd saved for me, climbed in, and tried my best to push it all away for eight hours, and wipe this day off the books.

CHAPTER 5
HELPLESS

I remember the day my father returned home from work early, rolled in a blanket of black soot and ash. He looked like he'd slid down through the chimney the entire 110 floors of the World Trade Center's North Tower. I was still small, relatively. My older brother, less so. We were just kids, really. Young, tireless kids mixed up in the chaos of becoming young men, so my mother and father did their best to keep things light.

My father's ivory white teeth gleamed in stark contrast to his charcoal-stained face as he smiled at us pleasantly. He was a goofy guy. He loved to play with us. My mother too. We were once a happy family, I remember.

Before we made the move to Connecticut. When we still lived in New York. When New York was still New York. When it was still dangerous. When it was still affordable to the people who built it and helped make it great. When it was what we now refer to as Old New York. Before Bloomberg. Before Giuliani.

Before my father sold his networking software company and mortal soul to a much larger corporation and went to work on the 110th floor of the World Trade Center's North Tower. Before my mother came to feel herself inadequate among the she-wolves of lower Fairfield County. And before my father's daily commute and long hours in the city evolved into overnight stays. Before all that, we were a happy family.

"What happened?" I asked my father.

We were in the kitchen of the yellow three-bedroom starter home that we rented while my parents hunted for a bigger place. We were rich now, sort of. We could afford it. But something happened to us when we left the city; to me specifically.

I had difficulty fitting in at school. I acted out. There were many scenes in our starter home. We were changing. Expanding. Our new model demanded a larger space to house the waste by-product of our spiraling, unstable nuclear family.

"We don't know for sure yet." He managed to maintain his large smile as he went on, "But they think someone tried to blow up the World Trade Center."

He lifted his right hand, palm pressed out flat like a mime trapped in an imaginary glass box, and grimaced. My father would do this before amending a statement that he had just made prior. It was an admission of guilt that he'd misspoke on some point. It was not something he enjoyed doing.

"Not the whole Trade Center, just Tower One." He again smiled and took the opportunity to shift the mood. "The one your dear old dad works in!"

He made a grand gesture with both arms raised up toward the sky, like Moses parting the Red Sea.

"It felt like an earthquake."

My old man played it down. He laughed and made jokes with me, my brother, and my mother all closely bound together in a fierce huddle in the kitchen of our yellow starter home.

"Your dad had to walk down a hundred and ten flights of stairs behind a guy in a wheelchair!" We stared at him wide eyed. He was our hero.

"What do you mean, 'behind a guy in a wheelchair'?" my mother inquired.

"Well, there were four guys bringing this guy down, and there was no way I could get around them."

A look of mild exasperation manifested on his middle-aged face.

"The guy held me up two hours! In the smoke! Couldn't see two inches in front of me!"

We laughed all together. It was a happy time. My father looked at my mother, adjusting his expression slightly to denote grown-up talk.

"I'll be home the rest of the week while they sort all this crap out." He then looked back at us with his enormous smile returned. "That means you guys get to have your dad around for a whole week!"

I was excited at the news, though my brother and I had, more or less, outgrown the need for paternal attention, as we'd been weaned off at such a young age.

"You mean you're going back to work?" I asked, dumbfounded. "But you said they tried to blow up Tower One." My puzzled expression communicated my struggle to comprehend the madness of returning to the scene of the crime, with the perpetrator of this random act of violence still on the loose.

"Well have they caught the guy?" I squeaked.

"Not yet," my father assured me. "But it's only a matter of time before they do."

"Well are there others?" I protested further, not quite ready to let the fear and anger go. "You know ... someone else that's gonna finish the job?"

"Oh, Norman," he replied dismissively. "I wouldn't worry about it too much. Doubt anyone's ever gonna try and pull a stunt like that again."

He pulled us in close and told us he loved us. It was a happy time, I remember.

CHAPTER 6
FURTHER

I awoke very suddenly from my morphine-induced coma to the sound and vibration of three great knocks. At first I thought it was the Sergeant Major's boot pounding on my door back at the hooch at Mehtar Lam. But as my eyes opened and came into focus, I made out giant industrial-size fluorescent lights way up above and rows upon rows of bunk beds all around. The Sergeant Major, having just kicked the leg of my bunk bed, was leering down at me. Piercing blue eyes sat high atop a rugged, midwestern visage. A look of irritated amusement enveloped his face. He stared at me a second before speaking. He both pitied and loathed me.

"How the fuck did you ever make it out of basic?"

I shut my eyes for a moment, half hoping I'd awoken to a dream within a dream. However when my eyes reopened, the Sergeant Major's full-on glare still fixed upon me, I became keenly aware that I was no longer dreaming.

"Somehow," I answered.

I rubbed my eyes, ran my hands over the spikey stubble of my shaved head. Having a shaved head really did simplify things.

I looked down at my feet and realized that I'd crashed out still in my boots and trousers. I'd managed to remove my blouse, but I'd fallen asleep in boots and utilities. As I rotated my body into a sitting position off the side of my rack, crouching slightly under the bunk just above, I heard Lieutenant Grey from across the room say, "Morning, Doc.

"Morning, LT."

The rest of the team members had dressed and were in the process of transferring to the chow hall for breakfast.

"You coming to chow?" Mortin asked me quietly.

My right leg was starting to kick involuntarily, and I could feel my jaw begin to clamp down. If I didn't address the issue promptly, a fever, chills, aching bones, and visual and auditory hallucinations would manifest in little or no time.

"Yeah, I'll be there in a minute, gotta hit the latrine," I answered.

He rolled his eyes.

"Yeah, whatever, dude. Do what you gotta do."

The showers and latrines that supported the transient tent were in a hygiene trailer to the rear. The trailer was put there to keep through traffic away from the Pat Tillman USO. I'd heard a story about a guy who got electrocuted in the shower, something about a faulty wiring job.

I walked up the four steel-grate steps into the trailer and moved quickly to an empty stall. My hands were trembling. The skin around the saline lock I'd secured to my arm was beginning to turn a violent blue. I thought about changing it, but my medbag was still locked up in the truck, and the sickness was beginning to take hold. I was sweating, and my heart was racing. If I didn't dose immediately, I risked losing the function of being able to dose at all.

As the hit passed through my vein and into my bloodstream, my heart rate dropped. I stopped sweating. I would have preferred to have nodded off in the stall for at least a few hours, until it was time for the next hit, but I was already on thin ice, so I gathered myself up and went in slow motion to the sink. I ran the cold water for a minute, doused my face, then looked up into the mirror. I saw myself disappearing slowly.

As I exited the latrine and made for the chow hall located on the west side of George Bush Avenue, just north of the Pat Tillman USO, the light was upon me again. Full, deep, brightness that washed over me as I swam upstream toward the chow hall, remembering to salute officers, and doing my best not to draw attention to myself. I had to don my ballistic sunglasses to keep the bright light from burning out my retinas.

On the way to the chow hall I stopped at one of the many MWR facilities that lined the road and signed in to use a Dell desktop. The Internet was fast, and I was able to check my e-mail, respond to my mother, tell her I loved her, that I was safe in the rear, then log into my Myspace page in under a minute. There was a message in my in-box from Gomez.

"Missed you last night."

Perhaps pride, or fatigue even, had kept me from making my late-night dash to the aid station back at Cobra. Or maybe I was too fucked up even to move. The details were fuzzy. But I responded to her without addressing the issue specifically.

"See you soon," I replied, before exiting the building.

I arrived at the chow hall just as the crew was finishing up breakfast.

"Go get some chow, then meet us at the trucks," the Sergeant Major said as he rose from his seat and approached me. "Ten fucking minutes, that's all you got. Zero five thirty we roll out, understand? We wanna be on the road by sunup." He grabbed my right sleeve with his left hand.

"What are you talking about?" I responded. "The sun's already up."

"Good one, Doc!" Lieutenant Grey howled as he pushed open the exit door of the chow hall, allowing the dark of the early morning to creep in. "Sun don't come up till at least six."

I resisted the impulse to remove my sunglasses.

"Ten fucking minutes," the Sergeant Major barked. "Zero five thirty. Be there." He looked at Mortin, who was finishing up a carton of skim milk, still seated at the table. "Make sure he gets there."

"Roger that, Sergeant Major," Mortin replied.

I ordered a western omelet at the grill and waited for the rest of the crew to file out of the chow hall before making a beeline to the coffee thermos. I poured myself a full cup, added one cream and two sugars, and stirred the mixture until it turned a light brown complexion, then sat down at the table across from Mortin.

The Kosovar refugee making my breakfast wore a black ball cap with the letters KBR embroidered in blood red on his head, a white apron around his flank. He hollered something at me as I sat down, but I ignored him.

"What the fuck is going on with you, man?" Mortin asked, concerned.

"Nothing, bro. Relax," I replied in an exasperated tone. "How much do those motherfuckers make?" I nodded in the direction of the KBR Kosovar, who'd begun to shoot me ugly looks across the dining area.

"I don't know, like eighty grand," Mortin said cavalierly, as though to him, money like that was a trivial sum.

"Tax-free?" I asked.

"Yeah," he answered.

I removed my sunglasses and looked at him square in the eye, which was difficult in my present condition, as the weight of my eyelids had begun to grow overbearing.

"These motherfuckers from fucking Kosovo got jobs with KBR, fucking came to Afghanistan, make three times our pay and never leave the fucking wire, and you're asking what's wrong with *me*?"

I pulled my cell phone from my right cargo pocket and observed the time. 0525. I rose to my feet, threw my half-drunk coffee in the trash, and then headed for the exit door. Before I pushed it open, I put on my black ballistic sunglasses.

"Dude, what the fuck are you wearing those for? It's pitch black outside," Mortin asked.

"In case it gets bright all of a sudden," I answered.

We moved silently, two abreast up George Bush Avenue in the direction of our parked vehicles. Bagram was a full-salute base, so every thirty feet or so, we would employ our learned military courtesy. In our pre-deployment training, we were taught not to salute officers downrange, as it would mark them for potential targets to enemy snipers. Bagram, however, was not considered downrange, and the only snipers on their side capable of making a kill shot from any real distance were out east in Kunar Province, all along the Korengal Valley, and out west in Kandahar and Helmand. Far away from here.

The chow hall was roughly a half mile or so from the shopping center where the vehicles were parked. We moved briskly. As we approached the entrance to the Ranger base, Camp Scott, on our right, I noticed two men walking toward us in the garb that was noticeably more militant than it was military. These men, I gathered, represented that cross section of souls which fell into that horrible gap—the negative, imaginary space. Between government and enterprise. The two of them looked nearly identical. They were both of Anglo-Saxon descent, and over six foot and wearing that ridiculous private security defense contractor get-up.

Their faces were clean-shaven, indicating that they likely did not belong to any SEAL team or Special Forces outfit. The one on the right struck me as particularly menacing. And though he, like myself, wore black ballistic sunglasses below his weathered grey ball cap, there was no doubt in my mind he was casing me, observing for weakness.

They turned left into Camp Scott, a section of Bagram reserved exclusively for the covert and clandestine services within our services. And while a part of me was curious about what sort of people comprised the elite forces, and what scrapes they'd gotten into with the enemy downrange, I was equally of a mind to keep my distance. The one on the right had impressed me. There was something ancient about his presence. Mortin didn't seem to notice either of them.

We caught up with the rest of the crew at around 0530. They had begun mounting the weapons and commencing the comms and routine vehicle maintenance checks. It was imperative always that our trucks be fully operational. There was no triple A road service to come get us in the event of a vehicle malfunction. One truck would have to tow the other unless, of course, both vehicles broke down simultaneously or were destroyed.

A disabled American Humvee in the middle of the road, any road, represented to the enemy an ideal ambush opportunity.

So we ran routine diagnostic checks before leaving post on every convoy mission. Or at least we endeavored to run diagnostic checks before each convoy mission. But we were not always one hundred percent all the time.

"Another minute and we'd have fucking left you," the Sergeant Major howled from the turret of his Humvee. "Lord knows I'd have liked to."

It was standard protocol that team members alternated positions in the vehicle, so that everyone would know how to do each job. Technically, shotgun was supposed to be reserved for the tactical commander, which, in name, was really just a fancy title for ranking guy in the truck.

However, in the operational sense, no one outranked the Sergeant Major, and no matter what, he either drove or gunned. Never rode shotgun.

"You and Doc ride with Lieutenant Grey," the Sergeant Major ordered Mortin. It seemed as though he was through making demands of me altogether.

"Back to the Meth Lab?" I asked.

"We gotta stop at Cobra first. Fucking ANA never left the goddamned base!"

I couldn't say that I was surprised. The ANA were known for their uncanny ability to fuck up even the simplest of orders.

I smiled to myself. Our return to Cobra would be fortuitous, I thought. I would have a chance to see Gomez, and I could stock up on dope.

As we exited the large parking lot of the shopping center and made a right out onto George Bush Avenue, I fell back against the vinyl seat and closed my eyes. My black ballistic sunglasses made it impossible for Lieutenant Grey to see me doze off, so I relaxed and breathed in deep. Just before I was about to nod off, I opened my eyes one final time.

We were passing through Bagram's outer perimeter checkpoint, the one manned by ANA soldiers. As we rolled by the guard shack to the right of the road, I identified a familiar face. It was Pat Tillman decked out in ANA fatigues, face hardened, truly looking the part. He gave me a look as if to say, "Don't breathe a fucking word of this to anyone!"

It all made sense. He was going undercover as an ANA soldier to root out the turncoats. Brilliant, I thought. I wondered if the Colonel knew, if he was in on it. From the little I'd known about him, it seemed like his sort of gambit.

Regardless, I was proud to be part of the mission, even if at the moment I played only a passive role. It was very hot in the truck, but despite the heat I managed to doze off after a while.

CHAPTER 7
RAMBO

As soon as we were clear of the outer checkpoint at Bagram Airfield and headed south down the highway that connects Bagram to Kabul, I rested my Kevlar against the four-inch-thick plexiglass front passenger-side window and allowed my heavy eyelids to finally close and stay shut.

I was listening to Lieutnenant Grey and Mortin go back and forth about the value in hooking up with fat chicks. And while I was compelled to chime in with my two cents about Gomez, I was sure that would have redirected the focus of the discussion back onto me, which was exactly the type of thing I was trying to avoid.

Instead, I was lulled to sleep by thelow vibrating hum of my kevlar as it made contact with the window as we passed over relatively smooth terrain.

Whether or not this particular pass had been part of the Old Silk Road, I was never certain. I knew only that the further I traveled down any road in-country, any paved street or goat path, I inevitably moved further and further away from whomever I was when this journey began.

With eyelids closed, I did my best to push away the ugliness; to find that curled-up, vulnerable feeling alongside a past lover in my mind, or safely nestled between two loving parents.

I tried not to think of the things that gave me pause: the injuries I'd treated; the hurt I'd seen. The discarded, severed limbs, strewn about haphazardly like so many scattered pick-up sticks.

I also could not repel the image or the memory of the meat. The red meat. And I was perhaps unwilling to admit or acknowledge how closely the flesh, the flesh of my fellows, resembled the hamburger meat from the grocery store that I used to buy on Sundays for my dad before his ordeal at the World Trade Center. Not the first one, but the second. The big one. The one where they finished the job.

There were noises too that I tried to rid my thoughts of. Loud, earth-shattering explosions that I'd felt in my guts, followed by chaotic sound collages of panicked voices screaming commands or crying out in horror. Sporadic machinegun fire, theirs and ours, that sounded like the Fourth of July on Montauk.

There were other, more profoundly sad sounds I'd heard, sounds I'd tried my hardest to exile from memory. Mothers I'd heard wailing over what remained of their sons and daughters after an ambush, an IED, or an airstrike; killed by their side, or by our side, or by some unknown mixture of both. Those thoughts were hardest to submerge or ignore.

I tried also to resign myself to the predictable fate that I too could end up this way, or worse. I could live. I could be burned alive in the fires of the jihad and live out my days a walking corpse.

I'd seen them in the burn ward at Brooke Army Medical Center, when I did my clinical studies. Horribly deformed men, burned beyond all recognition, stalking the halls and walkways of the burn unit, responding as zombies to the enthused voices of the doctors and nurse staff.

There was a certain measure of satisfaction to be gleaned from the awareness and the acceptance that some things were beyond my control. In fact, most things were. This deployment was a period of transition, I thought. I was transitioning away from something, and toward something else.

As the vehicle hummed along, Lieutenant Grey and Mortin kept up their banter. They'd changed subjects from fat girls to beer. Mortin was saying he only drank light beer because he was constantly monitoring his carb intake, and Lieutenant Grey was calling him a pussy.

"I'm constantly monitoring my carb intake."

"Pussy."

I came to with a start of fear to a loud clacking sound that reverberated through the passenger-side plexiglass window.

"What the fuck?" I shouted.

I could hear Mortin and Lieutenant Grey laughing through my headset.

"Relax, Doc. Some fucking hadji kid just threw a rock at the truck. No need to get excited," Lieutenant Grey reassured me.

"Yeah, no casualties here, Doc, you can go on back to sleep now," Mortin added.

The two of them cackled like a pair of hyenas. I looked out my passenger-side window and through the windshield to try and get an idea of what was going on. Our vehicle had been slowed by surrounding traffic to a near halt.

Fishmongers and beef peddlers in mule-driven carriages rode alongside late-model European buses. Some men listened to iPods, or cheap Pakistani replicas. A feeling of medieval sensibilities juxtaposed with glimpses of the modern world. We were back in Kabul.

"Fuck, what time is it?"

The cackling continued.

"Geez, Doc, what did you do, swallow a handful of fucking Ambiens"?

I wanted badly to lay into Mortin; to assail him at his weakest point. I wanted to point out his obvious flaws, and degrade him accordingly. But this was not possible to do, because when it came to deficiencies and shortcomings, with Mortin there was no low-hanging fruit. Any strikes against his character were not known to me or anyone else on the team, as far as I knew. Mortin was a good soldier.

"No, I didn't. What fucking time is it?"

"Twenty-one hundred."

The hadjis were all in casual attire. The men wore long man-dresses with large plain-colored shawls draped over their shoulders. The women, shrouded in their burkas, revealed to the world nothing more than their naked eyes. And the children threw rocks at our convoy. We were indeed back in Kabul.

Night had fallen in the time that I had slept, and with the night came an unseasonable cold. Lieutenant Grey had donned a set of PVS-7 night-vision goggles. The PVS-7 models were different from the PVS-14s. With the 7 series, the operator looked with both eyes into two separate lenses that merged into a single lens on the other end, eliminating his natural depth perception. With the 14s there was only one lens, so the operator used only his dominant eye. Though the 7s were probably more expensive, the 14s were better for operational use. We had the 7s, one set to a truck. It was nighttime in Kabul. Nighttime was always a more dangerous time.

"How fucking far are we from Cobra?" I spoke into the headset.

"Go back to sleep, Doc. We'll wake you when we're back in Kansas." Mortin couldn't help himself.

"Doc, we're making a pit stop at Phoenix," Lieutenant Grey interjected.

Camp Phoenix was located in downtown Kabul. Most other FOBs were built up in more defensible positions, but Phoenix lay in the thick of the rubble; its entrance sprawled out into a busy thoroughfare trafficked by street vendors, civilians, and people who just looked like they were up to no good. Many of them smiled, while many others held stern faces. I could never decide which were more troublesome.

"There's a white Camry's been following us," Mortin breathed into his headset.

"How far back is he?" Lieutenant Grey asked, a measure of subdued urgency in his voice. He was also an Iraq War veteran. He had seen and done and heard about things that Mortin and I could barely get ourselves to imagine. But fear still dogged him as it dogged the rest of us whenever the possibility of real physical harm presented itself.

I often thought that one day I'd just get over it; that I'd no longer be afraid. When I heard loud noises, explosions, or gunfire, I imagined, one day I would be unfazed. But that idea seemed to grow more hopeless the longer I spent in-country. In fact, things began to move in an opposite direction.

A great sinking feeling originating in my diaphragm started to take hold. Butterflies, as though I'd swallowed a whole swarm. An elevated heart rate and mild to profuse perspiration. Symptoms I would cite in diagnosing the condition of shock.

I began to experience waves and waves of controlled fear. I'd lied to myself so many times over the years, it was difficult to know what was real and what was false. The fear was real, I surmised. The threat was real also.

The Eleven-Fourteen up-armored Humvees that we used did not have rear windshields. Where the rear windshield would likely be on a different type of vehicle, a four-door sedan or even a pickup truck, on our Humvees, there was instead a hatch that opened up into the trunk area. The trunk space was separated from the main cab by a reinforced partition designed to absorb shock waves caused by blasts or penetrating explosive projectiles.

So, if anyone in the driver seat, or up front, or even in the back for that matter wanted to turn around and have a look at what was behind them, it would not have been possible. Relying on the eyes of the gunner, Mortin in this case, and the two giant oblong side-view mirrors on either side of the truck were the only ways of getting an idea of what was in our six position. The dearth of sunlight didn't help matters. Lieutenant Grey was donning our Humvee's only set of NVGs.

"How many cars between him and us?" Lieutenant Grey's voice began to rise gently in intensity.

"There's a minivan and two cars," Mortin answered.

He was now in fighting position, crouched forward in the turret, the .50-cal fixed on the white Toyota Camry to our rear.

Lieutenant Grey radioed the lead vehicle. "Horsemen One, this is Horseman Two. We have a possible suicide vehicle-borne IED three cars behind us, over."

"Roger that, Horseman One. Get his attention. Throw a water bottle at him, keep that gun on him," the Sergeant Major ordered. "If he gets too close, light 'em up, over."

The Sergeant Major's words were dispassionate, his tone flat. It took a lot to rattle his cage.

"Horseman Two, this is Phoenix TOC. Intel confirms a possible V-BID, white Toyota Camry in your vicinity, over."

"Roger that, Phoenix TOC," Lieutenant Grey responded.

I was always curious about the origin of this alleged intel. Where did it come from? What was the source? Why was there *always* a white Toyota Camry packed with explosives, riding around the traffic circles, hunting for a convoy to smash into and destroy?

"Doc, gimme a fucking water bottle, would you?" Mortin squawked. He was not a veteran of the Iraq War.

"Relax, dude," I replied. "Here's your fucking water bottle!" As I passed the projectile up and in the direction of the turret, Mortin reached into the cab, snatched it out of my hand, and rifled it at the white Camry.

"Got 'em!" Mortin shouted with glee. "Right on the fucking windshield! Bam!"

"How's he reacting?" Lieutenant Grey inquired. There was still tension in his voice, but he could not hide his obvious amusement. Throwing water bottles at other vehicles in traffic was one of the perks of the job. I thought to myself how difficult it would be, when I finally did rotate back to the States, to grind through the gridlock of Manhattan midtown rush hour traffic, the prospect of water bottle assaults on other vehicles no longer a viable option. It was not a happy thought.

"Slammed on the brakes. Now he's eyeballing me," Mortin replied. His voice trembled. He sounded like a puppy working itself up for the first time to a growl.

"Keep that gun on him," Lieutenant Grey insisted.

"Roger that," Mortin acquiesced.

The main entrance to Camp Phoenix featured a taupe-colored industrial steel sliding gate at its mouth. It was blast-proof, supposedly. The gate bridged the gap between two very old-looking brick walls. Two large stadium light fixtures lay on either side of the gate, flooding the ECP with unnatural light. This nearly blinded Lieutenant Grey, who was still donning the night vision goggles as we approached.

"Goddamned fucking floodlights!" he shouted as he ripped the goggles off his head forcefully, then, abruptly recalling their monetary value, placed them gently down on the center console.

Phoenix, like many of the FOBs now manned by US and Coalition forces, had been built and occupied by the Soviets during their decade-long campaign.

The Entry Control Point had a gravel road, and I could hear the tires crunch and grind the small pebbles into the earth as we approached.

We broke off from the flow of traffic and followed closely behind our convoy's lead vehicle into the ECP, when two Afghan National Army soldiers approached our trucks with long pole-shaped objects with mirrors attached to the ends. They looked like gigantic dental mirrors. They used these devices to check for explosives underneath both Humvees. This was standard operating procedure for larger bases like Phoenix and Bagram.

One of the ANA soldiers made eye contact with the fobbit who was manning a guard tower just inside the gate, at an elevated position. There were towers on either side of the gate, though the second tower was empty. The fobbit nodded in approval, and the two ANA soldiers began their scan.

"Is that fucking Camry still behind us? What's he doing now?" Lieutenant Grey asked.

"He's just sittin' there, mean-muggin' me," Mortin responded.

"I think you hurt his feelings, Mortin," I jabbered.

"Yeah, well, it's a dog-eat-dog world," he replied. This was one of Mortin's favorite euphemisms. He would use it to justify actions like the European colonization of the Americas, the wholesale slaughter of indigenous peoples, and throwing water bottles at cars in traffic in downtown Kabul.

"It's a dog-eat-dog world," I parroted.

The ANA soldiers completed their sweep of our vehicles and again looked to the fobbit, who rendered a second nod of approval. The two men then waved us on.

"Hang on a sec, looks like he's praying!" Mortin shouted.

"Get his attention, yell at him!" Lieutenant Grey shouted. "Throw another water bottle at—"

"He's rushing us! He's rushing us!" Mortin exclaimed as he simultaneously opened fire on the Camry. Our vehicle rocked back and forth as though it were up on hydraulics as Mortin expelled rounds from the .50-cal onto the white sedan. A hailstorm of percussive vibrations rippled through the cab of our truck. It felt almost as though we were the ones being fired on. Then the vibrations stopped.

"Fuck! Fuck!" Mortin erupted. "It's jammed! It's fucking jammed! The fucking gun is jammed!"

I heard shots from outside the vehicle and looked through the windshield to see the fobbit firing on the Camry with his M4 from the guard tower. Then I felt it.

The impact was not all that devastating. Nothing like I had come to expect. The blast that killed the five Army soldiers back at Mehtar Lam had been more intense, and in that instance, we had not even taken the hit ourselves. It had been the vehicle in front of us.

The Sergeant Major hailed our vehicle. "Damage report! Damage report!" His cage had been rattled.

"Sound off!" Lieutenant Grey shouted. "Mortin?"

"Here! The fucking gun is jammed!"

"Doc?"

"I'm okay!"

"We're all good," Lieutenant Grey responded. "What the fuck is that hadji doing? Mortin, shoot him! Use your fucking rifle!"

"It's in the cab! Doc, pass it up to me!"

"Use your fucking pistol! Shoot that motherfucker!"

"It fell out when he rammed us! Doc, pass me my fucking rifle!"

"Fuck this," I shouted. "I'll kill this asshole!"

"Stay in the fucking truck, Doc! Don't open that fucking door!" Lieutenant Grey hollered.

I noticed one of the ANA soldiers that had swept our vehicles for explosives approaching the pileup. I also observed the second ANA soldier drop his giant dental mirror apparatus and take off like a road hare into the busy thoroughfare of downtown Kabul.

The Camry had rear-ended us, and we in turn slammed into the Sergeant Major's vehicle, which had smashed into the gate. For whatever reason, the explosives in the car had failed to detonate.

Perhaps there were no explosives, I pondered. Maybe the hadji was just getting even with us for hurling a water bottle at his windshield. An unlikely turn, I thought.

The ANA soldier walked past the Sergeant Major's vehicle, then ours on the driver side, bypassing Lieutenant Grey who shouted, "What the fuck is *he* doing?"

Armed only with a black metal police-style baton, the ANA soldier swaggered up to the Camry's driver-side door. If he was at all frightened at the possibility of being martyred, he did well not to show it.

"He's grabbing the dude, pulling him out of the car," Mortin explained. "He's beating the shit out of him."

"Fuck yeah!" Lieutenant Grey hooted. "That's what you get, you dirty cocksucker!"

"He's really letting him have it," Mortin spoke again. A slightly concerned tone of voice shaped the words.

"Horseman Two, this is One," the Sergeant Major hailed our vehicle. "What's happening?"

"That ANA guard that scanned our trucks before is beating the shit out of that motherfucker who rammed us!" Lieutenant Grey answered.

"He's getting worked over pretty good, Sergeant Major," Mortin added. "He's not gonna last much longer, at this rate."

The large taupe-colored gate began to slide open, scraping against the front end of the Sergeant Major's truck. The two metals rubbing made a screeching, grinding sound like a garbage Dumpster unloading a bin full of trash.

Friction scraped the taupe paint off the section of the gate that rubbed against the Humvee, leaving behind a silver claw mark in its wake that caught the reflection of the floodlights and flashed brightly a few times.

Once the gate had opened enough for our Humvees to fit through, we barreled in at full speed and nearly took out a squad of soldiers who scattered like frightened mice as we crossed the threshold. "Everybody okay?" the Sergeant Major addressed the team.

"We're all good, Sergeant Major."

"Aye, Sergeant Major."

"Roger that, Sergeant Major."

"Good. Let's find out who put that motherfucker up to this before Rambo over there cracks his fucking skull open."

We dismounted right there on the spot, our vehicles left standing idly a few meters inside of the front gate. I grabbed my medbag from the back and my rifle and followed the pack.

The soldiers we had nearly run over appeared to be unarmed, which wasn't altogether unusual for a base like Phoenix. They disappeared from the scene, perhaps to retrieve their weapons.

"On me!" the Sergeant Major ordered.

We fell into formation, two columns fanned out in a V shape with the Sergeant Major in the adjoining position.

Our weapons locked and loaded, we approached the guard shack on the ground level, just to the right of the gate itself, then fell into a single-file column and followed the thin passage between the HESCO barriers that led from the interior of the base to the Entry Control Point. The space between the barriers created a tunnel that felt like a trench. A swallowed-up black hole.

"Raz, get up here!" the Sergeant Major commanded.

"Yes, Sergeant Major."

"Rest of you, stack up against the HESCO. Stand by!"

Stacking meant lining up body to body in extremely tight formation in preparation for an assault. It's a close-quarters combat tactic used for breaching doors and entryways to buildings more commonly practiced in places like Fallujah, Ramadi, or Baghdad.

The terrain in Afghanistan called for wider area tactics. This was to be my first stack outside of training. I was very excited.

I did my best to peek around the Sergeant Major's shoulder into the Entry Control Point just outside of the front gate.

The adrenaline from the incident had managed to distract my body's internal alarm system from its appointed purpose of reminding me that it was now time to dose. But with all the stillness and quiet inside the HESCO tunnel that linked the interior of the base with the ECP, I was alone with my senses as they unified in protest over my failure to administer the dope on schedule.

It was difficult to discern the conventional paranoia of acute opiate withdrawal from the overall fired-up fight-or-flight response that had been initiated when the hadji slammed into our Humvee.

Many of the symptoms—racing heartbeat, clammy skin, a feeling of impending doom—could be ascribed to either condition. It wasn't important, however, I thought. In either case, the treatment was the same.

With my uniform on, in full battle rattle, I managed inject a syringe full of Dilaudid into the saline lock and gently depress the plunger without anyone noticing. The darkness of the HESCO tunnel provided excellent cover.

The hit went in and worked its familiar magic. My knees went soft, but I held my balance, and I had to concentrate to keep my eyeballs from rolling backward into the chutes of my eye sockets. The fear dissipated like some foreign bacteria driven off by the administration of a heroic antibiotic. I was saved.

Looking over the Sergeant Major's shoulder, I could see into the ECP from the small HESCO tunnel. A figure standing beside the now smashed-up Toyota Camry was carrying on with a swinging motion.

My vision went in and out of focus and the light from the ECP slowly overwhelmed my sight.

I could not keep my body from shifting and swaying back and forth, side to side as though the ground beneath me was listing and pitching like a canoe in open water.

I hid this motion as best I could from the Sergeant Major as we stood, our backs to the wall of the HESCO tunnel, stacked and ready to roll. The huge girth of my medbag made it easier for me to lean back without slouching.

"What's happening Sergeant Major?" Mortin whispered.

"Shhhh!" he responded. "Raz," he went on, pointing to the ANA guard who continued to pulverize the corpse of our would-be assassin. "Tell him to stop."

Raz did as he was told, shouting from the HESCO tunnel into the ECP. He was good like that. He would have made a marvelous soldier.

The ANA guard shouted back something in Dari to Raz, then looked at the Sergeant Major and smiled. He dragged his pointed index finger across his own throat and gave a thumbs-up.

"Tell him to come here right now," the Sergeant Major whispered calmly. "Tell him to walk." His voice was controlled and soothing. "Tell him not to run."

Raz again shouted across the ECP, relaying the Sergeant Major's message. The ANA guard, with a look of cautious uncertainty, approached the HESCO tunnel. His footsteps made unmistakable crunching sounds as he crossed over the gravel surface toward our position.

When he came within striking distance, the Sergeant Major grabbed him by the collar and yanked him into the dark of the tunnel.

"Ask him why the fuck he beat that guy to death?" The Sergeant Major's tone went up a notable increment. "Doesn't he know we need intel from guys like him? How the fuck are we supposed to know who the bad guys are if we don't interrogate anyone?"

Raz translated the message and the ANA guard's face broke. It was possible only to make out the outline of his figure against the backdrop of the floodlights, but even that small amount of light was enough to read the expression draped across the guard's face.

His lips pursed and his eyes welled. He said something in Dari directed at the Sergeant Major and Raz translated.

"He say it make him very sad you no happy he kill dat man." He paused for a moment, waiting for the remainder of the transmission. "Dat man try to kill all you. Dat man a very bad man, and he kill dat man keep you safe, and now you angry." Raz looked back at his countryman with an expression that seemed to suggest empathy, and then back at the Sergeant Major with what looked to be an expression of guarded contempt. "It make him very sad."

The guard gestured with his hands and emoted with his face and body as he spoke. It was more of a performance than a dialogue.

The Sergeant Major raised his hand, palm facing out, and lowered his head slightly, and perhaps emoted a small measure himself.

"Tell him thank you very much for watching out for us. We appreciate it; we really do. Tell him we would do the same for him and his family. Tell him that's why we're here; to fight bad guys like the one who tried to blow us up."

Raz simultaneously translated as the Sergeant Major spoke. The ANA guard's face softened. The tears did not breach the lining of his retinas.

"But we have to find out," the Sergeant Major continued, "who's financing these operations, who's pulling the strings."

The ANA guard began to nod in agreement. Saving face was of utmost importance in Afghanistan.

"Doc . . ." the Sergeant Major started. "No . . . Mortin, go find those fucking fobbits. Have 'em call EOD." He pointed to the busted-up Camry. "We need to get this fucking thing cleared outta here now."

"Roger that, Sergeant Major."

The fobbits had dropped down and taken cover inside the guard tower when the Camry smashed into our truck. Had the explosives detonated, the whole ECP would have been leveled.

"EOD's on their way, Sergeant Major."

"Good."

The Sergeant Major grabbed the ANA guard by the arm, his hand around the man's bicep. He smiled at the Afghan. "Rambo," he said. "Can you believe the pair on this fucking guy?"

The whole crew laughed. Rambo laughed too. He was one of us. It was one of those moments of levity meant to insulate and distract us from the war. It was like the time outside the transient tent at Bagram, only more intense. We laughed louder and smiled harder because this time, the stakes were real. This time, we were all afraid.

PART II

CHAPTER 8
THE GOAT SCHOOL

The Goat School was located somewhere between the gently rolling prairie of the Hill Country north of San Antonio and the cedar wood pines of Wichita Falls. Somewhere deep in Comanche country. It could not have been anywhere outside the great border of the Texas Republic, because to cross the frontier it is a four-hour trek at least in any direction from greater San Antonio, and we had been no more than three hours on the bus by the time we arrived.

The location was kept secret, even from us, because if word got out among the PETA brigades and eco-freaks what cruel and unusual practices transpired at Goat School and where it was situated, a strong possibility prevailed that there would be a picket line of crunchy crusaders—occupying as close to the main gate as the armed sentries would allow—screaming bloody murder in protest over our treatment of the goats.

It had happened before at some post in Seattle or Wyoming—hordes of fired-up malcontents, scruffy and unwashed, in full revolt at the mouth of the base, signs waving, slogans being hurled, launched through the air and made more devastating through the projection of megaphones.

It was a near riot, we'd been told, so much so that the whole thing got shut down, moved in secret to a new, undisclosed vicinity; somewhere we could carry on with our training in peace.

Goat School would be the crucible for us thirty or so Army combat medics, or 91-Bravos as we were called back then. It was to be our final assessment; the culmination of several months of pre-deployment workup training, after which we would be deemed combat ready.

At Camp Shelby, in Mississippi, we'd undergone the bulk of our general advisor training—working with interpreters, routine exercises at mock villages way out in the woods, weapons qualifications (M9, M4, .50-cal, 240 Bravo, and Mark 19 automatic grenade launcher) breaching/room clearing, land navigation, and convoy operations. However, at the tail end of our workup, we were bussed to Camp Bullis, north of San Antonio, for what was to be additional advanced medical training.

At Bullis, the fundamentals of combat medicine—procedures we'd had drilled into our heads as fresh soldiers newly arrived at the Army Combat Medic School some years earlier—were reinforced through use and overuse of class lectures, PowerPoint presentations, and hands-on labs. We went over the three most common forms of preventable death on the battlefield and their corresponding treatments so many times that each of us could nearly recite the literature from the PowerPoint slides verbatim.

But when we did labs—mock combat casualty evaluations supervised by our instructors, where half the class dressed as patients doused in fake blood made up to look shot or fragged, while the other half tried to assess and treat the individual injuries—there was always a sense of loss and an atmosphere of disinterest because the wounds were artificial.

It wasn't that any one of us wanted necessarily to inflict harm on any other in our group, although certainly personal grudges and rivalries did surface from time to time.

Rather, we all yearned for that urgency of purpose that is native to all injuries in which death charges at us like a feral dog that must be beaten back by the steady hand of right action, calm under fire. We were not, at the time, seasoned veterans, but we knew this charade—in which we took turns writhing around on the grass outside the schoolhouse and alternated playing medic—wasn't serving our cause.

On the twenty-third day at oh-dark-thirty, we, carrying only our rucksacks packed with the most essential goods, were herded, half-conscious, onto a coach bus and whisked away into the unknown.

The ride went smoothly enough. The night, overcast and humid, did not twinkle with starlight. It instead absorbed our bus; opened like the cargo door on a C-130 transport aircraft into which we drove deliberately and peacefully as the darkness closed in behind us.

Some of us slept while others packed dips or drank whiskey. A few played on their phones or talked about girls, while some of us leaned back into the soft reclining grey wool seats of the coach charter bus to which we had been relegated and found that deep, troublesome half sleep—drooping eyelids, jaw cracked open, fixed gaze on the seatbacks to our front. A near catatonic state.

The night had ferried us safely from north of San Antonio into some other less observed, less populated corridor of the Lone Star State. A good sign that the Goat School's secure location had not been compromised came when we passed without incident through the checkpoint of the anonymous, unknown base. A guard in plain clothes waved us through. There were no demonstrators in place to derail our scheduled training evolution after all. We were going to have to go through with it.

I was half expecting to see tumbleweeds blowing by in the breeze as we debussed our transport, but instead was hit with a column of thick, moist autumn air on the way out. We had left Camp Bullis around two A.M., so I gathered that it was nearly dawn when we shuffled zombie-like down the steps of the charter bus, rucksacks in tow, and formed a long row shoulder to shoulder on the grass that bordered the road. We did this out of instinct mostly, but one of the higher-ranked soldiers, Sergeant Day, reinforced our movement with some good old-fashioned shouting.

"Move! Let's go! We don't have all fucking day! Line up, shoulder to shoulder! That means now!"

There is a time and place for rebuke in a military setting. Not quite mutiny, but a tempered rejection of the learned military courtesies. This was not such an occasion. We obliged the sergeant, moving slowly but with purpose. We were lined up parallel to the bus's left side, on the grass that bordered the dirt road we'd driven in on. The land dropped off sharply just in front of us, sloping downward at a sharp angle. There were several B-huts at various elevations built into the hill, fashioned in the archetypal log cabinstyle design. They were berthing units, I'd gathered. I imagined we Bravos would be divvied up and quartered, maybe six to a B-hut, or even ten. I could stand it, I thought. It would not have been the first time I'd made do with little or no personal space.

We were instructed at Camp Bullis to pack only the bare essentials. Sleeping bag, iso mat, one fresh uniform, rain gear, two canteens, a flashlight, and that was it. All other items vital to our training evolution were to be provided by our host camp.

Everything we brought with us, we stuffed into rucksacks that we now wore on our backs. My stomach growled indignantly, so I panned left to right, but saw no signs of a chow hall.

We were a good fifteen minutes in formation before a large figure emerged from one of the B-huts. I heard a screen door creak open, then crack as it slammed shut behind the large man now moving toward us.

"Y'all comin' from Camp Bullis?" A deep, hard voice with a strong southern dialect cut through the darkness.

A volley of expressions in the affirmative form ranging from "Roger that" to "Yes, sir" to "Aye, Sergeant" went out in response to the question.

"Who the fuck is in charge out here?"

By this time, the charter bus had pulled out and was making a U-turn. The space was tight, so it was difficult. Dirt from the road was stirred up into the air. The hum of the engine and of the wheels grinding into the road began to fade slowly as the bus drove off.

"That'd be me, sir," Sergeant Day replied.

The contour of his voice was southern in character as well, though not as deeply southern as the voice belonging to the large man who'd emerged from the B-hut.

"That a fact?" the large man replied, his affect, flat; his tone, wry.

It was near dawn now, and with the faint light came a degree of low visibility in which colors could not quite be seen, but shapes were clear enough. In this less than half-light, I made out the figure of the large man approaching our line, moving uphill against the grade of the sloping terrain at what felt like an aggressive speed. As he was about to make contact with two or three Bravos to the left of me, they jerked to either side, the one next to me nearly knocking me down, creating an opening in our phalanx. The large man's pace never slowed. He walked through our line as though it didn't exist. We all scrambled to turn around so as not to have our backs to him.

"Now hear this!" the large man shouted in a loud, dispassionately military persona as he simultaneously rotated his position 180 degrees to face us head-on. We Bravos snapped to attention and straightened out our line.

"You have been afforded the great honor and privilege of attending my school! In order to finish your pre-deployment workup, you must first complete my course!"

The large man seemed to be eyeballing us, scrolling from left to right in slow motion in what I deduced to be a vain attempt at sorting out the weak from the strong.

"If you fail my course," he continued, "you will not be able to deploy, which is, I'm sure, what most of you would rather see happen anyway!"

"Fuck that shit!" An initial repudiation of the large man's assessment was sounded by a Bravo a few bodies to my left, immediately followed by a chorus of angry voices. This was the appropriate time for rebuke.

"We fucking volunteered for this shit!"

"Ain't nobody up in this motherfucker that don't wanna be!"

The yelling had reached a fever pitch.

"Oh yeah?" the large man questioned. "That true for all of you?"

His head ceased to swivel as he locked it on my position and fixed his cold blue eyes on me. It was now light enough to make out color.

I of course said nothing, but stared back unfazed. I'd played this game before. It was not my first rodeo.

"How 'bout it, huh?" The man inched closer to me, his shit-eating grin spread ear to ear. He was now within arm's length. "Did you volunteer for this shit?"

"Actually, no. I was voluntold."

My fellow Bravos responded with controlled laughter, and the large man's face hardened. The laughter quickly died down, and the two of us stared back at one another but said nothing.

We remained in our stalemate for what felt like several minutes until a second figure appeared to face our formation. He was not as large or as tall as the first man, but he carried himself with a similar reserve. He had come out of the same B-hut, but had chosen to walk around our line rather than through it.

"I see you've met HM2 Dooley," the man said. His voice was hearty and smacked of midwestern sensibilities. It was clear too, not only from his tone but also his appearance, that he was older than Dooley and presumably superior in rank.

"I'm HM1 Book. We're your instructors. Welcome to Goat School."

There was a barely audible reaction of joy that passed through our line. Smiles and soft chuckles moved like a wave from soldier to soldier.

"You've most likely heard a lot of shit about this course, some of it probably true." Book's voice carried throughout the clearing. The sun had not quite risen, but its light pushed back against the darkness enough that I could now see clearly. The two instructors stood on the road facing our line. Behind them lurked a dense forest cut short by the dirt road on which they stood. Behind us, the terrain dropped and the trees scattered. Interspersed throughout the sloping meadow were B-huts. A fog that had been there all along was now visible in the growing light of morning.

"You listen up," said Book. "Do exactly what I or HM2 tell you to do and you'll all be fine."

"You motherfuckers'll be on a bus back to Bullis in no time," Dooley added.

The man to the left of me muttered something to the man on his left. I heard the sound, but was unable to make out the words. HM2 Dooley must have also heard the sidebar, because his face hardened and he shouted, "What the fuck is wrong with you goddamned idiots?! You haven't been here five fucking minutes, already you're fuckin' up!"

The two men, apparently taken by surprise, made the necessary adjustments to bring their bodies back to the position of attention. The one closest to me addressed the grievance.

"Sorry, sir."

"I'm not a sir! I'm H-M-fucking-two Dooley." Dooley was red with anger, which seemed a very natural look for him.

"It's just that . . . we've never . . ." The man paused. He was flustered. "What is an HM2, sir? I mean . . . I'm sorry, I have no idea how to address you . . ."

The two instructors looked at one another and howled with laughter. They were feeding off our confusion and uncertainty like sharks circling chum. Dooley took the initiative, clearing up the matter once and for all.

"We are Navy hospital corpsmen." He looked back at Book and continued. "HM1 Book is a first-class petty officer. So we address him as Hospital Corpsman First Class, or HM1 to shorten it up." Book glared back and gave a barely visible slow nod of his head in approval. Dooley went on. "I am a second-class petty officer." He paused at the line, rotating his head mechanically back and forth the full range of motion that his neck would allow.

Unsurprisingly, he again locked eyes with me.

"So what does that make me?" he spat out.

"I guess that would make you HM2."

"Very good! Smart boy, you're gonna do just fine out here."

I did not let my grin expire. HM2 Dooley turned his head to the left past his shoulder and addressed his superior.

"I want this cocksucker in my cadre, HM1."

HM1 Book was pinching a loaf of snuff from a can as Dooley's request registered in his ears. He did not look up as he responded.

"He's all yours."

It was at that moment that I realized HM2 Dooley was armed. In fact they both were. Each man had an M9 Beretta holstered on his right thigh. They were not the John Wayne–style, waist-level, belt clip-on holsters I had always thought that people who carried pistols were meant to wear. It was amazing, the degree to which my empirical knowledge had failed me.

"How many are you?" Dooley addressed the question to Sergeant Day.

"Thirty-three, sir . . . uh, I mean . . . HM2."

"Catching on, I see. Where's the rest of you?"

A few of our medics had managed to drop off between Camp Shelby and Camp Bullis either by successfully failing too many training evolutions or by citing some family or personal emergency situation that, in their minds, superseded their commitment to our country. Two or three at most. I'd managed to go the majority of the three-plus months without learning everybody's name partly because I thought it best not to develop an emotional connection with someone who could likely not make it back from the tour alive, but mostly because I valued my privacy.

"Two failed training at Camp Shelby and Camp Bullis, and one had a family emergency. Thirty-three is all there is, HM2."

HM2 Dooley pulled a sour face, disgusted with the attrition of our group.

"How do you wanna do this, HM1?" HM2 Dooley again craned his neck behind his left shoulder.

"Sixteen and seventeen."

"Who gets the extra man?"

HM1 zeroed in on me with his eyes. The enormous pinch of snuff protruded slightly from his bottom lip. I was amazed he was able to speak with it in.

"He's all yours, remember!" HM1 chuckled.

"Everyone to the right of him," HM2 Dooley pointed at me, "follow HM1 Book. Y'all are Cadre 1. The rest of you are Cadre 2. Spread out and stay quiet."

The men to my right filed in behind HM1 Book, who moved down across our line and headed toward the B-hut from whence he and HM2 Dooley had come some thirty minutes earlier. It was nearly full daylight. The sun shone hard.

The first cadre followed HM1 Book into the B-hut. They moved like well-disciplined soldiers, rucksacks firm and tight on their backs, not bouncing all around. They entered the B-hut carrying one rucksack each; then, almost immediately, each man exited with a second smaller pack in addition to the rucksack. They carried two bags, the larger rucksack and the smaller pack, which looked like a medbag, one on each shoulder. It looked to be somewhat painful, though I could see only through my peripheral vision as my cadre, the second cadre, was still on line at attention.

"What is the most common form of preventable death on the battlefield," HM2 addressed the cadre.

"Exsanguination of an extremity from a bullet hole wound or a laceration or amputation," Davis shouted back. He was a tall, slim black guy from Miami, queer as the day is long. Everyone knew. Nobody cared. It wasn't a thing, even back then.

The question he answered had been posed us countless times in Combat Medic School at Fort Sam Houston, and had been asked and asked again during our training at Camp Bullis.

"And what is the treatment for that injury?"

This question was also posed to the cadre as a whole.

"Apply a tourniquet four inches above the wound, tighten it until the bleeding stops. If the scene is unstable, move the patient to a more secure location, stuff the wound with a QuikClot bandage, then convert to a pressure dressing, loosen the tourniquet. As soon as the bleeding stops, start an IV of Hextend." Specialist Villalobos, a Filipino kid from San Diego, volunteered the answer, a sequence of responses that we had, each of us, committed to memory. These procedures had become mantras to us all.

"And if he starts bleeding again?"

"Tighten the tourniquet." The Cadre replied in unison to this last probe. If nothing else, our training had been thorough.

"What is the second most common form of preventable death on the battlefield?" This one, HM2 Dooley directed at me.

"Tension pneumothorax, collapsed lung secondary to a puncture wound to the thoracic cavity."

"Very sharp there, high speed. And what is the treatment?"

"Needle chest decompression. Using an IV catheter, poke a hole mid-clavicle in the third intercostal space between the second and third ribs on the injured side of the chest. Allow whatever air that's been trapped in the thoracic cavity to escape through the catheter, relieving the pressure within and allowing the lung to be restored upright. What else you got?"

"Ohhh!!!" The cadre erupted with cheer. Our instructor did not share their enthusiasm.

"Shut the fuck up, the rest of you! You think this is a goddamned game?" It was clear from his tone that he was no longer distant and dispassionate. It was now somehow personal.

"I was with Three-Five in Falluja . . . the second time! In November, right after the president got fucking reelected!" He sensed our confusion about the unit he'd referenced. "That's 3rd Battalion, 5th Marine Regiment for all you goddamned Army motherfuckers!" He had brought his tone down some, but was still yelling. "We were going house to house. That was how we did things back then. All it took was one IED and my whole fucking squad was down, every man, myself included." He looked down at his right foot.

"Some of them died right there, some died on the bird or later on in the hospital ship, and some survived. The ones that made it are alive today because I treated them! Because I had the will to act!" He brought his tone down even further and almost leaned in a bit to bridge the gap between himself and our cadre. "Knowing what to do in a situation like that doesn't come from God and it doesn't come out of nowhere either. It comes from training. You will get this, even if you have doubts. Do everything I tell you, and when the time comes, your instincts will take over. That's how training works. That's why our program is so effective. The procedures that we rehearse out here *will* give you the tools and the guidance *you need* to save lives, so pay fucking attention!"

The mood had been altered slightly in accordance with our instructor's show of good faith in opening up to us. There was an air of brotherly love that washed across our line as we tried to process the impact of HM2 Dooley's tragedy and the gravity of his wisdom. Our instructor took advantage of this dynamic. His head panned left, then right, until he finally brought his stare back to me. His eyes scanned my left breast pocket.

"Rogers."

"Yes, HM2."

"What is the third most common form of preventable death on the battlefield?"

"Airway obstruction from trauma to the head or face."

"What is the treatment?"

"Cricothyroidotomy." The whole cadre responded to the last one.

"Good," HM2 said as he began striding toward our line. "Now follow me."

He again managed to slip through a gap in our cadre line created by the same two guys who'd gotten out of his way the first time. We fell in behind him and moved downhill through the meadow to the B-hut where the first cadre had picked up their medbags. We moved into the B-hut, single file, to find that there were no racks, no place for berthing. There was only a Dell desktop workstation set up on the left wall, and a collection of medbags stacked against the wall opposite. Next to the pile of bags were a few torn-open green boxes of MREs. A few of the green oblong-shaped MRE bags littered the floor just in front of the boxes. Other than the computer and desk and the medbags and MRE boxes, the room was empty.

"Grab one medbag, three MREs, and one CAT tourniquet and form it back up on the road. Put the tourniquet in your cargo pocket." The first of our cadre had already picked up his medbag and begun digging through the MREs when HM2 Dooley shouted, "Just grab three MREs, the first three you see, and get back out on the road! Stop trying to get that fuckin' chili mac!" Everyone wanted the chili mac.

Without too much commotion, we were able to all acquire our supplies and equipment and form back up on the road seventeen abreast, each man now with a bag on each shoulder.

The weight was a little painful to bear, but I knew I could stay frozen in this position for hours if I had to.

"Rogers."

"Yes, HM2?"

"End of the line. Move."

"Moving."

My time in the military up to this point had conditioned me to respond with action, not thought, to commands of this nature. I swung around to the end of the line and the Bravos who'd been next to me closed in the gap.

"On me," HM2 Dooley called out, and with that we were off. There'd been many times in my career, too many to recall, when I'd set off, unclear as to my objective or purpose, scrambling to make sense of where I was or what I was supposed to be doing. And more often than not, it turned out that the simplest action was usually the right action. In this situation I was moving forward, one foot in front of the other, bringing up the rear as I had been ordered to.

The sun had risen and the heat was causing me to sweat. I pulled my canteen from the side pouch of my rucksack, which required a minor balancing act of the two bags on my back. We held column on the right margin of the road in case there was any vehicle traffic, though I didn't think there would be. It felt very much like we were alone in the wooded canopy.

After a quarter mile or so, a trail opened up from the woods on the right side of the road, and we entered. I soon realized that the Bravos up front had been breaking off from the trail and heading deeper into the woods on our left. I began to see what looked like some farm animals tethered to trees in the woods. Each makeshift enclosure was a good five hundred feet from the last, and roughly a hundred feet off the trail.

I saw Davis go off, then Villalobos. Then the rest of them, whose names I knew but did not care to recall. All of them eventually broke off the trail and moved through the dense forest to tend to their animals and await further directions from our instructor.

The last man in front of me turned left into the brush as HM2 Dooley pointed in the direction of his assigned area and ward. He then looked at me, grimaced, and made a nodding gesture with his head indicating that I follow him into the woods.

We did not speak as we moved through the forest, though we disturbed foliage and snapped twigs with our heavy boots. The woods became denser, and I realized that I could no longer see any of the other Bravos or their animals.

It felt like we'd been on the march for hours when I asked, "How much farther, HM2?"

"You'll know when we get there," he snarled.

I glanced at the pistol holstered on his right thigh. He always kept a good two steps ahead of me at any given time, and the terrain was uneven and difficult to negotiate. But we kept moving. Moving and moving. One foot in front of the next. No questions. No discussion. Just movement, one foot in front of the other.

And then the forest opened up into a circular clearing with a large weeping willow in the center.

A metallic chain dangled without tension from one of the branches of the tree. The other end of the chain was secured to a collar that wrapped around the neck of a shimmering white billy goat. The goat stared at us both. It had a brilliantly bright, almost blinding white coat and menacing blue eyes that were alert, though did not appear to take us as a threat.

"Put down your ruck."

"Alright."

I walked past the goat over to the tree. The goat did not change its footing, but it followed me with its head and eyes. I allowed my rucksack to slide gently off my left shoulder so that it made contact with the tree and remained upright. I rotated to the other side and began the same process with the medbag hanging from my right shoulder when HM2 Dooley snapped at me. "No! Keep your medbag on!"

Though I was never in my short military career accused of being a stellar soldier, I was no dirtbag either, at least not as I saw things. And while I took care to obey the orders of those appointed over me in accordance with the oath I swore, the soldier's creed, I also understood that I was no longer in boot camp. There was a finite amount of abuse I was willing to tolerate, and HM2 Dooley with his snide remarks and combat-cool swagger was dangerously close to exceeding the allotted quota.

He stood just beside the goat, petting and scratching its head. The goat blinked and leaned into his left thigh.

"Get over here."

"I'm fucking moving, can't you see that."

"You need to take it down a notch, Rogers. It's just you, me, and this goat way out in the woods, you know what I'm saying?"

I approached from the other side. I was now staring at Dooley, he was staring back at me, and the goat was between us. The chain jingled with the soft movements of the goat's head rubbing against Dooley's left leg.

"Are you confident in the interventions we went over earlier?"

"Yes."

"Do you think you have what it takes to treat casualties under fire?"

"I know I do."

He looked down at the goat and smiled.

"Beautiful, isn't she?"

"Yes, she is."

"Keep her alive for thirty-six hours, and you pass. If she dies . . ." He looked up at me and smiled again with that irritated, condescending look I was beginning to think was his default expression. "Then you fail. No deployment, no glory . . . which shouldn't be too much of a letdown for you, considering you were . . . '*voluntold*,' right?"

I knew that HM2 Dooley was the type of person who survived on the anger and doubt he inspired in others. I imagined that was the only thing he really had going for him anymore. But I would not oblige him in that way.

"I'll keep her alive."

His smile faded to a look of sincere, though guarded optimism as he nodded slightly.

"One more thing . . . "

"Yeah."

"Don't name her."

"What?"

"I said don't give her a name."

"Why not?"

"Just trust me, it's better that way."

"Whatever."

"What?"

"I said alright. Anything else?"

His condescending smile returned as he reached for his weapon.

"Yeah, good luck."

Dooley was still petting goat's head with his left hand as he simultaneously unholstered his M9 with his right and fired a shot into the animal's left hind leg.

"What the *fuck*?! Are you fucking *crazy*, man?!"

The goat made a sound like a dying baby's cry muffled by her shortness of breath as she capsized on the side of the wounded appendage. The chain jingled as she went down.

"Better get moving or this lab's gonna be over in thirty seconds!"

"Goddamn it!"

I pushed past Dooley to get position on the patient, then kneeled down beside her and grounded my medbag. Digging my two hands underneath her flank, I flipped her onto her right side so that I could get to work on the wound. As I did this, she continued to make horrible wailing sounds that I found difficult to ignore.

The wound Dooley inflicted had struck the femoral artery, which was undoubtedly his intention, causing the patient to hemorrhage large volumes of blood from her left hind leg. Our training indicated that a patient suffering this type of wound could bleed out in as little as ninety seconds.

The goat's leg was spurting blood like a volcano. Her shiny white coat was now dyed an indelible deep red in patches and splatter marks that went all the way up to her face. Her flank looked like a Jackson Pollock.

There was no time to go for the medbag. I reached into my right cargo pocket and pulled out the CAT tourniquet. We all knew that CAT tourniquet was a redundant expression, because CAT was an acronym for Combat Application Tourniquet, but we kept calling them CAT tourniquets the way people in civilian life continue to say ATM machine. Basic logic and reason overcome by the juggernaut of popular usage.

This trivial observation, however, did little to stop the patient from bleeding to death. It's a wonder what accounts for thought in a moment of truth such as this.

I slid the CAT tourniquet up the patient's leg, above the wound, which bloodied my hands and made it difficult to control the device. Once it was in place, I pulled the strap hard; then, using the winch, I tightened it till the geyser was reduced to a slow drip, like a faucet valve on full blast cranked suddenly shut. I then tightened it one more half turn and the oozing stopped altogether.

I grounded and unzipped my medbag and pulled the top part forward so it opened like a traveling salesman's display suitcase. In the top section I found a QuikClot bandage, which I tore open immediately and applied directly to the wound. The bandage was caked in a chalky substance that, upon contact with the patient's blood, immediately set off a chemical reaction that extracted the blood's moisture, causing it to clot instantly. I shoved the bandage as far into the wound as I could before the moisture from the blood began to set off the chemical change, causing my fingers to burn slightly.

I reached back into my medbag and pulled a second QuikClot bandage, which I then tore open and applied to the exit wound on the inside of the goat's leg. I set the bandage into the wound, same as before, only this time I did it without eyes, because I feared that turning her over again might have been too much for her. I instead reached around to the inside of her leg and stuffed the bandage into the opposing end of the canal left by the path and tremendous force of the M9 round.

There were risks associated with these clotting agents. The cauterizations often caused harmful burns, and I'd overheard trauma surgeons say that they make it difficult, sometimes impossible, to repair arteries on the operating table. However we were not surgeons, and our job was not to repair arteries or set fractures, or even suture. Our job was to sustain the life of the casualty until transfer to the next echelon of care, usually a medevac, at which point all responsibility of the patient's well-being shifted extemporaneously from us to them.

The cries had died down. The patient's head was wobbly as she lay on her side. Her remaining limbs began to twitch every ten seconds or so. Clearly, she had gone into shock and was circling the drain. She was panting, and her coat was wet with sweat and blood.

The QuikClot bandages had worked, it appeared, but the wound still needed to be dressed and wrapped.

I pulled from my medbag an Israeli bandage, which is really just a battle dressing attached to an Ace wrap. I pushed the dressing part of it down hard against the wound, then coiled the Ace wrap bit around the dressing and her limb to hold it in place. I made sure the tension was tight enough to hold the bleeding back, but not so tight that it would cut off the circulation to her leg. When I was finished I looked at the dressing, observed for any blood flow, and tested the tension of the wrap by sticking my index finger between the goat's leg and the inside of the dressing. I could not quite get a full finger inside, so it was good to go.

I then loosened the tourniquet and observed for blood flow a second time. There was none. I left the tourniquet in place, but with slack, in case the bleeding resumed and I had to tighten it back up.

Monitoring a wound like this is something that is done constantly until the patient is transferred to the next echelon of care, in this case, back to the clearing with the B-huts, provided she made it the next two days.

I heard a second shot way off in the distance, and when I looked up I realized HM2 Dooley was no longer around. I dug through my medbag until I found a 500cc bag of Hextend, the blood-plasma volumizing solution. The patient had lost at least a pint of blood, which made it very difficult for me to find a pulse, let alone insert an IV. I'd done IV sticks before, during the last phase of clinicals at Combat Medic School at Fort Sam Houston, then later on at the Brooke Army Medical Center ER. Way too many to count.

Also, we would give ourselves IVs the mornings after particularly brutal nights of binge drinking. All of us who worked in the ER would fix each other with IVs and infuse one another with solution—usually normal saline—to replenish the fluids we'd lost to alcohol-induced dehydration.

I had responded in the ER to bleeding laceration injuries in patients that had come in on gurneys, fresh from the scene of a motor vehicle accident, though this was the first time that I had been alone in treating a patient with a major hemorrhage wound like this one. Also, I had never treated a goat.

The fur made it difficult to find a vein, but despite the severity of the wound and my ignorance of the patient's foreign anatomy, I was able to set a saline lock into the left front leg. I knew the needle had struck her vein because of the flash of red that exploded into the valve when the blood came through the needle's catheter.

I then secured the IV tubing to the lock and hung the clear bag of Hextend from a small branch of the willow. The Hextend was clear like water, only a bit thicker in composition. I pushed the small wheel of the flow regulator all the way up with my thumb so the solution dripped out at a fast rate, like syrup from a Maine maple tree in spring, and after about a minute or so the patient began to show small signs of recovery. She was still whining and thrashing a bit, but she was alive.

I had stopped the bleeding, and put in an IV. The patient was no longer circling the drain, but she was in enormous pain.

I located a 10mg/5cc syringe of morphine sulfate in my medbag, uncapped the needle and drove it into the opaque yellow rubber stopper that jutted out at an acute angle halfway up the IV tubing. I already had IV access; there was no need to stick her twice. As I depressed the plunger with my thumb, I watched the patient react in real time to the administration of the narcotic. It was magical and surreal how quickly one small movement, one little push of the thumb, could remove such intense prolonged agony and replace it with bliss. There were two more syringes in the bag, I noted. This first one had done its job.

The twitching became less and less frequent until it ceased entirely. The patient's breathing pattern transitioned from short, shallow panting breaths to long, deep respirations. Her head lay off to the side, her blue eyes blinking but aware. Her perspiration had been reduced to a thin, moist layer, which was a normal reaction to the day's heat. The sun was now high in the air, and though the willow provided some cover, the warmth was still very intense, and I found myself sweating and imbibing large volumes of water. My first canteen was nearly empty, so I poured the last bit into the side of my patient's mouth. She licked her lips. The Hextend would help increase the volume of blood in her veins and arteries, though she would need drinkable water if she were to survive.

I heard a third shot off in the distance. It was farther off then the second had been.

I'm not sure exactly why I was so shocked when HM2 Dooley shot my goat. After all, the purpose of this course was to show us what a wound really looked like up close, and to make sure we knew how to respond. The goats were sacrifices. Their injuries served the larger purpose of our mission. We needed the practice. It made sense. I could rationalize it. Though the cruelty of it all weighed on me, and the sorrow and sadness I experienced made me feel weak.

I despised myself for allowing such feelings to take shape in my thoughts. To avoid obsessing on it any further I threw myself into my duties.

I lifted the patient's two eyelids, one at a time, and swiped a penlight across them both, ensuring her pupils were round and reactive to light. They both were.

I checked and rechecked her pulse, which eventually fell to between 90 and 120 beats per minute, the normal range for humans. Her coat was now dry and caked in the crimson of blood, which was thick and concentrated near the site of the wound and splattered in small spots along the rest of her left flank. There were even spots as far up as her face. Much of her blood had also stained my hands and blouse and had even struck my face and neck. But she was calm now.

The 500cc bag of Hextend suspended by a small branch of the willow above her head was nearly empty, so I changed it out with a second sack I grabbed out of my medbag. Her vein had swallowed the solution at an abnormally high rate due to the blood loss she'd sustained. I adjusted the drip rate on the second bag so that it would not empty as quickly.

I heard several more shots, each one farther off than the last, as I tended to my charge. It was not a good day for goats, I thought. But my patient, my goat, was going to live. I was sure of it.

I petted her coat, now stiff in parts from the coagulated blood spatter, though still soft in the swaths that were untouched by the hemorrhage. I petted her head and spoke to her.

"You're gonna be okay, goat. You're gonna make it; you're gonna live." She nuzzled gently against my hand with her head. I found it troubling and impersonal that I should refer to my patient by the name of her species rather than something more intimate. If she was going to live, she needed a name.

"You're gonna be okay, Sally. We're gonna get through this."

Sally was the name of a former girlfriend; the one I'd let slip away. Our time together had been brief but passionate. She had long, straight, shiny black hair with short bangs. Her complexion was fair and her body type was athletic. Her face was smart and pretty and her eyes were a deep blue or green depending on the light that surrounded her.

She was way out of my league, but I had managed to wrangle her through a series of verbal and physical exchanges. They were less about content, more about posture. I pulled it off, somehow. She fell for me.

It did not take long, however, for her to see through me. Our union was short-lived. But I loved her still, and I missed her and I knew that this would never change.

It was now close to dusk, and the heat had let up some. There was dense moisture in the air, which caused Sally and I to sweat. I had half a canteen of water left. The day's excitement had worn me down and I realized that I was very hungry. I dug through my rucksack and pulled out an MRE. Chicken tetrazzini.

The MRE heater required water to spark a chemical reaction which created the heat that cooked the meal. I chose to hold my water in reserve and eat the meal cold, which really wasn't much different from eating it hot.

The main meal was supplemented with crackers, a packet of peanut butter and jelly, two small slices of flat white bread, chocolate M&Ms, an instant coffee packet, and two small lemon-scented towelette wipes. I used the wipes to clean the dried blood off my hands. I had been tempted earlier in the day to use water for this purpose, but decided that it would have been a poor use of limited resources.

I crushed up the bread and the crackers into a grain meal and fed it to Sally. The right side of her face rested against the soft earth of the forest. She lifted it slightly and managed to scoop up the crushed bread and crackers with her lips, which tickled my hand a little. It reminded me of outings to the Bronx Zoo I'd taken as a boy with my family when we lived together in Old New York in the eighties.

When she was finished, I poured some water into her mouth from the side and she licked her lips and moved her jaw.

The sky had gone dark with rain clouds. The sun had not quite set, but I could see that a storm coming.

I procured my sleeping bag from my ruck and gently pulled it up underneath and around Sally. I then fashioned a small tarp from my poncho, affixed it to some branches of the willow to shelter her from the rain, and adjusted the drip rate on the second bag of Hextend to a very slow setting so that the bag would not empty overnight. There was a small amount of solution pooled at the bottom that would suffice.

If the bag empties and there's still negative pressure in the catheter, it is possible for the patient to take on an air embolism, perhaps causing a stroke. Losing her to such a gaffe at this point would have been unacceptable after all I'd done to keep her alive.

I climbed into the sleeping bag with the wounded goat so that neither one of us would develop hypothermia.

"It's okay, Sally. We're gonna get through this," I whispered into her ear. I knew she could not understand my language, but I knew also that my words had a calming effect.

"We're gonna get through this, I promise. I'm gonna bring you back home to Greenwich with me. You'll be back on your feet in a few weeks. This will all feel like a bad dream, you'll see. Everything's gonna work out, I promise."

Rain began to patter on the tarp above us, and though the odd drop was able to slip through and splash me or Sally, we stayed, for the most part, warm and dry. She twitched and kicked and moaned occasionally through the night, and when the morning came, I decided it was time for another dose of morphine.

As I rose to my feet and went for my medbag, which had also managed to stay mostly dry under the tarp, I heard the snap of twigs and the rustle of disturbed shrubbery.

"Goddamn, boy, what kinda shit did you get into?" HM2 was standing just over me.

"It's not what it looks like."

"Oh yeah? You got a loose understanding of the concept of battlefield medicine, son."

"Look, it was fucking raining out, and I didn't want her *or* me to hype out . . . "

"Yeah, yeah, I know. I'm just fuckin' with you. So how 'bout it, huh? She alive under there?"

"Yeah, she's alive. She's gonna make it."

"Show me what you've done."

I tore down the tarp, threw it aside and pulled the sleeping bag out from underneath Sally.

"You didn't name her, did you?"

"Course not."

"Good. I brought you some water." HM2 Dooley threw a one-liter bottle of Poland Spring water down beside my rain poncho.

"Thanks."

"Let's see what we got here." He squatted before Sally and began testing the tension of my pressure dressing, poking at the small space between her leg and the inside of the Ace wrap.

"Good stuff, looks like."

"Thanks."

"You put a QuikClot in there?"

"Yeah."

Dooley looked up and slightly left, furnished a quizzical expression, then glanced back at me.

"Those things work, but they cause more harm than good sometimes."

"I've heard that."

HM2 Dooley continued to check the patient's vital signs, observing her overall condition and the efficacy of my interventions. He applied light pressure to her carotid artery under her chin to check her pulse, which caused her to moan softly and avert her head in protest. HM2 Dooley gave a small nod of the head in my general direction that came with an expression of tempered approval. This was not a mocking gesture.

"How many bags did you give her?"

"That's the second one."

"Both Hextend?"

"Yeah."

"Change it out for a normal saline. She's dehydrated."

"Okay."

Unlike Hextend, normal saline did not pull water from the interstitial space between the skin and the blood vessels. It was just water with a little sodium. The infusion would not increase her blood volume as much as it would replenish fluid from the interstitial space that had been drawn into the bloodstream by the two bags of Hextend.

I grabbed the 500cc pouch of normal saline from my medbag as HM2 Dooley stared curiously at Sally. He was now right on top of her looking down at her left side. She lay on her right flank, unable to adjust her position since I'd flipped her over to treat the gunshot wound the previous day. I was standing a few inches from her head, changing out her IV. We were all three underneath the willow.

"We threw y'all in at the deep end 'cause downrange, that's how it is. You don't get time to prepare. When you get hit, it just happens. That's why we didn't even give y'all a chance to familiarize yourselves with the medbags we gave you. Have you figured out where everything is?"

"Yeah."

HM2 Dooley was talking to me straight finally. There was no animosity or distance between us.

"One thing we don't cover in this lab is burns." He looked off to his right as he spoke, focused perhaps on an unseen memory sprouted up from the flora.

"You ever see what burns look like up close?" he asked, his eyes fixed on the shrubbery dead ahead.

"I did my clinicals in the burn ward at BAM-C."

"Good old Brooke Army Medical Center!" he chuckled. "Yeah, a few of my guys wound up there."

"Oh. Well, what were their names? Maybe I knew them."

"It don't matter, they're all fuckin' dead now."

He examined Sally, pulling her eyelids open and observing her pupils.

"She's pretty calm. Did you hit her with morphine?"

"Yeah, but not before I got everything under control."

Dooley nodded his head in approval.

"You know you have to be careful with that shit?"

"Yeah, I know."

"No, seriously. That shit'll get over on you. You should only use it if the patient is on his way down. It's too tricky to tell sometimes, and you'll wind up doing more harm than good. That shit'll get over on you, be careful."

"I will, and I am."

"How many did you hit her with?"

"One."

"Really, I only counted one left in your medbag, and we gave you three, so you should have two. Where's the other one?"

"That's fucking bullshit! I only used one, and there were two left, I swear to God!"

"Don't sweat it, we'll worry about it when you turn everything in. But when you get downrange, you better keep a good eye on your supply. If everyone of those narcs isn't accounted for, that's a guaranteed court-martial. You can thank the Vietnam docs for that one. Apparently they had their fun, ruined it for the rest of us."

HM2 Dooley forced a smile over his face, and I was unable to decipher exactly which type of smile it was: one of camaraderie or contempt.

The Texas sun had risen high in the sky, causing the moisture from the previous night's rainfall to evaporate slowly. It was hot and humid.

"Make sure you're drinking enough water too."

"I'm alright."

"You know, Rogers," he turned to face me as he spoke, "this lab isn't just about keeping this fucking goat alive." He stroked Sally's head with his left hand the same way he had the previous day moments before he shot her in the hind leg. I found this disturbing, but said nothing. "The Army's spent a lot of money training, feeding, and paying your ass. You're no good to us dead."

"I thought you said you were in the Navy."

"I am, numb nuts." He smiled genuinely. "It's one team, one fight. You'll see when you get out there."

HM2 Dooley continued to nod slowly as he stroked the goat's head.

"Yeah, I think she's gonna make it. Rogers, you know where everything in your bag is, right? You know where your occlusive dressings are?"

"Yeah, they're in the bottom half, underneath the burn dressings."

"Very good." He did his best to look Sally in her eye as he spoke. She no longer protested his fondling of her. "Yeah, I think she's gonna make it."

While still in the crouching position, HM2 Dooley unholstered his pistol with his right hand and fired a shot into the goat's flank.

"No!" I shouted, and leaped over her and tackled him. "Stop shooting my fucking goat!"

My pounce caught him off balance, and I was able to briefly gain a mounted position on him and wrap my hands around his neck before he struck me in the head with his pistol.

The force of the blow knocked me over onto my back, and before I could make sense of what had happened, HM2 Dooley was standing over me shouting, the pistol trained dead on my skull.

"What the fuck is wrong with you, you stupid cocksucker!?"

He put his right foot on my chest and leaned in close with the pistol. His eyes were alive with hatred. I had tripped his switch and he was now upon me, bearing down with a loaded gun.

"Why do you keep shooting her?" I sobbed uncontrollably. "She can't defend herself, she's helpless, and I've fucking stabilized her!" I had come apart. Perhaps it was from the exhaustion of being at full capacity treating Sally for so many hours in the moist heat, then through the cold, wet night. Or maybe I was dehydrated and underfed. But whatever the cause, I had devolved into a blubbering mess, going to pieces on the soft earth of the interior wood.

"She was gonna survive. Why did you fucking do that?"

Dooley's face softened a hair, and he grabbed me by the blouse collar and pulled me up.

"She's not dead yet, go treat her!"

He threw me down onto my medbag, which I tore through to locate my occlusive dressings; flat, clear squares four by four inches in size and the consistency of Saran Wrap. Their purpose is to create a seal over a wound to the airway or respiratory system.

I peeled one open, and applied it to the hole in Sally's flank. I pressed hard around the squared edges, ensuring an airtight seal. The clear dressing was red with blood from the wound, but the blood did not bleed through to the other side. The seal was intact.

I then pulled a second occlusive dressing and peeled it open. With my left hand, I reached around to Sally's right flank and located the exit wound. Without flipping her over, I secured the clear plastic square to the wound, first with one hand, then ensuring the seal was intact by wrapping my other arm around her neck and applying pressure. I had both arms wrapped around her as though giving her a hug. In fact, I was hugging her.

"It's gonna be okay, Sally, trust me."

"What the fuck did you just say, Rogers?"

"Nothing, I didn't say anything." My voice was still full of hurt and trembling.

"Get the catheter out and finish this intervention."

HM2 Dooley's tone was distant and dispassionate. He was all business at this point.

Sally was still breathing, but her breaths had become laborious. She was showing a flail chest; the rise and fall of her chest did not sync up with the inhalation and exhalation of her breath. She displayed paradoxical motion, the hallmark of a collapsed lung. She had a tension pneumothorax, the second most common cause of preventable death on the battlefield. In order to fix it, I would have to poke a hole in her chest to relieve the pressure so her lungs could right themselves. Also, I noticed she was coughing up a little blood.

"Rogers, that means now! Move!"

"Alright!"

I grabbed a 14-gauge IV catheter from my medbag, uncapped it, and punctured the bloodstained fur of her flank through to the skin. The needle went in with a pop, and I felt a rush of warm air push out through the catheter.

"Now make sure the air doesn't get back in."

I pulled out a latex glove and a pair of trauma shears from my medbag and cut one of the fingers off, then placed the glove's amputated finger on top of the catheter so that air could escape, but could not get back in through the hole. For all our many innovative triumphs, our advancements in tactical medical equipment and procedures over the years, this was the best, most effective way to keep air out of the plural space.

"Rogers, you're lucky I didn't have you thrown in the fucking brig. You're even luckier I didn't blow your goddamned brains out. You've got six hours left on this lab. Keep that patient alive, and you pass. If she dies, you fail, and you stay home. You'll sit out the fucking war."

Air continued to squeak out through the catheter. Sally's chest began to slowly rise and fall evenly and in step with her breathing pattern.

"This is your chance to really do something with your life. Something extraordinary. Don't you want to be a part of something greater than yourself?"

"And end up like you?"

Dooley nearly had to take a step back as I answered his question with one of my own. His jaw about dropped and his eyes widened with great surprise. It was as though my words had pierced his lungs the way his bullet had torn a hole through Sally's.

"I'll see you in six hours."

He disappeared into the forest, this time without making a sound. I turned my attention back to Sally. She was in bad shape. I knew it was beyond my purview to put in a chest tube, but if I didn't get the blood out of her lungs, she would likely drown.

I found one in my medbag, and fastened a 10-gauge needle to the front end. Ten gauge is an extremely large bore size. A procedure like this is meant to be performed on the operating table under aseptic conditions by someone who is not only a medical doctor but also a trauma surgeon. My schooling amounted to twelve weeks at Combat Medic School at Fort Sam Houston and the twenty-two-day crash course in combat medicine at Camp Bullis.

I drove the tube through Sally's chest wall just underneath her armpit, the prescribed site for an insertion in humans. She jerked in horrible pain. I felt awful, but there was no turning back now.

The tube filled up with blood that poured out the opposite end onto the forest floor. When it looked like it was nearly finished emptying, I cut a finger off the same latex glove and placed it over the open end of the chest tube to keep air from getting back into the lung.

Airway, breathing, and circulation. ABCs. To manage those three things was to preserve life to the very best of our abilities, until transfer to the next echelon of care. The chest tube was an intervention well above my level of training and expertise. We had learned about the procedure, but had never trained or rehearsed one. I had no business putting it in, but I didn't know what else to do.

Sally was too close to the edge to administer morphine. If I didn't have to keep her alive for this stupid lab, I would have tied her off one last time and let her fade away in peace. It would have been the humane thing to do. Instead, I held vigil. I checked and rechecked my interventions, took vital signs, and even filled out a Field Medical Care Card, documenting her injuries and recording her condition.

When I realized I had reached the limits of what I could possibly do to keep her from expiring, I knelt beside her and bowed my head. I had never been taught before how to pray. I recalled while switching through radio channels in my car in San Antonio years earlier, and stumbling upon an evangelist station, that according to the Christian faith, all prayers were meant to be directed to God the father. But I had no idea who that was.

So I prayed to the God of mercy. I prayed to the God of eternal peace and forgiveness and wisdom and charity and second chances. I even spoke aloud:

"Please, God, don't let Sally die. Let me take her back home with me, back to Greenwich. I know things went wrong between us, but I still love her, God. Help me, I can't keep her out of my thoughts. She haunts me, oh God. Please see us through this trying time. Please let her live, help us try again, oh God."

I must have gone on and on like that for several hours, because when I sat up, I saw HM2 Dooley standing over Sally, petting her head gently and smiling.

Her head had perked up and she too appeared to be smiling. There was an even rise and fall of her chest. Her pulse was strong and within the normal range, and she was alert and responsive.

"I don't know how you pulled it off, Rogers, but looks like you're gonna pass."

"Really?" I could not contain my own smile.

"I can't figure it. Looked like for sure she was finished. You got some magic hands, huh? Those are gonna come in handy downrange."

"I don't have a litter. Will you help me carry her back?"

"Huh?"

"Back to camp?" I pointed in the direction of the trail that had led us out to the clearing the previous day. "I could manage it on my own, but she's still critical, and I don't want to risk it."

"What the fuck are you talking about?" A hard smirk appeared on his face.

"She's in critical condition. I've stabilized her, but we've got to get her on a medevac soon or she's not gonna make it."

HM2 Dooley laughed out loud. He put his hands on his hips and leaned back with his head and shoulders. Having been the source of many scraps and tussles as a youngster, I'd had it explained to me on more than one occasion, by more than one parent or teacher or camp counselor, the difference between someone laughing *with* you and laughing *at* you. HM2 Dooley was laughing *at* me.

"Rogers, we're not taking her back with us. This is the end of the line for poor old, what's her name? What did you call her?"

"I didn't call her anything."

"Bullshit, I heard you. Earlier today when I came out here, and just now, while you were praying, or whatever the fuck you were doing. And that's another thing. What the fuck do you know about God, huh?"

I paused for a moment in contemplation. *What did I know about God?*

"As much as the next guy."

"You think that's fuckin' funny, you Yankee cocksucker?"

"Whoa, chill the fuck out! What happened to 'one team, one fight'?"

I could tell this flustered Dooley, so I tried to reason with him.

"Look, I know its unorthodox or whatever, but I can take care of her. I'll take her to the vet, pay for it myself. I'll keep her around at my mom's house in Greenwich. She can stay there while I deploy, then I'll take her with me wherever I get stationed next. She doesn't have to die, please?"

HM2 Dooley reached for his pistol with his right hand.

"No, stop! Don't shoot her again, please!"

"I won't." Dooley unholstered his weapon, turned it around so that his hand gripped the barrel and the handle faced forward. He pushed the gun into my chest. "You will."

I had deluded myself into believing that there was another way.

"I can't." My head dropped forward, and I began to tear up.

"You have to."

"I can't."

"Take the fucking weapon, Rogers!"

But deep down, I knew all along what had to be done. Without looking up, I grabbed the pistol with my right hand and wiped the tears from my eyes with my left forearm.

"What the fuck is your problem, Rogers? The Army didn't fucking draft your ass. You signed on for this shit. What's your deal, son?"

I took a deep breath in and held it for a moment before exhaling.

"I didn't know it was gonna be this hard."

I looked up at Dooley, my eyes bloodshot and shimmering. I bit down on my upper lip to keep it from trembling.

"It's hard for everyone, Rogers. I told you not to name her, didn't I? You're soft now, but you'll grow hard. You will, I know you will. Now finish this, so we can get the fuck outta here."

I closed my eyes and nodded.

"Gimme a sec, alright?"

"Alright."

I walked over to Sally. She blinked and looked up at me, unaware of the inevitable conclusion to her epic trial. She had suffered as Jesus had suffered. And she would die as Jesus had died.

"You know, Sally, you were never there for me when I really needed you."

The goat sensed a shift in my tone, and rested her head back on the soft earth of the forest. It was a miracle she had survived to this point.

"You weren't there for me and you abandoned me when I needed you most."

Her eyes widened. I could sense her fear.

"And your family never liked me and I never liked them and you fucking abandoned me, you bitch! You fucking left me, you whore! You left me for that fucking captain you met at Cowboy's Dance Hall."

She was breathing rapidly now. She did her best to scramble with her good legs.

"And it's just as well, the two of you deserve each other! And I don't care if he *was* an officer, he was *still* white trash from Mobile or Pensacola or wherever, and you're *still* white trash from Bastrop County, and you don't belong in Greenwich, Connecticut anyway! I'm glad I never took you home with me, all my friends would've laughed at me. There's no place for Bastrop County white trash in Greenwich, Connecticut!"

For the first time, I heard the birds and the bugs and all the rest of the wildlife in layers of atmospheric sound. It was deafening.

"You did good, Rogers. Police up those IVs and bandages, grab your shit, and head back to camp. You'll be on a bus back to Bullis later on tonight. Don't worry about 'Sally' either. The coyotes'll get to her first, then the rest. Circle of life, brother."

HM2 Dooley had been going through my medbag. I assumed he was reorganizing it for the next group of Bravos to come through.

"Okay."

"Hey, where's your Field Medical Card?"

"I have it here."

I pulled the card from my right cargo pocket and handed it to Dooley. He looked it over, all the while nodding and looking back up at me every so often.

"Looks good, except for one thing. You only recorded one treatment of morphine. You forgot about the other two you pushed."

"But I only pushed one, I told you—"

"Be careful, Rogers," Dooley interrupted me. "That shit'll get over on you. Be careful."

Before I could respond, he was gone again, vanished into the thick brush of the forest like a Comanche ghost.

As I finished pulling off the bandages and separating the IV tubing, I noticed there was still one 10mg/5cc syringe of morphine sulfate in my medbag. I picked it up and stared at it curiously. Puzzled, I scanned the forest for signs that I was being watched. It would not have been altogether out of the ordinary for this last challenge to be the true test of Goat School.

In the end, I placed the syringe in my cargo pocket, finished policing up the area, packed up my medbag and rucksack with all perishable and nonperishable items and trash, and headed back in the direction of the camp, leaving the goat to rot in the high Texas sun, or be picked clean by the coyotes.

CHAPTER 9
BEER FOR MY HORSEMEN

The mood had shifted dramatically in the short time we'd been huddled inside the gate of Camp Phoenix from one of great fear and tension to full-scale jubilation and relief, as was commonplace for just after a scrape, or near scrape in which none of our own were killed or seriously injured. The night was cool and dry, and there was just enough ambient glow from the base's many floodlights for us to see each others' faces clearly.

We were gathered informally inside of the front gate, palling around and glad-handing, exchanging high fives and calling each other out for being terrified.

"I saw you in the tunnel, Harold, fingering your rosary, whispering something!" Lieutenant Grey howled as he laid into the captain. "You were sayin' a Hail Mary, weren't you?" We all got caught up in the hazing, like violent teenagers at a gang initiation. "You were prayin' to God we'd make it through!"

Captain Harold smiled smugly, as though he was privy to some great scheme in which, at a certain point, Lieutenant Grey would be made to answer for his blasphemous remarks. "That was my crucifix, thank you, I'm a Southern Baptist not a Catholic. And no amount of prayer could save you from what's in store."

At this the whole crew laughed in unison, Captain Harold included, though his laugh was more sardonic in nature.

"And Mortin, you with 'the gun is jammed, the gun is jammed!' Screaming like a little bitch! Fucking priceless!"

The boisterousness created a buffer between ourselves and the acknowledgment of how close to the edge we had come.

"What about fucking Rambo over here, beatin' the brains outta that cocksucker?" Mortin grabbed the ANA guard's right arm at the wrist with his left hand and raised it up as though the man was a prizefighter who'd just knocked out the reigning heavyweight champion of the world. The crowd went wild.

"How 'bout his buddy, took off running for the hills the second we got hit!" Captain Harold said. "So much for his career with the ANA. I'm sure he'll be missed."

Everyone laughed.

"And Doc, trying to jump out of the truck and take that motherfucker out like fucking *Die Hard*!" Lieutenant Grey added.

"Just doing my part. Preventative medicine, that's all that was."

The laughter teetered out abruptly after my joke, and the six of us were left standing in a circle in front of the two hastily parked Humvees, all staring at our boots or behind our shoulders or at the sky or anywhere at all except in the direct line of sight of anyone else in the formation. A moment of silence passed and the Sergeant Major took control of the situation.

"Doc, Mortin, take the trucks over to the motor pool. Tell the grease monkeys down there what happened. Tell them to do a full diagnostic on both trucks. Make sure they're good to go."

"Roger that," Mortin answered.

"Lieutenant Grey and Captain Harold," the Sergeant Major went on. "See about gettin' us some racks in the transient tent. We need six."

"On it," Lieutenant Grey responded. Captain Harold nodded his head.

"Raz, Rambo." The Sergeant Major put his arm around the ANA guard. "With me. We're gonna have to explain to EOD what the fuck happened out there." He pointed to the front gate.

"Meet up at the rec center above the PX at twenty-three hundred."

The Sergeant Major gave a look that we all took to mean our meeting had adjourned. With that, we stepped off in our different directions. I decided to take the opportunity to confront Mortin with some much-needed retribution for his many slights against my person.

"Mortin, man. You really fucked up, dude."

I said this in passing to him as we were both opening the driver-side doors to our respective Humvees, knowing full well that he did not have the capacity to formulate a response before I pulled off my gear, placed it up on the front right passenger side seat, and swung shut the enormous steel-reinforced door behind me. Mortin got in the lead vehicle, and I jumped in the rear.

This was the first time I had been asked to operate a vehicle since my driving privileges had been revoked at the request of the Sergeant Major after I'd rear-ended a minivan in downtown Kabul some months earlier.

I was easing into the comfortable middle part of my high where I was functional enough to carry out the task of bringing the Humvee to the motor pool, but still felt loose, and was a good hour or so, maybe longer, ahead of the shakes.

As the heavy door closed behind me, I shut my eyes, took a deep breath, and leaned back into the seat for just a moment. I didn't have time for a nod, but I wanted to get one great deep calming breath in while I had the chance. .

A moment later I opened my eyes and redeposited myself into the situation at hand. Both Humvees had been left running and the comms were still up so I put on my headset and hailed Mortin to continue the haranguing.

"Mortin, you read me?"

"Yeah, I hear you."

"Bro, what happened to your pistol? Is it still out there?"

"I don't know. Probably. The Sergeant Major told us to get the trucks fixed, so that's what we're doing. We can worry about my pistol later. I'm sure EOD or Sergeant Major will fucking find it. It's no big deal."

We rolled out in the direction of the motor pool, Mortin up front and myself pulling up the rear.

We were each alone in our respective trucks, able to talk to each other over the radio. It felt momentarily like we were on the outskirts of some podunk college town, communicating via cell phone, trying to find our way to some elusive after-party.

"You know where we're going, right?"

"Yeah."

"Good. I'm just making sure you're squared away, because, you know you dropped your pistol—"

"Fuck you!"

Though the location of Camp Phoenix was not considered downrange, it was still referred to as a Forward Operating Base, which seemed absurd. It was an echelon below Bagram or KAF in terms of size, but still housed anywhere from five hundred to a thousand military personnel and contractors, the latter of whom nearly all worked for KBR.

And while there were roads that were clearly designed to support the movement of vehicles, there were no sidewalks as there were at Bagram. Also, there were large tracts of land, particularly up by the front gate, that were flat and open and facilitated the comings and goings of both foot and vehicular traffic.

As we moved over the large, flat plain that connected the base's opposing wings, great big three-story apartment-style buildings appeared on our right side. These barracks housed the various contractors who made the camp hum. They were barbers and janitors. They kept up the fitness center and made sure the internet was working in the computer lab. And they made a shitload more money than we did.

"Get a load of the KBR digs," Mortin snarked over the radio.

"I hear they get fucking HBO and Showtime."

"Oh yeah? You heard that too?"

The motor pool lay on the opposite side of the base from the PX, just shy of a mile's distance, more or less. Attached to the large gravel parking lot was a two-story auto shop, complete with industrial-strength lifts to hoist Humvees and other heavy vehicles up for repairs.

The plateau on which we drove dropped off somewhat, creating a slight change in elevation as we pushed forward, keeping the base's front perimeter wall on our left side.

"Jesus fucking Christ!" Mortin hollered.

"What? What is it?"

"That fucking guy!"

"Who?"

"That fucking hadji! Jesus fucking Christ!"

It occurred to me that Mortin was still reeling from the gravity of what had gone down out in the ECP earlier in the evening, and that unlike myself, he had not been injected with a powerful sedative to help calm his nerves.

"Relax, bro. It's over."

I could hear him exhaling over the comms. I could almost smell his sweat and his fear.

"Try not to think about it. Think about something else."

"I don't fucking know how you're so calm all of the sudden, 'cause you seemed pretty fucking amped up a minute ago when we were all out there with that goddamned, motherfucking hadji!"

I knew that Mortin was smart, at least by military standards, but I did not suspect he knew what I'd been up to. And I felt his pain, I really did. I knew that anything I said to him in the interest of consolation would inevitably fall short or misfire. I knew also that there were other methods of coping with trauma, one in particular, that absolved all sins and transgressions, if only temporarily.

Perhaps if I knew Mortin better, maybe trusted him more, this would have been the ideal opportunity for me to sponsor his initiation into the dope game. But that would have required a great leap of faith on my part, and more importantly, a larger war chest of dry goods. I was running low on supply already without another vein to feed. He would have to settle for some of my generic, sentimental Hollywood bullshit.

"Bro, I'm still amped up. I've just been through it before, and I know that thinking about it over and over, analyzing it again and again in your head, is gonna drive you fucking crazy."

He let out a loud, audible sigh, one I was meant to hear, then let a moment pass before saying, "I don't fucking know, dude. That shit was *insane!*"

Just as Mortin was nearing the end of his rant, we arrived at the motor pool. We drove through the large gravel parking lot that was bordered by a corner section of the base's perimeter, into two adjacent bays of the auto shop. There were three more bays further down.

I killed the radio, pulled off my headset, powered down the Duke, and finally killed the engine, then opened the heavy blast door with my hand, pushed it open with my left arm and left leg, and slid out when the opening grew wide enough. I could never get over how heavy the doors were. Mortin did the same. We met in front of the trucks. The place was alive with mechanics and foremen all bustling around us busily. There were Humvees up on lifts in the bays over from where our trucks were parked, and there were men in grey jumpsuits, some with welding masks on their faces, welding, soldering, banging hammers, and turning wrenches. There were buzzing and clanking and whizzing sounds, and the occasional sortie of flying sparks that fired out from the workstations like bursts of tracer rounds.

A tall, thin worker bee with the top half of his jumpsuit unzipped and tied around his waist passed between me and Mortin, so I grabbed him gently on the inside of this tiny bicep.

"Hey bro, think you could have a look at our trucks?" I pointed to our Humvees.

The grease monkey, who could not have been much more than a day over nineteen, rolled his eyes, looked over his left shoulder at the mounting stockpile of unfinished work in his shop, then back at me, and in a deep Georgian accent asked, "What's wrong with it?"

Baffled somewhat, Mortin and I looked at each other. The rear vehicle had seemed fine to me, and I didn't hear him say anything about the other one on the drive over.

We had been commanded to bring the trucks to the shop, and so we had. We were guys who did things when we were told, not strategists. Ours was not to question why.

"Umm . . ." I pointed to the lead vehicle's front end, where the steel gate at the mouth of the base had scraped against when it opened and let us through.

"We got hit by a V-BID."

The boy's eyes widened and his mouth opened slightly. He began to scratch his shaved head with his right index finger.

"Then how are y'all still in one piece, and how come these trucks ain't blown to hell?"

Mortin and I made eye contact, and from this brief, unspoken exchange it was determined that having already initiated the dialogue with this youngster, it should be me that paints the picture of what had happened in the ECP.

"Well, we *almost* got hit," I went on.

The boy leaned back and panned left to right to take in a full view of both vehicles. Then he began a loop around each one individually. As he was walking he replied, "Aside from that little dinger on the hood and this little boo-boo on the bumper"— he pointed to the back of my vehicle—"neither one of these motherfuckers got a scratch on 'em."

He looked back at us, alternating his gaze from me to Mortin, Mortin to me.

"And what do you mean," he continued, "*almost* got hit? Did he hit a different truck in y'all's convoy?"

"No," Mortin chimed in. "He slammed into that one, which then rear-ended this other one, and pushed it into the front gate."

"Ohhhhh . . ." The boy nodded his head slowly as he thumbed an invisible goatee. "I don't see any frag marks anywhere. You say he hit you? Where at?"

"He hit us in the rear of this truck, like we told you. The explosives didn't fucking detonate, we don't know why. Our Sergeant Major's out there with EOD right now."

"You mean this just happened just now? At the fucking front gate?"

"Yeah," Mortin and I replied in unison, nodding our heads. We made identical faces, indicating our own surprise and disbelief.

"You say it didn't go off?" The boy looked up and in the direction of the front gate with an expression across his face that suggested both confusion and apprehension.

"That's what I said," I repeated. "Our Sergeant Major's out there right now with EOD. They've probably got him wearing that stupid suit with the huge goddamned collar."

The boy settled somewhat, but still appeared to be working out the details in his head.

"What about the driver?" He panned from left to right from Mortin to me with his tiny bird-shaped face. "Y'all shot him?"

I looked at Mortin and he rolled his eyes and shook his head slightly. He knew what was coming.

"Well, Mortin here was in the hatch, you see, and when he pulled his pistol out—"

"Would you shut the fuck up, Rogers! Jesus fucking Christ!"

I could not contain my laughter.

"The fucking fifty-cal jammed, my rifle was in the cab; I pulled my pistol, but when that motherfucker rammed us, it fell out of the truck." He looked at me with disgust. "There, happy?"

"I don't understand," the boy said. "If y'all didn't shoot him, who did?"

"No one," I answered.

"No one?" the boy parroted.

"That's right, no one. The fucking fobbits at the ECP ran and hid like little bitches when that cocksucker rammed us, and fucking numb nuts over here"—I gestured toward Mortin—"dropped his pistol after the gun jammed, so we had to rely on some fucking ANA guard to drag that piece of shit out his Camry and beat his fucking head in."

The boy's eyes widened and his face seemed to indicate a resolution to the mystery that had been puzzling him.

"Man, that's fucked up. I ain't never heard no shit like that before."

"Our Sergeant Major started calling him Rambo, can you believe that shit?" Mortin said.

"Well, the good news is," the boy said, "it doesn't look like there's much more than a scratch here and there on y'all's Humvees." He opened up the front passenger door of the lead vehicle, poked his head inside, then walked around and did the same with the rear vehicle. "Bad news is y'all don't have the new fire suppression systems installed yet, so we're gonna have to go ahead and put those in for you."

Mortin and I looked at each other.

"Well how long is that gonna take?" I asked.

The boy peered out over Mortin's left shoulder into the gravel parking lot of the motor pool where two columns of what looked to be six to eight Humvees sat parked in tight formation.

"A few days."

"Are you fucking kidding me? A few fucking days?" Mortin whined.

"Hey, relax," the boy shot back. "If it was up to me, I'd run a quick diagnostic and get you outta here in a minute. But it come down from on high, any truck comes into the shop gotta get the new fire suppression system installed."

"Yeah, dude, chill out." I put a hand on Mortin's shoulder. "What's your rush anyway? You in a hurry to get back downrange?"

"Y'all should be happy," the boy continued. "Too many soldiers gettin' burned up in them Humvees. This gonna help. If y'all get hit, like for real hit, this new system maybe keep y'all from gettin' burned alive."

"Alright," I said. "We'll see you in a few days I guess."

"Come by tomorrow, this time. It might be done by then."

"Cool, thanks," I said.

"Thank you," Mortin whispered.

We grabbed our weapons and put on our IBAs and Kevlars, and I snatched my medbag by one of its straps and pulled it from the front passenger seat of my vehicle and settled it onto my back. It was nearly impossible to move freely with all the gear on.

We contemplated removing the radios and bringing them with us, but determined that our loads were full already, and the minor infraction of leaving 4th Kandak gear in the trucks unsecured overnight would warrant only a mild tongue-lashing from the Sergeant Major. So long as we came back with our weapons, Kevlars, and IBAs, we would be good to go.

The march back to the rec center would take far longer than the drive over to the motor pool, though Mortin and I would go forward in silence, each man locked into his own meditative rhythm of movement.

The night was cool and dry, and for that I was grateful. The odd soldier or KBR worker would occasionally cross our path on the great plain that connected the base's two wings, but for the most part, we were on our own.

We came upon the complex in which the PX and rec center were both located at what must have been a little past 2300. Despite the relative coolness in temperature, we were both soaked through with sweat from the long haul. And although we'd been issued CamelBaks to help keep us hydrated, neither Mortin nor I had any idea where ours had disappeared to.

Inside the complex, there were a number of different shops and places to eat. On the ground floor there was a Pizza Hut, a sew shop, a store that sold pirated DVDs, and the PX. On the second floor there was a barbershop, a massage parlor, and a large open cafeteria with pool tables on one side and dart boards on the other that we all referred to as the rec center.

In the rec center there was a Green Beans Coffee counter, a little ice cream shop, and a fried chicken restaurant of some unremarkable American franchise. Taken altogether, the complex looked very much like an ordinary shopping center that could be found off either shoulder of I-95.

We entered through the main double doors in the center of the ground level and walked straight through till we found the staircase and walked up. Coming out of the stairwell, the rec center was on our right; the massage parlor, our left. I calculated that leaving the radios in the Humvees was in itself a small crime, but showing up an hour or more late for a muster on top of that would confound the issue unnecessarily. The massage could wait, I told myself.

Mortin and I more or less dragged ourselves the remaining feet of our epic journey from the motor pool, collapsing through the saloon doors of the rec center as though we'd been launched by catapult.

Toby Keith's "Courtesy of the Red, White and Blue" was blasting in the open space from mounted speakers in the four corners of the room. This particular song was very popular among the troops, and seemed to generate a lot of airplay. In fact, there was a whole loop of songs, all espousing a galvanized sense of patriotic ethos, that seemed to be on an infinite repeat cycle. Songs like "God Bless the USA" and "Small Town."

There was no real dancing going on, but the large uniformed bodies, mostly male and Caucasian, that meandered through the large room about the pool tables and dart boards would heave and hoe and nod their heads in accordance with the rhythm of the music.

There were, of course, females present, but the ratio of men to women greatly exceeded the known criteria for what may be called a sausage fest.

Many soldiers wore pistols around their waists or rifles across their chests bound to them by three-point slings, an ingenious design that allows a rifleman to dangle his weapon in front of his chest as though it was a sword suspended in the air, waiting to be drawn.

Many of the men also stacked their rifles against one another, creating miniature black graphite teepee structures, or leaned them against the walls. This was a bit unorthodox, but there was no danger of sabotage so nobody ever raised an eyebrow.

A bar that sold pints of Budweiser for ten bucks apiece stood next to the Green Beans Coffee counter, and though our General Order Number 1 forbade all US forces in theater from imbibing alcoholic beverages, this stipulation was not strictly observed.

And the rec center was not exclusive to US service members and contractors. There were present also soldiers from some of the other NATO countries that had committed themselves to assisting in our war.

In the chairs that appended the many lunch tables opposite the pool tables, they sat huddled in their little camps, talking in almost hushed tones. Ottomans, Greeks, Britains, Mongolians, emissaries of empires past, of one-time world powers, all gathered together here in the land that would not stay conquered for any of them. All that were missing were the Russians.

There was no real tension between the US and NATO troops that ever erupted into any violence, because at the end of the day we were allies, and had much more in common with each others' worldviews than with those of the Taliban, al-Qaeda, or even the host nation for that matter.

But there was a sense of unease, perhaps, that our allies felt at the way we carried on in the rec center as though we owned the place. And they might also have been somewhat bitter or envious that their own empires had come and gone, and that ours was very much in the now.

Mortin and I panted like like a couple of worn-out dogs as we each panned the room in search of our crew. They were nowhere to be found. We had each lost an estimated ten ounces of moisture to sweat on the long march to the rec center, but rather than replace the water we'd spent, we moved with purpose through the maze of gyrating human obstacles to the bar and ordered two pints.

"Oh, man, that feels good going down," Mortin said. I nodded in agreement, but did not take my lips off the glass until all of its contents had been drained into my stomach.

I could feel the alcohol enter my bloodstream almost immediately as a pleasurable rush of warm vibrations crawled up and down my body. The alcohol had created an instant buffer between my last hit and the onset of withdrawals, so I got my fill while I could before the Sergeant Major and the others made their way to the bar and put a stop to it.

"One more," I belched. The girl behind the counter, who I gathered was of Slavic descent, possibly a refugee of the wars in Bosnia and Serbia as many of the KBR staff were known to be, eyeballed me mildly. She knew the rules too and probably had a lot more to lose by breaking them, but she took my glass and refilled it without a word.

"Make it two," Mortin gasped as he slugged the remainder of his pint and slammed it down onto the bar.

The barmaid stared back at us both through her hard Eastern European features, her black ball cap pulled tight around her small head, the letters KBR stenciled in blood red on the front above the bill.

She handed us our drinks and collected the money in silence. Mortin and I clinked glasses and allowed an unspoken prayer for the lost to pass between us before once again putting the glasses to our lips and emptying them. This time Mortin finished first. He slammed his glass down on the bar and let out a loud burp.

"Oh yeah," he sighed after the air had all gone out of his gut.

I finished my pint and slammed it down next to his.

"You said it, man."

After the second beer, the wave really hit me and I felt good. It was nowhere near as intense as a hit of morphine or Dilaudid, and the sensation was not as pleasurable, but I wasn't complaining. A smile broke across my face.

"What?" Mortin asked. He had to shout over the loud music.

"Nothing, bro. I'm just relaxing, that's all," I shouted back.

He smiled, and for a moment it was as though we'd found that backwoods after-party we'd been searching for earlier in the evening.

I was not yet halfway through my twenties and Mortin had celebrated his twenty-first birthday just a few weeks earlier. We were kids, really. Just kids.

I thought for a moment about the people I'd grown up with, how they'd all gone off to fine schools, then found jobs on Wall Street or in law firms or medical practices.

I thought about their wide-open, gut-renovated factory lofts in Soho, or their six-room apartments up and down Park Avenue, where they would settle in with their spouses for a few years, until their own children grew legs and demanded more breathing room.

I imagined what their houses might look like, large brick Georgian Colonials interspersed throughout the dreamy landscapes of backcountry Greenwich, or grand Nantucket-style homes along the shore, when they finally came full circle and moved back to lower Fairfield County.

I thought about how far removed from that world I'd grown. The revolutionary in me cried out, *Injustice!*

But the clearer head, which nearly always prevailed, reminded me of all that I'd had, all I'd been born into, and all I'd let fall by the wayside. For my lot in life, the inevitable consequence of myriad poor decisions and overlooked opportunities, in the end, I had no one but myself to blame.

Out of the corner of my eye, I observed the advisors of 4th Kandak, led by the Sergeant Major, come barreling through the saloon doors of the rec center and toward Mortin and me, though I did not turn to greet them.

They moved all together through the mass of unwinding soldiers and arrived at the bar where Mortin and I had been posted up. I was good and loose at this point, as my tolerance to alcohol had been greatly reduced the months I'd been deployed.

The Sergeant Major stared at Mortin and me. From our faces, and perhaps also our inability to keep from swaying, it was obvious we'd been getting tight.

"What the fuck is going on here?" the Sergeant Major shouted. The music, which had changed to "God Bless the USA," was so loud, we could barely hear the question.

"Nothing, Sergeant Major. We brought the trucks to the shop. Dude said they looked alright, but he'd run a full diagnostic," I answered.

"Good, when are they ready?"

"He said check back tomorrow, but it might be a few days, because they've got to install the new fire suppression systems."

"The what?" I wasn't sure if the Sergeant Major didn't understand what I'd said, or if he simply couldn't hear me over the obnoxiously loud patriotic music.

"The new fire suppression system!" I bellowed. "Every truck has to have one."

"Oh yah?" he responded somewhat indifferently. "I meant what the fuck are you doing right here, right now?" He looked back and forth between Mortin and myself. "You know the goddamned rules!"

Mortin and I looked at one another as though we were two brothers who'd been caught syphoning off booze from our parents' liquor cabinet.

"Fuck it," the Sergeant Major said after a moment or two of not speaking. "Next one's on me!"

A cheer went up among the crew that was barely audible over the music.

"Hey sweetheart, can we get five tall ones?" The Sergeant Major leaned in over the bar and spoke loudly without shouting.

"I won't be needing one, Sergeant Major," Captain Harold snapped.

"Okay, make it four . . ."

"Sergeant Major." Raz put a light hand on the Sergeant Major's arm. "Can we have, too?"

I noticed at that point that our crew had picked up a stray. The ANA guard who'd come to our aid in the ECP was now with us ordering a beer in the rec center. Having Raz with us was in effect a slight security breach, though no one ever made a big deal about it. But bringing the ANA guard up here was a different matter entirely.

"Isn't that against your religion?" the Sergeant Major asked Raz.

"Yes, but . . ." Raz made a strained face, and the Sergeant Major took his meaning.

"Sorry 'bout that, doll. We'll have six."

The barmaid smiled and took the Sergeant Major's money, then started filling pint glasses.

"How did it go with EOD, Sergeant Major?" Mortin asked.

"Funny you should ask," the Sergeant Major replied as he turned his head side to side to make sure everyone was listening.

"The techs said the rig in the Camry was a fucking joke. Said it wasn't even a bomb."

Mortin and I pulled puzzled faces.

"They said there was no way in hell that thing could or would have gone off. There weren't even any explosives in it!"

"What do you mean, Sergeant Major?" I asked.

"Just what I said. It was amateur hour. Just goes to show how fucking useless these cocksuckers really are."

We took a minute to process the revelation.

"You dropped this," the Sergeant Major said to Mortin as he discretely handed him his pistol.

"Thanks, Sergeant Major," Mortin answered in a low tone, his eyes down.

Our drinks began to appear on the bar, and the Sergeant Major picked them up and distributed them to the crew with the exception of Captain Harold, who had voiced his opposition.

"To the fallen." The Sergeant Major raised his glass, signaling to us that we should do the same.

"To the fallen!" we echoed.

CHAPTER 10
KNOWING

It was two or three or maybe five days or more that we were held up at Phoenix, unable to leave post until the new fire suppression systems were successfully installed on both Humvees. Jeffreys, the teenaged mechanic who'd helped us get our trucks looked at, assured me each day I showed up to the motor pool that our vehicles would be ready the same time, the following day.

I certainly was in no position to make a fuss. Jeffreys was a good, solid kid. After the third day or so he opened up to me a bit. It turns out he'd grown up poor and hard in the Atlanta suburb of Marietta. Being born white into that particular environment was no great advantage. But unlike so many from his demographic, he did not harbor any ill will against his black neighbors. In fact, he did not hold any one group in contempt, not even the Afghans, which I'd found curious, considering he'd hardly ever laid eyes on them.

No one in his family had ever graduated high school. Jeffreys himself, had obtained a GED and, with his mother's written consent, enlisted in the Army at seventeen. To him, the service represented an escape from the dead-end cycle of petty crime, drug addiction, and domestic violence he was otherwise destined for. And though he lacked a certain polish or patina, he was no fool. He knew the military was his only way out, and he was happy to serve in combat, so he declared on several occasions, though he knew and I knew that twisting wrenches in the motor pool didn't exactly locate him in the direct path of any great danger.

He never asked about my origins, and I never volunteered anything. Instead, we yammered on a whole range of topics, from girls we knew to films we'd seen to where we'd like to be stationed after our deployments were over and we'd rotated back to the world.

And though our stories were quite different, in fact they were also remarkably similar. We had both sacrificed our personal freedoms and potentially our lives to serve here in this shithole. We both sought redemption, but for different reasons.

And the more people like Jeffreys—good, hard, strong-willed American boys—that I met along the way, the more I valued the collective wealth of human capital my country possessed. And the more I appreciated what I'd had, what I'd let slip away.

The reprieve at Phoenix also afforded me time to correspond with Gomez via Myspace at the MWR Internet café next to the chow hall. Things were really heating up between us, it seemed.

"Can't wait to see you!" she'd written.

"I'll be there soon, leave the light on for me." I responded.

The allure of Gomez's warmth and the understanding that this deployment would one day be over were the only substantive truths that kept me going. My habit was just for routine maintenance.

I'd begun, out of necessity, to ration my intake of morphine and Dilaudid. By this time, the morphine alone could no longer do the trick. I'd managed to get my hands on a bottle of tramadol, a synthetic opioid, which helped somewhat to mitigate the crisis, but was not a long-term solution.

The Troop Medical Clinic at Camp Phoenix was staffed mostly by Navy corpsmen, many of whom had seen intense combat with the Marines in Haditha, Ramadi, and Fallujah, and some who had never before been deployed at all.

Each time I entered the B-hut, I was first greeted as an encroaching rival, then observed as an inferior specimen, and then finally classified as a third-tier medic whose presence was tolerated but not by any means appreciated. Navy corpsmen believe they're God's gift to combat medicine.

I offered several times to assist the doctors in seeing patients at sick call, but was never afforded the opportunity. Instead I was handed a broom and told that if I wanted to help, I should field day the clinic.

Field day, I learned, was Marine-speak for clean the shit out of everything, sweep and mop every surface until they shine like deliverance.

The corpsmen, at least the ones who'd fought in Iraq, were really just Marines in Navy clothing.

I didn't mind being tasked with sweeping and mopping up the floors of the clinic because it allowed me access to the med shelf in the back of the B-hut next to the gurneys and the hospital curtains without drawing anyone's attention.

And though I didn't care for the condescending looks the corpsmen sent my way as I went about my chores, I knew in the end it would all be worth it.

The bottle of tramadol that I nicked was on the med shelf behind some anti-inflammatories and allergy medications. I knew that it would not be missed, at least not right away.

But the true prize lay in the narc locker, a simple cabinet secured with a standard padlock.

I knew there would be a plethora of hard-hitting intravenous narcotics behind that cabinet door—enough to keep me riding high till we made it back to the Meth Lab. But only the medical officers and the head corpsman had keys, and as far as I knew, they carried them on their persons at all times, linked into the chain necklaces that also held their dog tags.

This would not be a simple quid pro quo like it had been with Ghazzi. I could not bribe these men with porn. They had all the porn I had and more. I would have to procure a key from one of them.

The medical officers were impossible marks. There were two of them. Both Air Force, and both highly impersonal. They slept in the officers' berthing, a threshold I dared not approach without a legitimate reason. Their keys were well beyond my reach.

The key, on the other hand, that belonged to the head corpsman, HM1 Burke, was the only real option. Burke was a six-footer, a big, burly man in his late twenties, I estimated. His hair—what little he had atop his nearly shaved head—was a very light blond hue. His eyes were ice-colored, like the eyes of an arctic wolf.

He was hard; there was no denying it. He'd spent six years in various infantry battalions of the 1st Marine Division. He'd been out to sea with the Marines, and had twice deployed to Iraq. He was there for the ground invasion in March 2003. He didn't talk very much. He didn't have to. His hard silence was enough usually to compel those around him to behave accordingly.

As far as I could tell, he kept the key on him at all times. I learned this the hard way, by stalking his movements, appearing out of thin air in places where I knew he would also be.

Burke grew weary of my presence after one too many coincidental encounters, and shot me a look outside the chow hall that communicated with perfect clarity the value of his unspoken words.

I stayed away from HM1 Burke after that, but continued to frequent the TMC after I'd met with Jeffreys at the motor pool, or Myspaced Gomez from the MWR room.

While we were at Phoenix, life became somewhat docile and serene again, and I was reminded of the time I'd spent at Camp Cobra before I was assigned to 4th Kandak.

The only real concern I had was for my vanishing supply of narcotics. I had to both increase the time intervals between treatments and lower the dosage in order to make the hits last until the next re-up.

Occasionally I would see Pat Tillman moving freely about the base. Every time he would be incognito, dressed one day as an Air Force general, the next as an ANA or Romanian Army soldier.

And always, he would cast a knowing glance in my direction, and I in his, and from this small, almost negligible interaction, I would know that however minor or inconsequential a role I played presently, in the end, I would be an integral part of a major mission in the Afghan war. One for the record books; possibly a definitive climax that would usher in a unilateral victory for Coalition forces.

We were desperate for such a triumph in America; a successful, well-justified campaign that might steam clean the stench of Operation Iraqi Freedom off our soiled hands.

After all, it was *we* who were struck first by the terrorist horde. And the attacks of September 11 weren't even the first or second or even third time they'd hit us.

There was the first Trade Center bombing, then the twin attacks on our embassies in Kenya and Tanzania. Then there was the suicide dingy that tore a hole the width of the Lincoln Tunnel through the belly of the USS *Cole* in the Gulf of Aden, off the coast of Yemen.

The campaign in Iraq had since confounded the issue, but we were in the right in Afghanistan. We were justified in our invasion. And only a complete military victory over the Taliban and al-Qaeda could defray the tragedy of Iraq. I knew it. Pat Tillman knew it. There was something big about to go down, and we would both be key players, I was certain.

I also noticed the sweeping, pulsating light that beamed on at a great distance several times during my walks through the base. I wondered if the light had something to do with the mission. I had asked Pat Tillman about it as we passed the football back and forth outside the HESCO barrier at Bagram talking about what a pussy Tom Brady was, but he was reluctant to discuss the details. It was probably not the opportune moment to disclose such information, I thought.

Rambo, the ANA guard who'd come, baton wielding, to our aid in the ECP the day of our incident, had been elevated in rank. I noticed that he had been issued a pair Army Combat Uniform fatigues, the grey, digi-patterned-style blouse and trousers that were by now infamous the world over; the same uniform that we wore.

On his nameplate read the word "RAMBO" in big block letters. I suspected the Sergeant Major had something to do with that, but there was no way of knowing for certain.

And he had been issued a weapon, something very unusual for an Afghan that guarded a Coalition checkpoint to have.

Because the entryway to Camp Phoenix literally opened up into downtown Kabul, there was not enough room for two checkpoints. Most other bases had an exterior entry point guarded by ANA soldiers, then a Coalition checkpoint, almost invariably guarded by Americans. The ANA guards that manned the outer checkpoints were armed with Kalashnikovs. This was normal.

The absence of an outer checkpoint at Phoenix created a unique situation, and the leadership thought it best not to issue firearms to the ANA guards, for whatever reason. Perhaps they considered it somewhat of a security risk. I couldn't say for certain.

But Rambo, through his selflessly brave act the previous week, had earned the respect and trust of the higher-ups, and had hence been issued an AK-47 of his own.

Inevitably, the day came when our trucks, now fitted with the finest in fire suppression technology that money could buy, were ready for pick up.

"Looks like your little vay-cay come to an end, brother," Jeffreys chided me at the motor pool. "Time to get back to work, earn ya keep!"

"Don't fucking remind me, dude," I said. We both laughed. It was a nice time. Jeffreys was a good man.

Our vehicles had been parked out in the gravel parking lot beside the giant garage, where men at work carried on busily as though there had been no pause or interruption to their labor from the moment Mortin and I had come by to have our trucks inspected.

I took one of the Humvees to the TMC for the purpose of loading a dry ice cooler into the trunk space, during which time I also made my farewells to the staff of corpsmen who did little more than raise their eyes to mine and nod. This gesture was a ruse on my part, a carefully timed maneuver I'd executed to get an idea of exactly how many of them were around, and might be loitering about the premises after dark.

HM1 Burke shot me an especially cold glance as I stood in the middle of the treatment room, and with that I set myself to the task of moving the cooler. I also grabbed a few Ace wraps, some Israeli bandages, a few splints, some Kerlix gauze, and some tape. No one seemed to mind. There was no shortage of medical supplies at Camp Phoenix.

I eyeballed the narc locker one last time before heading out to the truck, dry ice cooler in tow.

Back at the transient tent the crew lay sprawled out in their racks, uniforms relaxed, boots removed. Lieutenant Grey was laid out in a bottom bunk, legs crossed, with his laptop opened and balanced across his chest. Shrieking, histrionic moans shaped by what sounded to be Russian or Ukrainian accents emanated from the machine. The voices sounded familiar to me.

"What's up, Doc?" Lieutenant Grey asked without removing his gaze from the screen.

"Doing alright, I guess." I looked around at the crew, each man in his own unique temporary world.

"What are you watching, LT?"

"It's the one with all those Romanian bitches," the Sergeant Major inserted himself into the conversation from the rack next to Lieutenant Grey's. "From the thumb drive you gave me before we left the Meth Lab. The one with all the butt lickin', remember?"

"How do you know they're Romanian, Sergeant Major?"

Some chuckles arose from soldiers of other units with whom we shared the tent.

"'Cause of the way they twist and bend like they grew up in the fucking circus!"

More laughs.

"In my mind they were two Ukrainian college students who got freaky in a dorm room one night during the Orange Revolution."

"Nope, sorry. They're two just two plain old Romanian sluts who love to lick pussy. Sorry to burst your bubble, Doc."

"No worries, Sergeant Major."

"I like this kind of girls," Raz reported from an unseen corner of the tent.

"What the fuck difference does it make where they're from?" Mortin joined the discussion from the bunk above the Sergeant Major's.

"Context," I replied.

"Context? What the fuck are you talking about, *context*?" Lieutenant Grey asked, taking his bespectacled eyes off the computer screen for the first time and looking up at me.

"Yeah, Doc. What the fuck are you saying?" A soldier laid out in the top rack across the squad bay from Mortin, no one I'd ever before seen or spoken to, repeated Lieutenant Grey's initial challenge.

"Those videos that you watch," I paused, "that we all watch … they're designed to take you out of your world. They're fantasy, that's why we love them so much; because they can never truly be."

The faces around me appeared somewhat puzzled, as though they were struggling with the concepts I'd laid out, but were not altogether dumbfounded.

"It's innate to our being, this desire to be deceived," I continued. "But the deception must be somewhat plausible, otherwise we'll tear it apart in our minds."

A cool silence hung heavy in the tent. I felt both strong and wise for the first time in a great while.

"Man, they're just two bitches taking turns going down on each other, that's all." The soldier in the top rack broke the silence. "Why you gotta read all that into it, Doc? Why can't you just enjoy it for what it is, two pretty ladies getting to know each other a little better?"

At this the room exploded into heavy laughter, the kind reminiscent of the moments inside of the front gate just after our mishap with the would-be suicide bomber. Everyone in the tent within earshot of the soldier laid out across the bay from Mortin was in stitches, with the exception of myself and Captain Harold.

"You know, Doc is right," the captain entered finally into the dialogue. "Though I myself choose to abstain from the viewing of such filth, I believe there's a lesson to be learned in what Specialist Rogers said about man's innate desire to be deceived." The laughing softened to a dull roar.

"And the bit about the deception having to be at least somewhat credible, otherwise our comprehension will break it down—that made real sense to me, Doc. Thank you for sharing."

"Aww, isn't that sweet?" the Sergeant Major mocked.

"Good to know, Captain Harold," I sincerely replied. "Good news, by the way." I addressed the gathering as a whole. "The Humvees are ready. I know you're all in such a hurry to get back downrange."

"Alright," the Sergeant Major grunted as he raised himself up from the bottom bunk. "Listen up. Police up your gear, everyone. Vacation's over. Doc and Mortin, bring the trucks over to the rec center parking lot." He looked at his watch. "It's too late to roll out today; we'll never make it back before dark, and I don't wanna take any fucking chances out east. We leave tomorrow. Reveille is zero four hundred. We're at the trucks four thirty; zero five, we roll out."

"Roger that," I said.

"Good to go," Mortin said.

"I'll be back in a few minutes," Lieutenant Grey said as he got up from his rack and headed for the porto-shitter outside, laptop in tow, with the video he was watching still playing. The climactic moans of the two Eastern European girls died down slowly as he moved away from the group toward the tent's exit.

"Filth," Captain Harold said as he got up from his bottom bunk to stretch.

With the exception of personal weapons, IBAs, and Kevlars, no one had any major items to carry back to the trucks. After all, we'd left the radios and the crew-served weapons locked up in each truck's cab.

So after Mortin and I finished bringing the two refitted Humvees—one of them containing a dry ice cooler and fresh medical supplies—to the parking lot beside the rec center, we strolled unhurriedly through the base back toward the tent.

I had been fighting the onset of withdrawals for at least a few days by this point, but, to my knowledge, no one from the team was yet aware of my dilemma. Mortin and I refrained from bantering on the walk back, and I took the quiet opportunity to try and convince myself that the withdrawals weren't real.

Every junky approaches this challenge in his own way, because at some point, in the life of every addict, sooner or later the dope runs out. Lower-end fiends, bums, street walkers and the like face this obstacle more frequently on account of their lower economic status and inability to hold onto or accrue any measure of sustainable wealth beyond the next hit. They are hence grittier, and able to more easily access the place within themselves where the pain and horrors of dope sickness can be ignored or tolerated.

But hop heads of the upper echelons, men and women, boys and girls—for whom the question of monetary means is no question at all—face shortages of product and failed acquisitions themselves, and must, in their own way, come to terms with the inevitable truth that without the dose to which they have become intrinsically accustomed, they are in for some real terror.

I myself chose to focus on the positive. I was still in possession of two 10mg hits of morphine sulfate: one auto-injector and one syringe. I could tolerate the sweats, the fear and paranoia and feelings of impending doom so long as I could believe there was a light at the end of the tunnel.

When we got back to the tent I broke off from Mortin and headed for the latrine trailer to dose. I used the syringe, jabbing the needle through the worn-down little yellow rubber stopper connected to my saline lock. The contraption had been fused to my left arm for longer than I cared to acknowledge. Early signs of infection, a very light green color outlining the shape of my vein and an overall look of consigned flesh around the area, were evident. The site was sensitive to the touch.

I pressed down on the plunger as hard as I could with my thumb so the pressure would force the liquid morphine through the blood clot that had formed inside the saline lock. I knew this was an incredibly dangerous and foolish thing to do, but I did not have a spare syringe to flush the site with normal saline on me, and the sickness was beginning to take hold.

An unbelievably sharp pain ripped through my arm, up to my shoulder and down to my fingers. It felt as though I'd shot myself up with sulfuric acid. A fierce burning and tingling sensation, like I'd smashed my funny bone against a brick wall.

"Ahhhhh!!!" I shouted. Then the drug began to calm my nerves, and I slumped backward on the toilet seat so that my back rested against the hard plastic tank. I stayed there a minute and breathed very heavily.

The hit was not strong enough to incite a full-on nod, but it did help stave off the symptomatic progression of withdrawals.

I lay in my rack that night, unable to sleep, as the euphoria of the hit evaporated from my being into the open tent like waves of body heat. And each degree of pleasant bliss that dissipated as the drug continued to slowly wear off was replaced by an increment of elevated discomfort. I could feel my muscles tighten as though they were tethered to a winch that would, every so often, be ratcheted up a quarter turn.

I swallowed my last handful of Tramadols and drifted somewhat into a contested middle ground between sleep and consciousness.

I could tell from all the futzing around in the tent that it was 4:00 A.M. or somewhere thereabouts. The sound of zippers zipping, bootlaces rustling through eyelets, and heavy breathing in the dark informed my sense of things that it was now time to wake up and get moving.

I tore myself from the rack, dressed quickly, and assembled my gear. My skin felt like it was crawling with spiders, and the fear I had come to live with it for a long time now was especially intense.

There was, in fact, a hybrid of two great fears; the first being the elongated, natural fear of physical harm that had stalked me from the moment I received orders to deploy.

The second, and by far the more urgent of the two presently, was the neurological apprehension caused by my body's unmet demand for more opiates. Real opiates.

Each small movement required great effort, though it was crucial to avoid making strained faces or expressing pain in any way. The last thing I needed was the Sergeant Major on my case even more.

We walked to the trucks in silence, each of us in a mind-state known only to those who've been conjured from sleep in the early morning hours to carry out a duty or task for which they will not be duly compensated or recognized. It was a thankless job in many ways, this business of war.

But forward we went, placing one foot unmistakably in front of the next. I was grateful that the others looked so poorly, as it meant I would fit in more easily as one of them and not call unnecessary attention to myself.

The air was crisp and cool, and bright shimmering stars dotted the sky like grains of silver dust blown over a canvas stained in black oil paints.

"Same trucks as before, everybody," the Sergeant Major spoke up as we arrived at the rec center parking lot and began the process of unlocking the vehicles, mounting weapons, and doing comms checks.

"No need to go changing things, we're just headed back to Mehtar Lam. I got a call from the Colonel late last night. He's fucking pissed off we've been on the road so long. Turns out he's been up Peeve's ass trying to figure out what we've been up to this whole time."

We all laughed. No one recognized the leadership of Major Peeve. It was in everyone's best interest that he'd stayed back at the Meth Lab. He'd have only gotten in the way, and God forbid we got into a scrape, I doubted seriously he'd have had the sense to execute his own response, let alone lead the crew in any type of defensive action.

"We need to get back right away," the Sergeant Major went on. "Should be there by lunch time. Who knows, maybe we'll get lucky with some Mongolian barbecue."

This was, of course, a joke. Mongolian barbecue wasn't even on the menu at the Army-staffed Mehtar Lam chow hall. More likely there would be a platter of boiled burgers or steaks, baked potatoes, and whatever else.

Sunlight began to flood the sky, the stars began disappearing. It was light enough to see clearly, but not quite sunup. The pre-convoy tasks seemed to drag on and the Sergeant Major occasionally yelled or snarled something awful at the crew, though not at anyone specifically, in order to hasten our departure.

The marching order was Captain Harold in the driver's seat, the Sergeant Major in the turret, and Raz in shotgun for the lead vehicle, and myself in shotgun, Mortin up top, and Lieutenant Grey behind the wheel bringing up the rear.

As we pulled into the ECP, this time facing the opposite direction, I noticed Rambo smiling and waving on the port side of the convoy, his AK-47 already caked in a thick layer of red dust.

The Sergeant Major waved back from the turret of the lead vehicle, and Mortin waved from the the rear. Then Rambo made a stopping gesture with his hand directed at Lieutenant Grey.

The steel gate closed behind us and sunlight caught the scrape mark where it had rubbed against the Sergeant Major's Humvee during the botched vehicle-borne IED strike. I observed the flash of bright light reflected by the gate's scar through the oblong passenger side-view mirror. I wanted to wait until we were well off the base before hitting myself with the 10mg auto-injector, but with every second I could feel the sickness getting worse and worse.

As we were rolling out, Lieutenant Grey hailed the lead vehicle. "Horseman One, this is Two, hang on a minute. This 'Rambo' dude is trying to tell me something."

"Roger that, make it quick. We don't have time for this bullshit," the Sergeant Major responded.

I saw through the thick plexiglass driver-side window Rambo make a come hither gesture toward Mortin, who was in the turret. What happened next was difficult to comprehend.

All perception is inherently flawed. When we first experience something, when it happens in real time, we're not able to evaluate it properly because there's simply too much going on. And in the moment, we do not have the benefit of hindsight.

But when we reexamine an experience through the lens of memory, the mind cannot reproduce the urgency of the event, no matter how hard we try to recall it. In either situation, in real time, or in memory, our perception of things is imperfect.

What, according to memory, might in retrospect feel like an obvious warning sign—a certain look in Rambo's eye and his posture as he stood tall out in the ECP—may in fact be a contrivance implemented after the fact by an unreliable narrator doing his best to make sense of a moment in which things went horribly wrong. There's simply no way of knowing for certain.

I heard the shots, seven or ten rounds fired off in rapid succession by the fully automatic weapon of the ANA guard Rambo, who had days earlier beaten a man to death with a riot baton for slamming into our vehicle in a white Toyota Camry.

I heard Mortin scream through the comms, though his scream morphed suddenly into a kind of choking, drowning sound, almost as though something had lodged in his throat.

More shots followed. It was difficult to say who exactly was firing from my position in the front seat.

Mortin collapsed onto the steel grate of the gunner's platform in the cab, clutching at his throat with both hands. His legs were suspended by the thick leather strap. It looked like he'd fallen backwards off a swing. I leaped into the back and tried to figure out exactly where he'd been hit.

Thick spurts of fresh blood began to burst through his closed hands and I realized that I would not have much time to work.

"Mortin!" I screamed. "Mortin! Mortin! Mortin!" I must have called his name a hundred times as I dug through my medbag for an occlusive dressing.

"Fuck!" Lieutenant Grey screamed.

The problem was twofold: he had been hit at least once in the throat, an area that is vulnerable to both hemorrhage from a ruptured jugular vein or carotid artery, as well as a compromised airway secondary to puncture of the trachea.

"Mortin! Mortin!" I continued.

"Fuck! Fuck!" Lieutenant Grey shouted. "We're fucking trapped! Fuck! Horseman One, this is Horseman Two, we're fucking pinned down right here, pull forward and let us the fuck out, over!"

"Mortin! Mortin!" I shouted at the top of my lungs.

Finally, I managed to get the occlusive dressing over the wound in Mortin's neck, which was quickly filling up with blood. I had to fight him to remove his hands from his throat.

"Horseman Two, this is One. There's traffic backed up to the exit up here, we can't move forward! He's hiding out behind your back left tire. The fobbits are trying to get him, but he's dug in right there, over."

The trouble with neck wounds is that they require firm, steady pressure to arrest any blood flow from the laceration. But it's very easy to apply too much pressure and crush the patient's airway.

"Fuck!" Lieutenant Grey shouted. "Fuck!"

I was able stop the bleeding and keep the airway open using an occlusive dressing. With some gauze, I wiped off the blood around the edges of the square-shaped plastic sheet, and taped the corners down so it would stay. All the while Mortin continued to hack up more blood through his mouth and struggled to breath.

"Morphine," he pleaded.

"What?" I asked.

"Morphine," he said again, between gurgles and blood bubbles.

"You're gonna be alright, dude, just trust me. You're gonna be all good, I promise."

"He's asking for morphine, Doc!" Lieutenant Grey shouted from the driver seat. "Hit him with fucking morphine already!"

I heard the Sergeant Major hail the TOC over the radio. "Phoenix TOC, this is Horseman One. We're in a firefight in the ECP, over."

The shooting outside continued. As far as I could tell, the Sergeant Major had opened up the 240 Bravo just a hair. But he was using his rounds sparingly, I imagined, because one shot through the windshield of our truck could take out all three of us in the rear vehicle.

"Roger that, Horseman One, we've got a QRF team on their way out to you now."

There were shots coming from the guard tower also.

"Don't tell me how to do my fucking job!" I shouted back at Lieutenant Grey. "He's fucking critical right now; touch and go!"

"Morphine," Mortin gasped.

The noise of the gunfire penetrated the armor of our Humvee. Inside the cab it sounded like firecrackers.

"Phoenix TOC, this is Horseman Two," Lieutenant Grey shouted. "Where's that fucking QRF team, over?"

"Morphine," Mortin begged.

"Doc, give that fucking kid some goddamned morphine!" Lieutenant Grey screamed.

Shots, presumably fired from the guard tower, began to rain down on our truck's sloping hatchback.

"Goddamn it!" Lieutenant Grey shouted.

"Mortin!" I screamed.

"Morphine," Mortin implored me.

"Doc, if you don't hit that fucking kid with some morphine, I'm gonna climb back there and do it for you, and then you and me are gonna have some fucking issues, you hear me!"

"Horseman Two, this is Horseman One. We hit him . . . he's still alive out there, but we got him, I'm sure of it, over."

"Morphine," Mortin groveled.

"I don't fucking have anymore!"

"Roger that, Horseman One. That's a good copy, over," Lieutenant Grey answered the Sergeant Major, then turned back around to face my direction.

"What the fuck are you talking about, Doc? You haven't treated anyone since that fucking hadji kid back at Mehtar Lam, and that was weeks ago!"

There was a level of recognizable betrayal in his voice. "How did you go through all your issue unless you been using it yourself, huh Doc? Fucking answer me!"

The shots outside the truck had become fewer and farther between, but there were still some volleys here and there. The fight was winding down.

"I've got one left." As I said the words, I felt the full force of my withdrawal symptoms take hold as I came to the realization that only this 10mg auto-injector of morphine sulfate lay between myself and total ruin.

And my friend and colleague lay beside me less than halfway through a slow, painful death. I pulled the hit from my cargo pocket and stared at it until the literature printed in a ring around its shape began to blur.

"Morphine," Mortin gagged. He tried to lift his hand but was unable.

"Doc!" Lieutenant Grey shouted.

"Aghhhhh!!!!!" I cried out loud as I slammed the last hit of my stash into Mortin's thigh and watched the pain melt from his face.

CHAPTER 11
BECAUSE

Almost immediately after I'd deposited the ten milligrams of morphine sulfate into Mortin's thigh, I felt the full fury of my own withdrawals come on so strong that I had to seal my mouth shut with both hands to keep from vomiting all over my patient. Sweat and fear and a dull ache that seemed to radiate outward from my bones. A part of me secretly wished to trade places with Mortin.

He was a goner, I could tell. I'd seen enough casualties in the late stages of trauma to know when it was over.

Lieutenant Grey kept shouting at the Phoenix Tactical Operations Center to open the front gate so we could drive to the TMC, but they steadfastly refused on account of the active firefight still ongoing in the ECP. With the gate closed, as far as they were concerned, the situation was contained.

"We got a kid fucking dying back here, open the fucking gate!"

"We can't, sir, not while there are still shots being fired in the ECP. It's against SOP. I'm sorry, there's nothing we can do. There's a QRF team on their way out to you now. Stand by, over."

"Open that fucking gate!"

"Not while that insurgent is still firing on us."

"He's no goddamned insurgent, he's the fucking ANA guard you idiots gave an AK-47 to!"

"We didn't give an AK-47 to anyone, sir. We're just following orders."

"Fuck this!" Lieutenant Grey shouted as he hurled the little black comms box with the toggle switch at the passenger-side window, threw the truck into reverse, and hammered his foot down on the accelerator.

My body slammed into the back end of the driver's seat.

We made contact, and I heard a loud thump, and what sounded like a shriek, but the gate did not give, so Lieutenant Grey pulled forward, nearly smashing into the Sergeant Major's vehicle, and then threw the truck into reverse a second time, making another run for it.

This time the truck caught air on the back left side. Mortin and I were thrown upward momentarily, and then dropped back down on the hard steel plate of the gunner's platform. It felt as though we'd gone over a speed bump.

"Careful!" I shouted at Lieutenant Grey. "I don't want his dressings to come undone!"

"Roger that," he responded. "Hold onto him, we're gonna hit it again."

Lieutenant Grey pulled the truck forward a second time, shifted into reverse, then held the brake pedal and accelerator down at the same time. I could feel the tires spinning as the Humvee's back end fishtailed slightly from side to side. The hard rubber of the tires ground into the gravel surface, and I heard and felt tiny gravel pebbles being thrown up into the undercarriage by the spinning wheels.

"Horsemen Two, what the fuck are you doing, over?"

"Horseman One, Mortin's been hit and these fucking fobbits won't open the goddamned gate, so I'm opening it for them!"

With that Lieutenant Grey released his foot from the brake and we lurched backward, caught air on the left side again Then struck the gate at full speed, knocking it backward off its hinges.

"Horseman Two, I think you got him. I say again, the shooter is down. It looks like a real mess. We're right behind you, we'll see you at the TMC, over," said the Sergeant Major.

We rolled over the crumpled gate on the ground, spun around, shifted gears, and began to move forward. I did my best to keep Mortin from being thrown all over, but it was impossible. The fast, unpredictable movement of the vehicle exacerbated my illness and nausea.

By the time we made it to the TMC, the corpsmen had been alerted to the situation and had brought a gurney out to the entrance of the B-hut. Lieutenant Grey stopped the vehicle and we went through the motions of transporting Mortin from the truck to the gurney and then into the TMC. There was blood on the steel platform and blood on my boots and on my uniform, and all over Mortin.

One of the corpsmen called in a 9-Line medevac, citing the category of his condition as Urgent Surgical.

I went along with them, racing to get him onto the gurney, though I was sure that by this time he had stopped breathing.

"Let's go, let's move!" HM1 Burke shouted. I think that was the first time I'd ever heard him speak.

"Get him inside! Check those interventions, get an IV started!"

"I hit him with ten milligrams of morphine," I said aloud.

"You what?" Burke questioned me.

My sickness was becoming intolerable. The intensity of the situation had elevated my anxiety to an unstable level. And with Mortin now in the hands of the corpsmen, I found myself slipping off to a space in between the TMC B-hut and another B-hut that housed some administrative element of the war.

When I knew I was alone I reached for my pistol with my right hand. This was not the way I had imagined things would end.

It felt, at that point, as though my life had been a great dig. As far back as I could remember, I'd been digging and digging myself deeper into a spiritual and emotional void that had no clear end in sight. The drugs were really just the manifestation of an innate need to hide from a whole host of weaknesses and other character defects. The morphine was an advanced digging tool.

Though presently, I found myself stuck deep in the hole I'd spent my life tilling, without the necessary gear to dig further, and with no possible means of escape. I began to feel the hole closing in. Sand rained down I thought to myself, this is it.

I gripped my pistol in its holster, closed my eyes, and breathed deeply. But when I went to pull it out, it wouldn't budge. I tugged again, then noticed a hand, not my own, holding tightly onto my blouse's sleeve at the wrist.

"Hey Doc." I turned my head slightly to the right to see who it was interfering with my exit strategy.

"I think you dropped these."

The man yanked my hand off my pistol and pushed a handful of syringes and auto-injectors of Dilaudid and morphine sulfate into my opened palm. I recognized the texture of the drugs immediately without even having to look at them.

"Thank you, Captain Harold," I said.

"No sweat, Doc." He smiled and put a hand on my shoulder. "It must have been really difficult for you to see Mortin get hit like that." He made a sad, empathetic face. "Why don't you take a minute, get sorted out, then come back to us." He said it with a slight nod of his head, as though he was reaffirming his own suggestion.

"Okay," I said.

Then he disappeared. I didn't care where he'd gone to; it didn't make any difference. I'd gotten what I needed, and I was grateful. I didn't question the motives or the origin behind my gifts. I didn't have time to. Every fraction of my focus was committed to the mission of getting the dope into my system immediately.

I chose one of the Dilaudid syringes, unzipped my blouse, and pushed the needle head through the saline lock's little yellow stopper and threw myself back against the wall of the B-hut as the rush overwhelmed my senses.

The hit burned and tingled, put the pain was no match for the strength of the dose. I swore to myself I would change out the saline lock before we left post.

I took a minute to get myself together before returning to the TMC. I donned my black ballistic sunglasses and made sure they weren't crooked on my face. My head felt like a thousand-pound bowling ball, bobbling and swiveling on the axis of my C-spine.

When I resurfaced, I observed the mood had altered dramatically. The great sense of urgency was gone, replaced by a solemn, thick silence. Heads hung low; I did my best to take stock of the situation.

"Where the fuck did you go?" I heard a voice shout at me.

"I couldn't look at him like this, I'm sorry," I answered.

HM1 Burke approached me and his affect softened. He put a hand on my shoulder.

"I get it, bro, I've been there."

I felt a great swell of sadness engulf my abdomen, and without realizing it, I began to weep. A few silent tears slipped down under my sunglasses, followed shortly by fits of sobbing.

"That occlusive dressing you put on was perfect," he said comfortingly. "And you did the right thing hitting him with morphine. There was no way he could've survived. And you made his last few moments a little more tolerable."

I continued to cry openly.

"You're a good medic, Rogers," he went on. "Your crew is lucky to have you."

After a minute or so, I grabbed hold of myself and got it together.

"Where is he now?" I said.

"He's bagged up in the TMC. We changed the 9-Line from Urgent Surgical to Expectant, so it'll be a while before the bird gets here if you wanna go in and say good-bye."

I took a minute, breathed deeply a few times.

"No that's alright. I'd rather not."

"I understand."

Several hours passed by in relative quiet. Our two Humvees remained parked out in front of the TMC and the occasional curious soldier or contractor walking by would approach the scene to get a better look, and upon examination, either stick around and try to be useful in some way, or continue on about their business and not concern themselves with the matter.

The base went black. All nonessential comms were shut down. The MWR computer lab was temporarily closed. This was business as usual following a casualty. The black-out policy had been put in place to ensure the victim's next of kin was notified before any news outlet caught wind of the incident.

And oftentimes the deaths out here went under noticed or ignored completely back home, overshadowed by high death tolls in Anbar Province and other regions of Iraq.

Mortin was from Texas. One of the rich Dallas suburbs, I believe. He was an unusual specimen for the enlisted Army, in that he was able to effortlessly speak in complete, grammatically sound sentences. Perhaps that was why we were friends.

Evenings at Camp Cobra, before I'd been assigned to 4th Kandak, we would meet in the chow hall and make turkey sandwiches and confess our true hatred of the Army and the dumbass, down-home farm boys who ran it. There had been an understanding between us that we had more in common with one another than either of us did with anyone else we'd met in-country. He'd only been dead a few hours, but already, I missed him terribly.

The inside of my arm, where I had installed the saline lock, was beginning to ache. I knew that I could no longer put off the task of changing it out, but there were too many bodies, alive and dead, in and around the TMC. I would have to wait.

Mortin had been in the bag a few hours already by the time they brought him out. It was decided that he would be carried to the medevac rather than wheeled on a gurney, because the terrain was too uneven for the gurney's wheels.

It was decided also, in the unspoken language of head nods and steady eye contact, that the advisors of 4th Kandak, 1st Brigade, including our interpreter, Raz Mohammed, would be the ones to carry him to the helicopter.

We tried at first to hoist the bag up to shoulder level and carry Mortin in a dignified way, as though we were pallbearers at his funeral ferrying him high in the air to his final resting place.

But the bag's design made this effort cumbersome, so we settled on each grabbing a side or a corner of black leather and carrying him at waist level.

The Sergeant Major and myself supported the front left and right corners respectively, while Captain Harold and Lieutenant Grey each held up a back corner. Raz Mohammed supported the right flank. An unknown soldier held up the left side.

We moved quietly toward the reverberating vortex of the medevac bird. The aircraft was a Huey, the so-called workhorse of Vietnam. The airfield lay roughly a quarter mile from the TMC, next to the motor pool.

As we moved forward, a procession of Navy corpsmen from the TMC and other soldiers and airmen who'd gathered outside followed at a short distance. Contractors and soldiers who obstructed our path got out of the way and stood at attention. Those who were in uniform saluted.

The cyclone of wind and dust kicked up by the tremendous force of the aircraft's rotary wings grew more intense with every step we took. Dirt and small pebbles began to strike me, and I had to raise my arm up to my face in order to keep from inhaling the flying debris.

As the bird came down we moved toward it, established eye contact with the crew chief, then passed the black leather bag to the flight medics onboard. The whole interaction took only a few seconds. The bird did not even touch down. There were no words exchanged, and even if there had been, the sound of the blades tearing through the air like the wings of a giant humming bird would have drowned them out.

And then he was gone. Hoisted into the aircraft, whisked away to Bagram Airfield for processing, then on to Landstuhl, Germany, and eventually to Dover Air Force Base in Delaware, the place of reception for every military service member killed in-theater.

They would drape an American flag over his coffin, and high-ranking military officials would salute him as he deplaned the aircraft.

He might be alone, or perhaps with a small group, or if there was a particularly large battle or an extremely well-timed IED strike in Fallujah or Ramadi or even elsewhere in Afghanistan, he might be consolidated into a larger unit of casualties.

It made sense logistically to bring as many bodies home in one trip as was humanly possible. Sometimes, the corpses would wait on ice in Bagram, Baghdad, or Landstuhl until there were enough of them to fill the cargo space of a C-130.

It was more efficient that way, and it created fewer opportunities for news agencies to film and broadcast the ceremonies.

We watched the bird disappear into the late afternoon sun, the fury of its engines and fan blades fading to a low hum as it drifted off into the distance.

We then looked at each other, but said nothing. Now, we were five again. The loss was great emotionally, but in the operational sense, we were now short one man in an already small crew.

And though we had not set out from Mehtar Lam with Mortin on our team, we had since come to rely on him for his expertise with the radios and helping out with much of the heavy lifting.

Going forward, all of the necessary low-end, menial tasks would fall onto me and only me, the first of which would be scrubbing down grated steel plate onto which my friend Mortin had bled to death.

It would have made more sense to clean the blood off right away before it coagulated into thick sticky globs. But it would have been bad form not to wait until Mortin had been handed off..

In the interest of redefining my role within the crew I took the initiative and began the cleansing process on my own, without being told to. The corpsmen from the TMC of course helped. It was not the first time many of them had sanitized the interior of a Humvee, nor would it be the last.

We carried on in silence. I was grateful that the wounds inflicted on Mortin did not sever his major organs or shatter any major skeletal structures. There was no brain matter or skull fragments. There was only blood.

We used spray bottles of 409 and regular sponges to scrub away the stains. The consistency of dried blood is not unlike that of dried maple syrup. But for the obvious difference in color, cleaning the grated steel plate was like cleaning a breakfast plate gunked up with maple syrup and the occasional bit of leftover pancake.

When we were finished, the plate shined brightly as the waning sunshine funneled down through the hatch.

There was also some blood on the truck's back left corner and on the tires, from when we ran down Rambo, which we managed to take care of with a garden hose.

Once the truck had been cleaned thoroughly, I knew which it would have to be brought back to the motor pool. The back hatch had been penetrated with a salvo of 5.56 rounds presumably fired by the fobbits in the guard tower. Thankfully, none of the large gas cans tethered to the vehicle's back corners were struck during the fight.

Also, there was the possibility of structural damage from the impact when the truck hit the front gate.

And, unrelated to the truck, there was the gate itself which, having been torn off its hinges, had created a major security breach that would undoubtedly rouse the interest of the garrison's higher-ups. This was bad news for Lieutenant Grey, and bad news for 4th Kandak.

But whatever problems that might have arisen from the gate being forced open were well above my purview. In fact, *my* job was to ensure both vehicles remained operational. So I drove, one at a time, to the motor pool, (although I was certain there was nothing wrong with the Sergeant Major's truck) and solicited the expertise of my new friend Jeffreys, who had by this time learned of the demise of my old friend, Mortin.

"Geez, man, I don't know what to say," Jeffreys shouted over the din of the auto shop, his eyes welling up with sorrow and fright. "Was just a few days ago y'all two were standing here, tryin' to get me to have a look at y'all's trucks."

He looked like he was one or two deep breaths away from breaking into tears.

"It's alright, dude. We're gonna be alright," I said as reassuringly as possible over the noise.

"What can you do for me here?" I pointed to the hatchback pockmarked with small bullet holes. It looked like a silhouette target after a full day on the range.

"We'll get you a new one, gonna take a few days," Jeffreys replied, his voice shaky and uncertain as he turned away from me, closed his eyes, and put his thumb and middle finger on the bridge of his nose.

"I'll check back tomorrow," I hollered. "What about the other one?"

"There ain't nothin' wrong with it," he shouted back.

I went through the trunk space and removed the medical supplies, MREs, and the dry ice cooler that had been torn up by the strafing.

"Fuck," I said as I took to cleaning once more. Jeffreys had disappeared to some unseen corner of the motor pool to clear his senses, I imagined.

When I was finished dumping out all of the dry ice that leaked out of the cooler and bits of tortellini and beef steak that had been shot out of the MREs, I located a bottle of pink-colored disinfectant and a pressure washer from one of the many steel bins that dotted the motor pool and sprayed the empty trunk space after I'd lathered it up with a light coat of the pink soap. It had a sweet strawberry smell, which stood out against the heavy odor of grease and metal that enveloped the auto shop.

For good measure, I applied a second light coat to the steel rotary plate that I had, more or less, just finished scrubbing down with the corpsmen back at the TMC. I chuckled to myself at the passing thought that had Mortin been here with me now, I'd have told him to do it.

The pressure washer's powerful stream fanned out like a triangular blade and struck the steel plate with a roar of sound as the final traces of DNA that linked Mortin to our Humvee were eradicated.

I moved briskly through the camp till I reached the TMC. When I went inside, it was mostly dark. There were a few fluorescent lights on that illuminated the white fabric hospital curtains that partitioned the spaces around the gurneys into mini patients' quarters.

The B-hut was empty except for HM1 Burke, who came up to me and said in a very sincere, wholesome midwestern voice, "Doc, I know this is rough on you. I've been there myself. If there's anything you need, don't be shy about asking."

In my head I could hear myself say, *Why, now that you mention it, HM1, I could really use that key to the narc locker that you fucking carry with you 24/7*, but I knew better.

"Thank you, HM1," I said.

"No problem," he answered.

"Actually, HM1, some of my supplies got shot up in the fight. I could go for a re-up of some bandages and shit like that."

"Take what you need," HM1 Burke said as he headed toward the front door of the B-hut. Just before he was about to open it, he turned to me and said, "Just padlock the door on your way out." He reached for his dog tags a moment, then let his hand fall back down by his side.

"You won't need a key," he said. "The lock is open, hanging off the latch outside the door. Just make sure you clamp it shut."

"Roger that," I said.

When he'd gone out of the B-hut, I moved toward the bins and shelves near the gurneys and grabbed a fresh IV kit complete with saline lock. When I'd gotten my kit prepped up and ready to go on one of the gurneys, I moved to the sink opposite the med shelf and began removing my old saline lock.

The whole site surrounding the inside of my left elbow had become tender to the touch, and had begun to turn an unpleasant, green color. I tore the flat, clear sticky plastic Tegaderm dressing which held the lock in place from my arm. It felt as though I'd ripped off a layer of skin.

Shooting, burning, and tingling sensations rang up and down my arm. All this, I thought, and I haven't even pulled the tube out yet.

I knew there would be no way to extract the device from my arm without causing intense pain, so I opted for the fast, hard approach to get it over with quickly. I grabbed ahold of the little yellow stopper, which had by now been punched through more times than the hatchback on our Humvee, and yanked the contraption free of my arm.

"Ooowww!!!" I did my best to muffle the sound by turning my head and forcing my face into my right shoulder.

A spray of blood and pus splattered against the sink's mirror, and it looked as though I'd exploded a giant pimple. I held my trembling left arm over the sink as I squeezed blood and purulent drainage from the site of my disengaged saline lock. Next, I ran it under the faucet for a minute, lathered it up with a glob of antibacterial soap that I gathered from a dispenser on the wall next to the mirror, then ran it under the water a second time, wiping the area clean with my right hand. The whole ordeal was extremely painful, and extreme pain was an indicator for Dilaudid.

I dried off the wound by dabbing it with paper towels. When it was dry, I applied a thin layer of antibacterial cream to the site and closed it up with a giant Band-Aid.

It was difficult to set the saline lock in my right arm, not only because of how much pain I was still in, but also because I was not left-handed. I missed the vein a few times and had to stick myself more than once before I observed the red flash shoot into the chamber.

I cleaned it off with an alcohol swab, then locked it down with a Tegaderm dressing. The dressing was clear and taut against my skin except for where the tube stuck out of my arm like an unnatural tiny appendage.

I then flushed the flash chamber with ten cc of normal saline to ensure that I did not give myself a stroke. Things were really coming together for me, I thought.

With proper care and attention to detail I could shrink my habit to a manageable level and maintain it till my deployment ended, after which I would quit once and for all. There was no real future this way, I was beginning to realize. But first things first.

I came to laid out on the gurney as though I was a patient in a hospital. The Dilaudid syringe was sticking out of the saline lock I'd stuck in my right arm a few hours earlier. The fluorescent lights overhead were blinding.

I didn't have much time before the corpsmen would arrive at the TMC for morning sick call, so I wrangled myself up from the supine position, shook my head violently back and forth several times, and began field daying the TMC.

I didn't go all out in my efforts to clean because I didn't have a lot of time and also because I was still quite fucked up.

And though it was dark outside, I could sense the sun would soon rise and the day would begin, and I would be in serious trouble if anyone caught me in here all smacked up.

I pulled the spent syringe from my right arm. It tingled and burned a little, but I was not concerned. I put the needle in a red sharps container beside the sink and grabbed my rifle and whatever other personal gear I'd let spill out during my nod, though I was certain I would forget something, so I checked and rechecked the area around the gurney several times before giving up and exiting the B-hut, padlocking the front door as HM1 Burke had asked me to. Before I left, I eyeballed the narc locker. This morning would not be ideal for a breach, so I made sure to leave one of the back windows unlocked before heading out.

The next few days were a relative blur, and I was grateful that the crew members gave me some time and distance to grieve the loss of my friend Mortin, which made it much easier for me to administer a regimen of morphine and Dilauded.

Occasionally, Captain Harold would pat me on the shoulder and say something like, "Hang in there, Doc," and I would half smile, nod my head, and stare back vacantly.

I had informed Gomez about Mortin, and she offered her condolences, though I got the sense that she was pulling back from me. After that initial exchange, several of my Myspace messages to her went unanswered, and I presumed that she had found a new friend, or several. There was no way of knowing for certain what she was up to.

And I was too distracted by what had happened to Mortin and by the spike in my opiate usage to really dwell on it. It was what it was, a temporary austere romance that had run its course.

I had noticed, also, that a number of my friends from back home had sent "friend requests" to my e-mail address for a new website called Facebook. *What a joke*, I thought. *It'll never catch on.*

One morning as I made my rounds through the camp, I was approached by a familiar figure. It was Pat Tillman, this time in a Marines green and black woodlands digi-patterned battle dress uniform. He came up from behind and walked alongside me without ever making eye contact. The need for discretion was clear.

"Heard about your buddy," he said in a low tone. "I'm sorry."

"Yeah," was all I could come up with in the way of a response.

"Going forward," he glanced very slightly in my direction without turning his head, "it's gonna be the real deal. Some hard-core shit." He paused a moment. "Are you sure you're up for it?"

"Yeah, of course," I said without hesitation. "I'm up for it, fuck yeah!"

"Good," he replied.

"One other thing."

"Yeah?"

"The Colonel . . . "

"What about him?" I asked, but there was no response. "It's just that I wish I knew what was going on . . ." I said as I rotated my head forty-five degrees to the right to face him, but he had already vanished like a spirit.

I continued with my usual check-ins at the motor pool and spoke to Jeffreys pretty regularly, who seemed to take Mortin's death very hard.

The Sergeant Major passed the word that the Colonel had called him again, this time to express his empathy for the loss of Mortin, which also represented a loss for his command, but also to remind us of our need to return downrange to Mehtar Lam and to the war.

I was again down to my final syringe of morphine when word came that the hatch on our Humvee had been replaced. I took the opportunity to say good-bye to Jeffreys, to wish him well and all that.

I'd forgotten to load a fresh dry ice cooler and additional medical supplies into one of our Humvees the night that I changed out my saline lock at the TMC, partly because the Humvee that I had grown accustomed to riding in was in the shop having its rear hatch replaced, but also because that night I had gotten extremely fucked up and had awoken just before morning sick call hours.

I took the present time to correct this mistake, making for the TMC in my newly re-hatched Humvee, then loading the items in question without communicating directly with any of the corpsmen, who were all busy working.

The Sergeant Major informed the crew that we would be leaving Camp Phoenix the following morning at 0500, which meant reveille at 0400, weapons mounted and comms checked at 0430, same as the other day we'd tried to depart, but for one small difference.

We were now a man short, and as much as we tried to go through the motions of operating our small unit of the great war machine as though nothing had happened, it was impossible not to feel an overwhelming sense of loss with each small movement.

Mortin was our comms guy. He loaded the crypto, the encoded layer of protection which made it impossible for our enemies to intercept our radio transmissions. Normally this task would fall to me, but I was terrible at it so Lieutenant Grey picked up the slack, because in addition to being an excellent cavalry officer, he was also a versatile, adaptable soldier who understood the nuances of this newfangled combat environment from the ground up. In fact, he adored this lifestyle. He lived for it.

And so as we set about completing the necessary systems and weapons checks the morning of our departure, we did so with Mortin's ghost looming over us, in our hearts and thoughts and all around us, whether or not we made mention of it to one another.

"I've gotta grab something," I said to the crew as they hurried about the two vehicles, punching in codes and making minor adjustments to the weapons' mounting systems. The trucks were parked side by side in their same respective spots as they had been that morning, a few days earlier, when we'd planned to leave originally.

"From where?" Lieutenant Grey shouted.

"I'll be right back," I hollered as I walked down the sloping platform of our new rear hatch and then dropped down.

Before anyone could question me thoroughly I was off in the direction of the TMC to address the needs of my own personal maintenance.

I slipped through the window that I'd left unlocked and approached the narc locker. I was no cat burglar. This was to be a smash and grab then get the fuck out of Dodge type operation.

I was reminded of the film *Drugstore Cowboy* and I laughed to myself. Burroughs would be proud, I thought.

I pulled my pistol from its holster, gripped it at the barrel so that in my hand it looked like a hammer, and struck the padlock with the butt end. The lock cracked open and I screamed out, "Yahtzee!"

I opened the cabinet door and emptied its contents into a small supplemental med pouch I'd brought with me. The score was huge. One box of a hundred morphine 10mg auto-injectors in plastic shrink-wrap, and nine bottles of 1000mg morphine sulfate. The concentration was 50mg/1mL. The math confused me, but I figured I could sort it all out later on.

I also obtained twelve bottles of Dilaudid, 500mg at 10mg/mL. More math.

I did my best to reset the lock onto the latch of the narc locker cabinet, but it was useless. It might not cause an alarm right away, but sooner or later, someone was going to notice it had been broken into and emptied.

I had a real need to put distance between myself and Camp Phoenix, because I knew that even if the corpsmen at the TMC implicated me as the culprit in this crime of passion, which they undoubtedly would, as long as we made it back to Mehtar Lam, we would be under the protection the 1st Brigade leadership, and the whole thing would get swept under the rug.

Similarly, Lieutenant Grey had an interest in fleeing as quickly as possible to avoid being charged with misconduct or whatever else for his reckless breach of the front gate. But he too would be immunized by crossing the great barrier of unstable, violent territory that lay between Kabul and the wild east. There was, after all, a war on. And through the fog of war, we don't always observe the jungle from the vines. Things happen, and in the grander scheme, a broken-up narc locker and a busted-down gate was not worth prosecuting.

We might have been due for a stern talking-to by the Colonel, but that would take place downrange, on our turf. And there was no guarantee, after all, that we would even make it there alive anyway, so the situation was, in a way, trivial to begin with. There were no guarantees. Mortin's death could be attributed to that philosophy.

Our sins would be ignored if not absolved so long as we were not around to stand trial, so with that in mind, the advisors of 4th Kandak, 1st Brigade pushed through Camp Phoenix in a formation of two Humvees, myself in the gunner's hatch and Captain Harold at the helm this time, with the Sergeant Major at the rear gun, Raz Mohammed in shotgun, and Lieutenant Grey in the driver seat of the rear vehicle hollering at us over the radio to push faster as we blew through the ECP—through the gaping hole that we'd created days earlier, causing the unarmed ANA guards to scramble like frightened pigeons to either side of our convoy—in the direction of the Old Silk Road that would lead us back to FOB Mehtar Lam.

CHAPTER 12
GONE, GONE, GONE

It was just before dawn by the time we finally left post, and the early morning hour meant there would be little or no traffic obstructing our path as we moved through the ravaged, bombed-out remains of downtown Kabul. I always found it inane that though we had been at war here for nearly six years, the lion's share of the damage the city had sustained did not occur on our watch.

At first I found the scene to be off-putting and imposing. But the more time I spent in-country, the more I realized that the blown-out buildings and shot-up street signs were really just the appropriate indicators of this land's character. It was a region destined to be at constant war; a place where armies went to die. The rubble no longer felt strange. It now seemed the proper aesthetic.

We had left post without notifying the Phoenix TOC, a transgression in and of itself, to make certain we would not be held up at the last minute for Lieutenant Grey's smashing down of the front gate days earlier, or for any other crime that may or may not have occurred during our short stay at the base.

Our planned visit to Camp Cobra had been scrubbed on account of our need to get back to Mehtar Lam before the

Phoenix brass started inquiring as to our whereabouts, so we pushed east through downtown Kabul, moving freely in the twilight hours of morning.

Though it was still dark somewhat, it was not so dark as to require the use of night vision goggles. The air was brisk. I observed vendors readying their store tents for the day's work. There were only men on the streets, no women or children.

"Well, at least now we know why that fucking V-BID didn't go off," Captain Harold snarled.

"Come again?" I said, puzzled.

"That Camry, it was a damned decoy. They sent that poor hadji on a fool's errand, and that Rambo fella knew it."

"Still not following." I had managed to shove off while in the turret without giving myself away, and I was too fucked up to make sense of what the captain was saying.

"They set that guy in the Camry up, put him in the car with bogus explosives so that the Rambo fella could get to him and look like the hero."

"Yeah?"

"It was all a show so they'd give him that AK he used to shoot Mortin in the damned neck with."

"You think so?"

"I know so," he said confidently. "I know how these mongrels think." Captain Harold was once again fired up. "You'll see, Doc. Things ain't always as they seem. You'll get it one of these days."

"I hope so."

Doing my best to keep an eye on potential troublemakers, I allowed my mind to drift carelessly into the abstract. I thought about Gomez. It was just as well we were forgoing our visit to Cobra. No need to encounter the legion of Joes she was probably sucking off in the aid station after dark.

And as much as I tried to avoid thinking about it, my thoughts inevitably wandered back to Mortin. He was so young. And why had it been him up in the turret and not me? Dumb luck, I suppose.

And I thought once again about the Embedded Training Team's advisory mission and how futile it had become, if ever it had been a justifiable use of resources. It was hard enough to get the ANA soldiers to form a line for chow or sick call or God forbid clean their weapons, let alone execute complex tactical maneuvers or practice battlefield medicine. We couldn't even count on them to show up on time for our convoy from Cobra to Bagram some two weeks earlier. And now we couldn't trust them not to turn their weapons on us.

"We're meeting up with the ANA just before the switchback," the Sergeant Major hollered over the radio as though he'd somehow heard what I'd been thinking. "Raz just got off the phone with your boy Ghazzi, Doc. They're supposedly pulled over on the side of the road waiting for us."

"Waiting to fucking ambush us?" I asked.

"I doubt it," the Sergeant Major said. "But keep that gun on the ready in case of any funny business."

My uniform and flak jacket were still stained with Mortin's blood as we rolled through the docile war zone on our way to rendezvous with the soldiers we'd been sent here to train.

"You know, I don't know what the fuck we're even doing out here, Captain Harold," I protested. "There's just no fucking way in hell these motherfuckers are ever gonna be a serious army. Just ain't gonna happen."

"Hmm," Captain Harold obliged.

"And how many of them are already fucking working for the other side?" I was dispassionate in my speech, owing largely to the dose of Dilaudid I'd self-administered earlier, but also out of a sort of prolonged helplessness that I'd more or less come to accept.

"Doc, I think you're reading too much into this. True, these mongoloids are good for nothing heathens, predestined for the Lord's wrath, but it's a good thing that we're over here doing what we're doing." There was a chipper quality to his voice. "There's definitely value in having our guys over here, no doubt." He paused for a moment, then added, "And Iraq, too. What's the point of having the world's greatest military if we don't flex our muscles every once in a while, right? Think about all we spend on defense. If we didn't get to clobber some jerk-off country every ten or twenty years, all that money would be a colossal waste. If you got it, use it. That's what I say."

My humanist education—as instilled by the Greenwich public school system—had manifested in me a tenacious resentment of our nation's military policies and posture, citing as a basis the unjust war in Vietnam. And for a long time, or at least what had then felt like a long time, I embraced this ethos.

But as a sortie of hijacked passenger aircraft careened into the World Trade Center's Twin Towers, causing them to crumble, I began to acutely reexamine my beliefs. And in the heartbreak of that moment, when it was clear that there was no going back, all that humanism that I'd come to know as insoluble truth dissolved from my thoughts.

So when I listened to Captain Harold and others like him (as I had indeed encountered many others like him), I did so through the hybrid of my two selves: the former and the latter. The younger, more wide-eyed self who'd believed in the doctrine of confrontation as a last resort, always listened though rarely spoke.

The part of me, however, that wanted revenge on the dark regions of the earth tended to agree with men like the captain, because, although a strike against a suspected insurgent safe house in Fallujah or Baghdad or even out here might not be the justified response to the attacks of September 11, it would at least be a response.

I wanted to believe in what I was doing, but I had doubts. I didn't know what to think and I was beginning to feel like that hadji who'd been issued a car full of false explosives and sent in blindly to ram our convoy from behind, like meat on a stick.

"You know, this was supposed to be the *good* war," I sighed.

"It'll all work out in the end, Doc, so long as you have faith."

There was a break in our discourse and I leaned back into the turret and breathed deeply. The air temperature was beginning to climb. I did my best to prepare myself mentally for the brutally intense heat of the lower elevation. We would first have to traverse the switchback, descend its nine ledges into the depths of Laghman Province.

"You know, I watched them come down," I said finally.

"What's that, Doc?"

"I said I saw the Twin Towers fall; I was there."

"Really?"

"Yeah. I was nineteen."

"What were you doing there?"

"Well, I'd already failed out of community college, so my dad had gotten me an internship at his company. September eleventh was supposed to my first day, but I was late to work, so . . ."

"Oh man, I'm sorry, Doc. That must've been rough."

"I saw the South Tower come down. I was right there when that fucking debris cloud blew up. I was on TV too, CNN or something. They had a camera crew set up when that whole thing went down."

"Really?"

"I must have watched it over and over a million times. You could see the cloud swallow people up like a sandstorm."

"Yeah, I saw it on TV too. You were there for that?"

"Yeah." I breathed in a moment. "My dad used to take me up there when I was little, six or so."

"Where?"

"Up to the top of the Twin Towers. The hundred-and-tenth floor, the North Tower. Tower One."

"Oh yeah?"

"You wouldn't believe what it looked like up there, Captain Harold. It was like the view from heaven."

A brief silence followed as we made a left-hand turn onto Route 1, the road we had started out on some two or three weeks earlier. The only real road in Afghanistan. The Old Silk Road.

The sun was rising to the east, which was right in front of us. It stained the sky and cloud cover a soft cotton candy pink, and we drove headlong into the growing light of day.

I broke the silence finally. "I don't understand really how the towers collapsed."

"Easy. The planes hit, caused a fire. The fire melted the girders, and the one floor collapsed onto the floor below it, and so on, and so forth."

The captain's tone was very matter of fact, leaving no room for discussion or dissent.

"Yeah, I know," I replied. "I've heard all that shit, and I guess it makes sense." I paused a moment. "But I was *there*," I went on. "I literally watched the South Tower come down, and I know it sounds crazy, but it looked like the building just imploded."

Captain Harold breathed heavily into his microphone.

"Oh Doc, don't tell me you're one of those."

"One of what?" I questioned.

"You know, one of those conspiracy theorists—truthers, I think they're called now. Whack jobs, basically."

"Oh, no. Not at all," I countered. "It's just that I know what I saw."

"Doc, don't you love America?

"Haven't we already been through this, Captain Harold?"

"I know you *say* that you love America, but I'm not sure that you really mean it."

At this I took umbrage.

"Captain Harold," I started in a scolding tone, "I am the descendent of Polish Holocaust survivors and Sicilian sulfur miners."

"That a fact?" he chided me.

"Yes, it is. My father built a computer software engineering firm from the ground up in the eighties, before it was the fucking hip thing to do. My brother and I wanted for nothing growing up. If anyone loves America, it's me, you hear me? I fucking *love* America!"

I had allowed myself to get somewhat riled up during the debate, and had to hold back to keep from full-on shouting at the captain.

"Well that's good, Doc. That's what I like to hear. Wish there were more like you from your generation."

"There are plenty of people like me," I retorted. "And there are other ways to demonstrate patriotism besides military service."

"Oh yeah?" he challenged me. "Then why did you enlist?"

It was a great question; one I'd contemplated countless times on my own. In my rack in boot camp, then at Combat Medic School, and nearly every night since I'd been deployed. Why had I joined?

"Because I didn't know what else to do," I answered finally.

"I'll take that for what it's worth," Captain Harold responded.

"Well, thank you, sir," I mocked.

It was now full daylight, and I could see three ANA trucks pulled over on the right shoulder of Route 1, just before the entrance to the switchback. They were milling about, running around the vehicles playing games. They were children, really. They uniformly behaved as such. And though I was little more than an overgrown child myself, I was certain there was much I could teach them if they would only·listen and do what they were told.

After all, I was their advisor. It was my role to guide them, to introduce them to the art of battlefield medicine, the way I'd been shown and reshown.

"They're up here on the right," the Sergeant Major hailed our vehicle. "Doc, you see your boy Ghazzi?"

"Roger that. I see him. He's running around like a goddamned dickhead."

I heard the Sergeant Major laugh on the other end.

"We're gonna pull behind them, then they're gonna take the lead, just like last time."

I was a touch relieved to learn that we wouldn't ride out in front of the ANA soldiers. Whatever distrust of them I'd harbored at the onset of our voyage had been amplified tenfold by the attack against Mortin.

And as we cruised up to their haphazard assembly of vehicles, weapons, and man-children, I fixed my weapon on a group of three or four of them. I was now operating the 240 Bravo, which did not command the same level of firepower as did the Ma Deuce, but its accuracy was known to be more reliable.

I was certain that if I chose to squeeze off a burst and decimate the area target before me, things could go one of several ways.

They could fire back and kill me and perhaps the captain and Lieutenant Grey and Raz Mohammed and the Sergeant Major in the rear vehicle. This was an unlikely outcome.

I could get them all and even the score a little, but face a general court-martial if the crew decided not to go along with my account of events, which would of course name the ANA as the instigators.

Or, I could get them all, get the crew to back me up in claiming that the ANA had fired the first shots, and continue on with my deployment as though nothing had ever happened. It would not be a difficult sell, especially with what had happened to Mortin still fresh in everyone's mind. The crew would have it out with me. Especially the Sergeant Major. We might come to blows, which would be devastating for me physically, but in the end, I believe he would have my back. Raz might be a problem, but we could take care of him if we had to. This was the likeliest of scenarios.

The only problem is that we were still within the grasp of the Phoenix garrison, who in all likelihood were already trying to track us down and bring us up on charges for our loose conduct. For that reason, I thought it best not to open fire on the ANA just yet. Not before we got back to our home turf, or at least nearer to it. Once we crossed the threshold of the great switchback and descended once again into the sweltering low country. Then, they would be fair game, I thought.

"Ayy Doc!" Ghazzi ran up to our Humvee as we pulled alongside the three ANA trucks on the right shoulder of Route 1. "Yoo haff kandi?" he asked me full of hope and cheer.

I had kept my weapon trained on him just in case, but I was not staring him down, so he didn't feel threatened.

"No, Ghazzi," I answered firmly.

His face went pouty, and I pointed to the ANA trucks and said, "You go now."

He acquiesced, childlike. Slumped shoulders and head hung low, he sauntered back to the ANA truck from whence he came, and mounted up.

The Sergeant Major in the rear vehicle just behind ours began shouting and pointing in the direction of the switchback, indicating to the ANA that he wanted them to lead the convoy. This was, after all, policy.

The ANA soldiers eventually saddled up and pulled off the shoulder onto the road headed east. The sun was high in the sky as we filed in behind them. It seemed as though we were finally, after all this time, headed back home.

PART III

CHAPTER 13
DOWN

The three ANA trucks that had been pulled over on the shoulder made their way onto the road, and Captain Harold and I in the lead Humvee and the Sergeant Major, Lieutenant Grey, and Raz Mohammed in the rear vehicle filed in behind them.

"Weren't there four of them when we left Mehtar Lam?" I asked Captain Harold. "They're short one LTV," I continued.

"You're right, Doc, good eye," he answered, before hailing the Sergeant Major.

"Sergeant Major, the ANA are short one truck. What do you want to do about it?"

"Nothing. Fuck 'em. They don't have their shit together enough to get their people where they need to be, there's nothing we can do for them. Keep rolling."

It was anyone's guess, really, what had become of the missing LTV. They could have sold it, with or without the M60 weapon system rigged up to the bed. They could have ridden south, deserted to Pakistan, or west to Iran. Or they could have gotten to the switchback, to the high ground ahead of our convoy this morning, and set up an ambush. This was an unlikely possibility, but there was no way of knowing for certain what they were up to.

All we knew was that when we came west initially, there were four ANA trucks with eight to twelve soldiers attached to each, leading our convoy. And when we left Bagram, the advisors of 4th Kandak, 1st Brigade numbered six, including Raz Mohammed. And now that we were headed finally back east to our base of operations—a relative sanctuary from which we had set out with no real defined operational purpose—we were short a man, as the ANA were short a vehicle.

It was a quick ride from the shoulder to the switchback. The morning sun had risen, and I put the air temperature at a tolerable ninety-five degrees Fahrenheit. Beads of sweat had begun to accumulate on my forehead like tiny drops of early morning dew.

I drank from one of the three Dasani water bottles that I had lined up like mortar shells on the ledge of the turret in order to launch at civilian vehicles that obstructed our path or came too close our truck.

We passed FOB Policharki on the left, the last man-made structure, aside from the road itself, that separated Kabul from the lower elevation.

Two great cliffs on either side rose up like giant stone castles, peering down onto our convoy as we passed between them. Entrenched tactical positions were numerous on both sides. If we had been fighting the Vietcong, it could have been Dien Bien Phu all over again.

But we were not fighting the Vietcong. We were fighting the Taliban, and al-Qaeda, and the Haqqani network, and the Pakistani ISI. We were fighting the Chechens, and the Iranian Revolutionary Guard. We fought against Palestinians and Jordanians and Libyans and Saudis and Egyptians and everyone else who followed, like practitioners to the morning prayer, an international call to jihad against the American invaders.

We were fortunate in that, at the time, the war in Iraq served as a more powerful magnet for such holy warriors, though in Afghanistan, we too encountered our fair share.

But what menaced us most, what gave me cause to fear, was the uncertainty of our Afghan allies' loyalty or resolve. The men who were leading us on a return convoy through this great valley, down, down, and further down to the depths of the low country, simply could not be trusted or relied upon. For all we knew, they were leading us into a trap.

So I kept my weapon locked on the vehicle directly in front of me. Every so often the soldiers, eight or so in the bed of the pickup on either side of a mounted M60 machine gun, would stare back at me. Sometimes they would smile, while others, they'd preserve hard faces.

My affect never changed. I remained not hostile, but indifferent. Black ballistic sunglasses shielded my contemptuous eyes and kept me from making enemies out of alleged friends.

As we passed between the two great cliffs, the ground on the left side dropped off sharply into a large valley with what looked like a river or lake down at the bottom. On the right side was a large wall.

The air temperature went up a noticeable few degrees, and I took another swig of water from the Dasani bottle.

"You feel that?" I asked Captain Harold.

"Feel what?"

"How much hotter it just got."

"Doc, I got the AC on. It's nice and frosty down here." Captain Harold chuckled. "You'll be alright."

"I know. I'm not worried. I was just saying."

"Uh-huh."

The wall on the right side grew upward and slightly overhead as we pushed forward, creating a sort of half tunnel. From this vantage point, the sun was obscured, though there seemed to be a second light source way down in the valley on the left side of the road.

The heat and moisture continued to intensify, and I perspired heavily and attempted to recover the lost water by finishing the first Dasani, chucking the empty bottle into the cab, and opening up one of the reserves.

We were still descending the first level of the switchback when I said to Captain Harold, "My God, do you feel that heat?"

"I told you, Doc, I got the AC on. Quit your belly achin'."

I was too flustered to bother arguing with him, and I understood that with the distance to Mehtar Lam still at least a few hours' ride from our present position, the opportunity to initiate a new argument down the road would undoubtedly surface.

"Sergeant Major," I hailed the rear vehicle. "Do you feel that heat?"

"Yeah, I feel it."

The road had become a ledge, falling off dramatically on the left side of the convoy. The lake or river in the valley below seemed to be incredibly far down.

"I don't remember it being this hot."

"Welcome to Afghanistan."

I found the Sergeant Major's remark to be a bit degrading even for his particular style of rhetoric, because I had been in-country a full six months longer than he had, and was no stranger to the wrath of the Afghan sun.

"Yeah, I get it, Sergeant Major. I know it's hot." We continued to move at an elongated downward angle for what felt like several miles. "I'm just saying, it feels *really* fucking hot today."

"Yeah, it does," he answered.

After a good hour or so on the top level, we came to the first hairpin turn. The ANA trucks up front led the way. One thing their soldiers knew how to do was drive. The treacherous passes were no great obstacle for them. Captain Harold, on the other hand, had to slow our Humvee to a near halt in order to negotiate the one hundred and eighty degree turn.

But he managed to execute it, and after a few minutes, we were able to catch up with the ANA trucks that had continued forward without slowing down. Lieutenant Grey kept up behind us, no problem.

We had essentially made a U-turn, when we rounded the corner. The second level of the switchback was even steeper than the first, and the heat grew more intense with every inch we rolled forward.

"I don't remember it being this steep," I said to Captain Harold.

"Doc, just watch the high ground, will you?"

I finished the remaining Dasani water bottle and continued to sweat profusely. The ANA trucks moved briskly, and we began to straggle. The air became thicker and moister, and my visibility started to decline. Condensation formed on my sunglasses, and I had to wipe them off periodically in order to see.

The Sergeant Major hailed our vehicle. "Horseman Two, this is One, how's your visibility, over?"

"It's alright," Captain Harold responded. "Getting worse."

"How 'bout you, Doc?"

"Same here."

"Just keep following the ANA, they know the road better than we do."

"That's what I'm afraid of," I snapped.

We advanced to the second hairpin turn with the third ANA truck a good fifty meters ahead of us. I saw its tail whip around the turn at full speed and duck out of sight as it moved onto the third level. Captain Harold, lacking the control to pull off such a maneuver, again slowed down, allowing the ANA trucks to pull even further ahead of us.

By the time we began our descent onto the third level, which was even steeper than the second, the third ANA truck was barely within sight. The air had begun to turn a light orange color as we moved farther away from the sun and closer to a second, unknown light source.

"Get up on them . . ." I heard the Sergeant Major shout before static engulfed the channel. White noise ripped through my headset, and I let out a shriek.

At the third turn, the ANA had completely disappeared from sight, and I could barely see ten feet in front of my face. The heat was unbearable. The air was turning a deeper red the further we descended, and our ability to communicate with the rear vehicle had been disrupted, either by the low elevation or by the great wall of the switchback, or by some unknown, unexplainable force.

"We need to catch up to the ANA!" I shouted at Captain Harold.

"I know, Doc. But I can't see three damned feet in front of me!"

I began to fear that the ANA had planned this; that they'd pulled away from our Humvee, perhaps rendezvoused with the missing LTV to set up an ambush. Maybe they sensed my desire to fire on them. I had done my best to appear professional, but I wasn't always able to keep my feelings in check. Maybe they saw this strike as a means of survival. Us or them. That was certainly how I felt about things.

The sun had become completely obscured behind the great wall of the cliff face, and whatever light that gave us the benefit of limited sight seemed to be emanating from a source in the deep valley below.

"Captain Harold?" I hollered. "Captain Harold!" I said again. "Fuck!"

I removed my headset and threw it violently into the cab. Our radio had failed. I was dizzy with exhaustion, and had not dosed since before we'd entered the switchback. And as much as I craved a hit to ease the horrible discomfort, I feared that if I indulged this whim, I would not maintain consciousness. And at this stage of the game, consciousness was paramount.

A short while later, my vision was overwhelmed completely by the red haze, though I could tell when the vehicle changed directions and descended onto the subsequent level. But I lost track of exactly which level we were on. It could have been the fifth, or the sixth, or perhaps the eighth or ninth.

My senses all blended together, and all I could feel was a dense, red heat as though my skin was burning. I cried out, but my voice was muted. I began to weep. I could feel my body melting, my spirit wilting.

I reached for my pistol once again, but I could not tear it loose from its holster. I searched my body frantically for a blade or a sharp edge that I could use to open my throat with. My Leatherman utility tool was in my left cargo pocket, so I pulled it up and out and drew the blade. I rubbed my thumb against it gently to make sure that it was sharp enough. This is it, I thought.

Just as I was about to drag the blade across my throat, my vision began to return. I made out the three ANA trucks pulled over to the right side of the road, the soldiers all sitting down

Indian style on the ground with their hands on their helmets in the position of surrender.

Guarding them were a group of soldiers wearing tan uniforms with hoods that obscured their heads. Their faces too were covered by flaps that zippered all the way up to their eyes. A small space between the hood and the flaps created a visor through which they were able to see. They carried Kalashnikovs.

What looked like a full army—tanks, artillery, armored vehicles, and legions of ground troops—blockaded the road. One of the soldiers stood atop a tank that was out front of the formation, his right hand extended outward, palm flat, indicating that we halt our convoy. I took him to be the ranking officer. Beside him on the tank stood a brutally large man whom I understood to be his second in command.

A river of molten lava sloshed along to the left of our Humvees at a distance of thirty meters. The heat coming off the liquid fire was unbelievable. It seemed that we had located finally the source of the light.

Captain Harold ground our vehicle to a halt, and Lieutenant Grey and the Sergeant Major and Raz Mohammed pulled alongside us so that we were both facing and within shouting distance of the soldier standing on the tank.

CHAPTER 14
REDS

The Sergeant Major's truck stood lined up next to ours, side by side, as though we were gearing up for a drag race. His .50-cal was at the low ready, as was my 240 Bravo. Because we were facing a blockade of soldiers and machines whose intentions were unclear, we did not want to appear hostile right off the bat.

The soldiers of the blockade on the ground as well as others on top of tanks and armored personnel carriers all wore the same tan-colored desert drab uniform with their hoods pulled over their heads and the flaps of their blouses zipped up all the way to the hoods. It was impossible to see their faces.

At first, I made them for soldiers of an obscure NATO member country, the Bulgarians or Czechs or the Danes even. But I quickly dismissed this notion on the grounds that no NATO country, whatever the cause, would have the gall to halt a US convoy.

I thought then that they must be some Army Ranger crew or SEAL team or some other elite forces unit. That would explain their posture. But the uniforms were a design I had never seen before. And the elite forces that I had seen and spoken to from time to time didn't wear uniforms anyway. I was puzzled.

The sky was a deep blood red. It must have been overcast, because the sun was not at all visible. To our left, large bubbles rose up to the surface of the molten river and broke apart, releasing flames and gaseous vapors that elevated the air temperature in noticeable increments. It was a deep volcanic atmosphere at the low elevation, though there were no cavernous walls nearby or ceilings overhead. The road, which had been paved when we'd ridden west some three or four weeks earlier, was, for some reason, now a dirt road, with brown soil and large rocks set deep into it.

We had successfully negotiated the switchback and descended the great distance to the low country, only it was not at all as I had remembered it.

The ranking officer of the blockade who stood atop the tank out in front of their formation let his hand fall back from its outstretched position to his side after we halted. He stared, or I imagine he stared, at the Sergeant Major and me for a minute or so. It was impossible to know what his eyes were doing behind that hooded cowl. The large man at his side stood facing us as well with his weapon also at the low ready.

"What are you doing here?" A muffled voice escaped the beige hood of the ranking officer. The dialect was not American.

"What do you mean, 'what are we doin' here'?" the Sergeant Major snarled back, bewildered. "We're driving down the fucking road! Who the fuck are *you*? What the fuck are *you* doing out here?"

It was then that I noticed the red patches with a crossed gold hammer and sickle emblem on the right shoulder of each man's uniform.

"We are soldiers, like you." The officer paused a moment. Flames erupted from the river. "And like you, we have been here a long time."

The man then pointed toward the ANA soldiers in the surrender position on the road's margin. "Who are they to you?" he asked the Sergeant Major.

"They're with us!" the Sergeant Major shouted. "We're their advisors!" he went on.

"Oh, I see."

"You got a lotta nerve taking them prisoner!" The Sergeant Major was furious. I noticed him thumbing the butterfly trigger and scanning left to right, trying to get a figure of how many guns they had and where they were positioned in case things got out of hand.

"They are not prisoners. We were holding them here for you."

"Oh." The Sergeant Major blushed a little. "Well ... uh ... thank you," he almost whispered.

"What are you doing here?" the officer repeated.

"I told you, we're training them so they can take over responsibility for the country's security after we leave." The Sergeant Major pointed to the ANA soldiers who were smiling, wide eyed, watching the exchange like small children watching a puppet show, their hands still on their helmets in the position of surrender.

"Do you really think they will be able to accept this great responsibility?" The officer's tone was less grating, more empathetic.

"It doesn't matter what I think," the Sergeant Major gruffed. "We got orders." Sensing a slight change in the dynamic, the Sergeant Major then asked, "What are you folks doing out here?"

"We had a treaty with the old government."

"The Taliban?" I asked.

"No," he replied. "Before them. When the revolution broke out, after numerous requests, we were finally deployed here to stabilize the country and establish a ruling class that remained sensitive to our nation's ideals."

At this, the entire army of hooded soldiers laughed wildly.

"Why are they laughing?" the Sergeant Major asked.

"Because this justification for the war is something that has been burned into our minds. But we know better. We know there is only one reason a country invades another country, and that is because it can."

"Oh." The Sergeant Major and I nodded.

"Why is your country at war in Afghanistan?"

"There was an attack against one of our cities a few years ago. Many people were killed."

"The perpetrators of this attack, they were Afghan?" the officer asked.

"No," I answered.

"I'm confused," he continued. "Why is your country at war *here*?"

"The men who attacked our country trained here under the protection of the local government." The ANA soldiers looked on at our discussion in childlike wonder as the Sergeant Major spoke. "One in particular, he masterminded the whole thing."

"Was he Afghan?"

"No, he's Saudi," I answered.

"Ah, yes." The officer went on: "I've heard of this man. He is our enemy as well. I thought he was your ally, no? Oh well, no matter. These things change from time to time. We understand. What has become of him?"

"Nobody knows," the Sergeant Major replied. "Last we heard, he was down south by Tora Bora. But that was years ago. It's anyone's guess where he's holed up now."

"What's going on up there, Doc?" Captain Harold asked.

"Nothing, we're just talking to these guys."

"We need to get back to Mehtar Lam now. Tell those bozos to clear the road!"

"The Sergeant Major is still talking to their head guy," I responded.

There was a short pause, and the two leaders, the Sergeant Major and the hooded officer, understood that they were not enemies.

"We have been in this godforsaken country longer than I care to remember," the hooded officer said finally. "And I fear that we will be stuck here for all time."

"I'm sure that isn't true," I said, trying to make light of the situation.

"They say this land is cursed, you know," he continued. "The soil has a thirst for the blood of warriors." He paused a moment. "Don't get stuck here."

The Sergeant Major nodded his head.

"We need to pass your blockade to get back to our base," the Sergeant Major said in a tone that sounded soft for him. "And we need to take them with us." He pointed at the ANA soldiers seated with their hands on their helmets.

"Be careful," the officer warned. "They're not to be trusted."

The Sergeant Major nodded slightly, then made a come hither gesture at the ANA soldiers, and they got up and went to their trucks.

The large hooded soldier that stood next to the one in charge turned his head to face me.

"There's a light that comes off this river." He pointed to the moving body of molten lava on our left side. His accent was American. "But it's not the light you're after."

The man unzipped the upper part of his blouse, revealing his face. It was Pat Tillman, going native once again, this time embedded with a foreign army.

"Keep following this road." He pointed east. "There is another light, one you'll rather follow."

I nodded my head in acquiescence. The ANA mounted up, and the soldiers of the blockade began to pull their ranks and their vehicles off the road, creating a space in the middle just large enough for our convoy to slip through.

"Good luck," the hooded officer said. "I hope you find what it is you're looking for."

The Sergeant Major waved his hand in friendship, and again we were off, three ANA trucks up front followed by Lieutenant Grey, Raz Mohammed, and the Sergeant Major, then myself and Captain Harold this time pulling up the rear.

CHAPTER 15
DR. BRYDON

Our convoy pushed slowly through the blockade of Red Army soldiers that parted in the middle as we approached, freeing up the road to make way for us.

I swung the turret around so that I was facing the rear, and watched as the soldiers and mechanized units who had opened their ranks to allow our passage quickly closed back up after we'd moved through. And after a short while, as we cruised east in the direction of FOB Mehtar Lam, the great mass of men and machines grew smaller and smaller until they disappeared from sight entirely.

I pushed a syringe full of Dilaudid up through the saline lock into my vein discretely, as I had always done, though I was beginning to feel as though it didn't matter whether or not Captain Harold was aware of each time I dosed. Out of courtesy, I kept it hidden from him as best I could.

The sky grew an even deeper red, until it looked as though the heavens were bleeding out, and the cloud cover suspended up above was keeping the hemorrhage from spilling onto the road and onto all of us.

The river of liquid flame sloshed on to the left of the convoy at a distance of roughly thirty meters. Every so often the current would force a small wave to crash against the near bank, causing a blinding splash of red-hot lava. The heat was unbearable. I reached into the cab and picked up another three Dasani water bottles, opening one and drinking from it, while setting the other two on the ledge of the turret to be used possibly as projectiles against any meddlesome civilian traffic. Though we hadn't seen any civilians in a long time.

"Horseman Two, this is One, are you seeing this?" the Sergeant Major hollered over the radio, which had begun to function once more, though the transmissions came through muddled.

"Seeing what?" Captain Harold asked.

I swung the turret around to face front, momentarily leaving the rear exposed, to try and get a look at whatever it was the Sergeant Major was going on about.

"I don't see anything," I said.

Then the convoy began to bear right on the road slightly, and slowing down quite a bit, we came to surround on the right side some horribly deformed-looking beast hobbling along at very low speed.

"I see it now," I said.

"Me too," Captain Harold said.

"What the hell is it?" I asked.

The Sergeant Major, after some effort, got the attention of the three ANA trucks and held up his fist in the air, almost like a Black Panthers salute, indicating they halt their vehicles, which they did, and we also did.

After close scrutiny from an obstructed angle, I observed that the creature to the left of our convoy, between ourselves and the river of molten lava, was in fact two creatures: a horse and rider.

The steed looked to be of Arabian stock, and was white in color except for the many crimson-stained splotches caused by blood spatter from several arrows stuck into its hindquarters.

The thin arrows bounced and gyrated with each belabored stride the animal made.

The rider had at least two arrows stuck in him as well. There was one poking out his left shoulder, and one driven into his right thigh. A slow but steady stream of blood had trickled down his right leg to his boot and was dripping off his heel in little red droplets.

He was slumped down on the neck of the beast, barely able to keep himself from falling over. He wore a red tunic with white laces and tan trousers that had been browned and sullied by the blowing dust and by the blood from his wounds and also from the wounds to the horse.

The Arabian pushed on a few more brave steps before collapsing forward, taking the rider down with her. The red-frocked man lay on top of the horse's carcass a moment before moving his head side to side slightly and releasing a deep, pain-filled moan. From the tenor of his voice it was evident that he'd suffered for a significant length of time.

He wore a matching tan safari-style pith helmet that had succumbed to the same manner of discoloration as had his trousers. There was blood trickle around his right ear and what appeared to be magazine pages stuffed into the helmet on the right side.

"Doc, go see what's up with that guy," the Sergeant Major ordered me.

"Alright."

I swung the turret back around so it was facing behind us. We staggered the vehicles so the Sergeant Major's weapon could encompass the convoy's rear into his field of fire, in case anyone tried hitting us from behind.

I then climbed down over the hood of our Humvee, dropped onto the brown dirt road packed in with large and small stones, and moved over to the disheveled heap of man and horse.

"Ooooohhhhhhh," the man moaned.

I crouched beside him as he rotated his head slowly to the right and brought his gaze to mine. Blood had been caked to the right side of his face, stiffening his mustache. His head bobbed and twitched as he moved it.

"Are you alright?" I asked.

Flies buzzed around the arrows stuck in the dead horse's flesh.

"Savages!" he cried out. "Bloody heathen savages!"

The man began to weep lightly, and I reached over to put a hand on his shoulder, but he cried out in pain, "Ooooohhhhhh!"

I retracted my hand and stumbled back a step.

"Bloody savages!" he went on. His accent was high British with a hint of Scottish undertone.

"What's going on, Doc?" the Sergeant Major yelled from the turret of his Humvee. "We can't be dicking around here all goddamned day."

"I don't know," I said. "He's fucked up pretty bad."

The ANA, true to form, began to dismount and mill around. They had a hard time keeping still or following simple directions.

"Hey!" the Sergeant Major shouted. "Get back in the trucks! Hey!"

"Savages!" the wounded man exclaimed. "Bloody Afghan savages, the lot of them! Keep them away from me. Oh dear!"

The man protected his head with a boxer's guard while straddling the dead horse's neck.

The Sergeant Major ordered Raz out of the vehicle and told him to tell the ANA soldiers to get back in their trucks, which he did, and with minimal fuss, they obliged.

"Doc, let's move! Grab him and get back in the truck. He might have some intel!" the Sergeant Major shouted.

"Give me a minute," I called back. It was always about the intel.

I knew what had to be done. As much as it killed me to give up any of my stash, I knew that this man, whomever he was, could not be moved without the administration of an anesthetic.

I hit him with a 10mg auto-injector of morphine sulfate and watched the pain dissolve from his expression. His whole body went limp and I knew I would not have much time.

I grabbed my medbag from the Humvee and dug through it till I found a vacuum-sealed pouch of QuikClot, the hemostatic agent, which I set to the side on top of the horse carcass.

I also pulled two Israeli dressings and my Leatherman. Removing embedded foreign objects is outside the purview of any first responder. However, riding the injured man in our Humvee with two arrows stuck in him was out of the question. The bumpy ride would cause the projectiles to dig around in the flesh, perhaps opening up a new hemorrhage.

So I opened the Leatherman's blade, ran it over a flame from my Zippo lighter for sanitization purposes, and got to work loosening the arrowhead from the man's thigh. He kept still, fully nodded out, as I tinkered and wrenched inside his leg.

I had the QuikClot just beside me, and when I'd finished cutting out the arrowhead and removing the weapon from the wound, just as I'd imagined it would, the hole began filling with bright red arterial blood.

As quickly as I could, I tore open the pouch of QuikClot and poured its contents into the gash. It looked like brown sand, absorbing the red blood. There was no flash or sizzle as the blood's liquid plasma made contact with the grainy substance, triggering the chemical reaction that instantly cauterized the wound. And I knew that it had worked because the bleeding stopped immediately. After a minute I plugged the hole and wrapped an Ace wrap around his leg.

I repeated the procedure with the wound on the man's left shoulder, and like the first time, he made no great protest as the morphine kept him cool and loose.

"Savages," he whispered as I finished bandaging his shoulder.

"Let's go, Doc!" the Sergeant Major shouted.

The ANA soldiers had begun to dismount a second time, and Raz Mohammed was again called out of the Humvee to herd them back into their vehicles.

"I'm almost done, Sergeant Major!" I shouted back.

I raised the man so that he was sitting upright on top of the dead horse, and while I was doing this, the pith helmet fell from his head onto the road, along with a magazine that had been wedged in between the helmet and the right side of his head.

I picked it up. Its pages had been glued together by blood from a deep gash, but I could still make out the title on the stiffened parchment. It read *Blackwood's Edinburgh Magazine*. The date and volume number were smeared and illegible.

"What happened here?" I said, pointing with my eyes to the wound on the right side of the man's head.

"Savages! Bloody no good, lying savages!" he cried out, staring now at the ANA soldiers.

"Don't get them all riled up," I said. "Hold still."

The cut was deep. Part of the man's skull had been sheared off.

"It was cold this morning." He spoke with his eyes down, as though recalling a horrific trauma. "I put the *Blackwood's* underneath my helmet to keep warm."

"I see."

I grabbed another Israeli dressing from my medbag and tied a modified Barton bandage around his head. This meant applying a direct dressing to the wound while looping the Ace wrap around the head then underneath the chin, taking care not to constrict the airway.

When it was all finished I picked up the helmet and placed it gently on the man's head over the bandage.

"There you go," I said. "Now you're all fixed up."

"Thank you, good sir, oh thank you so kindly," he replied.

As he stood up for the first time, one leg on either side of the dead, I noticed a great red stain in and around the area of his crotch.

"Oh my God!" I said in disbelief, pointing to the man's nether region. "What the fuck happened?"

He lowered his head as though moving in slow motion until his eyes focused on the red stain where his trouser legs met in the middle. He then resumed crying.

"Savages," he whimpered, covering his eyes with his left hand, while pointing with his right to a small satchel tethered to the dead horse's saddle. There were flies buzzing around the pouch, and it too was stained crimson.

I reached down, untied the satchel, and opened it up to look inside.

"Oh, God!" I turned my head to the right and nearly retched from the stench and also from the shock. I had seen much barbarism in my short life, but never anything so personal.

"Savages," the man whispered through his tears.

I walked over to him and placed my hand gently on his good shoulder.

"When we get back to base, we can fly you out to Landstuhl or the States, get this sewed back on."

"Doc, let's fucking go!" the Sergeant Major shouted, though this time I ignored him.

The eunuch continued to weep, and I did my best to comfort him.

"Don't worry about it, dude. They can sew it back on. Believe it or not, in our country, this sort of thing happens more than you might think."

"Oh, the bloody savages!"

"I have to dress the wound before we can take you into the Humvee."

"Into the what?"

"Drop your trousers."

After some deliberation, the eunuch obliged and lowered his trousers, and I dressed the wound as best I could, using some Kerlix, Ace wrap, and a generous amount of medical tape.

The man pulled up his trousers and I carefully transferred the contents of the bloody satchel to an airtight sealed Ziploc bag and then wrapped it loosely into an Ace wrap bandage and placed it in the dry-ice cooler in the trunk of our Humvee.

"Let's get you in the truck," I said, guiding him at the shoulder with my hand as though he were a geriatric patient, and I his ward nurse.

He was still quite lit up by the time we got him inside and I had to help him remove his helmet. I was careful not to disturb the head wound as I placed the headset around his ears and adjusted the mic so that it was right in front of his mouth.

"What is this bloody thing?" he queried, thumbing one of the earphones.

"It's so we can all hear each other. Gets pretty loud in here sometimes."

I secured the patient into the vehicle, then closed the rear door and climbed up into the turret and put on my own headset.

"Horseman One, this is Two, we're ready when you are," I hailed the Sergeant Major.

"Good to go, Two," he answered, "rolling out now."

I saw him make a few grand gestures in the direction of the ANA trucks and holler some rhetoric to get the convoy moving, and after a few moments, we were on our way east again, headed back to the Meth Lab, three ANA trucks up front followed by Lieutenent Grey, the Sergeant Major, and Raz Mohammed, then myself, Captain Harold, and our new, dismembered patient and passenger rounding out the back of the column.

"What did you say your name was, friend?" I asked over the comms.

"Brydon."

"What's that?" Captain Harold inquired.

"Dr. William Brydon, assistant surgeon to the Bengal Army, British East India Company."

CHAPTER 16
THE COMPANY

The convoy moved along at cruising speed, bumping and pitching along the Old Silk Road, as sweat escaped my body in thick torrents.

I thought it would be a good use of our time to try and learn something about our most recent addition to the crew. Why was he riding that broken-down horse? Who had shot him up with arrows? What was he doing out here all alone?

"Brydon," I said.

"It's Dr. Brydon, sir. What may I call you?"

"Doc."

"Very well, Doc."

The truck rolled over an especially large rock in the road, and I was thrown forward in the turret.

"You're a surgeon?"

"Assistant surgeon."

"With the British Army, right?"

"Bengal Army, British East India Company."

"I'm confused," I said. "You're a soldier, right?"

"I am; a medical officer."

"Which country's army do you serve?"

"I serve the crown, Her Majesty's Empire."

"So, you're a British soldier?"

"Sort of."

"What do you mean, 'sort of'?" I questioned rather exasperatedly. "You either are or you aren't."

"The Company serves the interest of the Crown, but it is a privately held entity."

"You mean a corporation?"

"If you will."

"You're telling me that your *corporation* has a standing army that serves the interest of the *state*?"

"No, Doc," he answered. "I'm telling you that we have three, one for each presidency. Mine is the Bengal Army." His tone was triumphant for the first time. "But the Company has the right and the obligation to wage war and govern on behalf of Her Majesty, the Queen."

The sound of wheels grinding and pistons firing droned on in the background.

"That doesn't seem fair," I said.

"Ha! What's fair got to do with it?" Dr. Brydon said.

"You'll have to excuse the Doc, Dr. Brydon," Captain Harold chimed in cheerfully. "He's still in the process of figuring out what exactly makes the world go round."

"Well," Dr. Brydon continued. "I'm sure he'll know soon enough."

"I'm sure you're right," Captain Harold answered.

An hour passed by without any words spoken. Then another hour. Then two more. Then Dr. Brydon spoke.

"I say, Doc, have you any more injections?"

I didn't respond.

"It's just that," he continued, "I fear the effects of the first injection are coming to an end, regrettably, and I'm in a great deal of pain from my many injuries."

"You hearing this, Doc?" Captain Harold asked.

"Yeah, I'm hearing it," I answered. "I'm sorry you're in pain, Dr. Brydon, but I have only a limited supply of anesthetics for the whole crew. And I've already dipped into our chest to accommodate you, and you are not one of us."

"Yes, I see," Dr. Brydon went on. "It's just that I seem to be the only man to have suffered any injury, and—"

"I said no!" I shouted. "I don't have enough to go around!"

There was a stiff, uncomfortable silence, and then Dr. Brydon said, "Very well, I understand."

Another hour or so passed and there seemed to be no change in the sky's color and the sun was completely obscured. I found it puzzling that we had been several hours in the truck, and there was no indication that the day was any closer to being over than when we had set out.

"Ooooohhhhhhhh," Dr. Brydon began to whine.

"Dr. Brydon, are you alright?" Captain Harold asked.

"I'm fine, it's just that ... ooooohhhhhh," he continued to moan.

"Can you tell us about what happened to you?" Captain Harold asked. "What were you doing out there on that horse?"

"I would love to tell you chaps all about it, it's just that ... ooooohhhhhh!" He let out a howl. "It just hurts so bloody much to talk at all!"

I knew what he was getting at. I had run game on my fair share of doctors and medical professionals to obtain what I needed; what I craved. If anyone could recognize the manipulative plays of a dope fiend, it was me.

There were, however, his severe injuries to consider. The doctor had been wounded in more than one place, and it was quite possible that his desire for more morphine was a legitimate, normal reaction to the level of pain he had experienced. At least initially.

I reached down and stuck him with a second auto-injector of morphine sulfate, then quickly popped back up into the turret and hit myself with a syringe full of Dilaudid.

I suddenly found the doctor to be much more agreeable and came to accept our whole situation out here on the road, beneath the blood-red sky in this awful heat, with a renewed sense of tolerance.

It was always like that for me. Things would get pent up to a point where I felt like I was ready to burst, then I would steal off somewhere and with a hard dose I would release the tension all at once. And it worked, until it didn't, and I would stop for a while, then start up again. But once I got back home, I swore, away from this bottomless hell, I would give it all up for good.

"Tell us what happened, Dr. Brydon," Captain Harold said softly. "We need to know."

Dr. Brydon took a deep, audible breath, then spoke.

"Oh, the savages," he muttered. "We set out from Kabul, 4,500 men and officers, mostly Indians and Gurkhas. Except for the officers, who were all British born, of course." He chuckled, then continued.

"There were twelve thousand women and children, the wives and families of the men." He paused. "Oh, the savages."

"What happened?" I asked.

"Elphinstone, that senile buffoon, he marched us down through the pass, surrendering hostages for 'safe passage.'" He inflected his tone to indicate sarcasm. "Then the tribes fell upon us; first with muskets and arrows, then with talwars and scimitars, rush after rush, advance after advance." He paused. "Savages!" he cried out.

"Go on," Captain Harold urged.

"It was six or seven days we were on that bloody road, and all the while the savages from every tribe we passed by came at us and fought. They kept demanding more prisoners. It was the women they wanted! Bloody Afghan savages! In exchange, they kept offering safe passage, and Elphinstone, that fool, kept handing over more and more of the women and children, and eventually surrendered himself, the coward!"

"Where were you headed?" I asked.

"Jalalabad, the garrison there."

"We're headed that way now."

"Yes, I know," he answered. "East."

"Did you fight back?" I asked.

"Bloody well yes, we fought back!" Dr. Brydon shouted. "But the savages had the numbers and the high ground, and we were mostly made up of women and children. Weak, defenseless, women and babies. Oh, the savages!" he continued.

"We made a final stand at Gandamak, twenty-five officers and forty-five soldiers, mostly of the 44th East Essex Regiment of Foot. They cut us down like bamboo rods, and took captives of those who surrendered."

"What happened to the captives?"

"Oh, it was horrible what they did to them."

"Tell us, Dr. Brydon. We need to know," Captain Harold insisted.

"Those who surrendered were promised safe quarter. But when they were brought back to the camps and villages, the savages had their way with them. The men were strapped down, their mouths forced open, and the Afghan women squatted over their faces and urinated into their mouths."

"What?" I asked."

"I say, the soldiers who surrendered were drowned in the piss of those filthy Afghan whores! Oh, the savages!"

"How did you make it out alive?"

Dr. Brydon took another deep breath and answered.

"I don't know. By God's grace, I escaped. I am the only one left from the column. All others were killed or captured. The Crown will have its revenge and the Company will have its revenge!" Dr. Brydon shouted.

"I don't doubt it," I said.

Several more hours passed, and though I could not see the doctor to know for certain if he was crying, I could feel a frailty in his voice as he breathed into the microphone of his headset. The sky remained red and unchanged, and sweat poured out of me in great sheets as I alternated between sitting and standing in the turret.

"What sort of goods does the Company trade in, Dr. Brydon?" I asked, finally.

"Oh, a great number of things, really. There's the tea, salt, saltpeter for gunpowder. That's a favorite with the Crown!" he laughed. "Also, the indigo dye, the silk, and the cotton as well. There is no great shortage of treasures out here in the East Indies. I suppose that's why we've taken such an interest."

We road over a small bump and the Humvee jumped up a little.

"Then there's the opium. They've tried outlawing it in China, but we were able to get around that. There's a wonderful return on our investment in the opium." His tone seemed to perk up whenever he spoke of the Crown or the Company. Especially the Company.

"In fact, many believe the opium to be the underlying cause of our campaign here in Afghanistan."

"Is that right?" Captain Harold inquired.

"Oh well, not officially, of course, but many in the highest ranks believe it to be true."

"What is the official reason?" I asked, curious.

"Oh well, it's what they call the Great Game; this notion that the Russians will move inevitably further south, and if allowed to, invade India, the Jewel of the Empire."

"Hmm," I said.

"Yes, but there's also the opium to consider. It's true, there's plenty growing wild in India, but it's been my experience that you can never have too much, don't you agree, Doc?"

"What's that?" I asked, puzzled.

"From the medical standpoint, I say. Surely a man of medicine such as yourself can understand and appreciate the immense value and power of the opiates." He paused. "Purely from a therapeutic perspective, I mean."

I didn't answer.

"Oh, Doc knows all about it," Captain Harold replied. "He is a subject matter expert; we're lucky to have him as our doc."

"Oh, rightly so. I do agree."

There was a long period of silence, and I found myself submersed in my thoughts. I could see the Sergeant Major's vehicle in front of me, and could barely make out the third ANA truck in the convoy, but my mind was elsewhere. I was not upset. The Dilaudid had made certain of that, but I knew something was terribly wrong.

And then I saw it. The flash of bright, sweeping, pulsating light. It still looked quite far away, but it radiated from the same point of origin. Only we were now closer to it. It was still off to the east, in the direction of FOB Mehtar Lam. This was the light that Pat Tillman had talked about at the blockade with the hooded soldiers. This was the good light.

"If the Chinese have outlawed the opium trade, what gives you or the Company the right to subvert their laws and sell dope to the people?" I asked.

"Oh, my dear boy," Dr Brydon said. "You mustn't look at things in such a nasty light."

"He's still very young," Captain Harold said. "He's still learning how the world operates."

"Did it ever occur to you that perhaps the Chinese leadership favors the illegal trade of opium because it can publicly denounce the drug and its connoisseurs as vile and unfit, whilst at the same time reaping massive profits from its illicit sale?"

The doctor posed this question with an air of indignation.

"If the drugs are harmful," I answered, "as we both know they are, then it's the responsibility of the state to make sure that they're kept off the street. I can't imagine that a government would play both sides like that," I responded.

"Well, all I'm saying is that if there is a demand for a product—in this case, opium—and a government makes the sale of that product illegal, all they've done is made the market for said product that much more profitable to the traders," he announced in an informed tone. "And if the profits do reach an obscene level, as they inevitably do in this kind of business, then there isn't a government on earth comprised of men that are able to resist corruption from the trade."

"Our government isn't like that," I said defiantly.

"Oh really?" said Dr Brydon.

Captain Harold said nothing.

CHAPTER 17
THE GREAT KHAN

My uniform was now drenched with sweat from the many long hours we'd spent on the road. The heat seemed to intensify the further east we moved. Had it not been for the many doses of Dilaudid, I'm not sure I would have made it through.

The doctor had kept quiet, no doubt thanks to the second morphine injection I'd given him, and though I was dismayed at having shared with him any narcotics in the first place, I was grateful he'd gone this long without requesting a third.

Captain Harold too had stayed silent, most likely entranced in the monotony and repetition of life on the road in eastern Afghanistan.

I could see that up ahead the road descended further and twisted and turned to the left slightly and came right up alongside the river of liquid flame. As we approached the drop-off point, I saw what looked to be a long, black, serpent-like shape that stretched on for miles and miles, almost to the point of origin of the bright light. The shape adhered to the curves in the road, and seemed to move forward aided by millions of tiny black legs like a giant millipede.

"Horseman Two, we're slowing down. There's something up here on the road, over," the Sergeant Major said.

"Got it," Captain Harold answered.

I could see the Sergeant Major waving both arms around, making grand gestures almost like jumping jacks in the direction of the ANA trucks. Once he got their attention, he indicated that they pull off to the left shoulder and halt, which they did, amazingly.

"Horseman Two, pull up alongside us," the Sergeant Major ordered after the way had been cleared by the ANA trucks.

"Roger that," Captain Harold replied.

We slunk up next to the Sergeant Major's truck and halted, and I was able to discern clearly what it was I'd seen earlier.

I observed a command element of mounted cavalrymen, adorned in dark, shiny metal plate and chain-mail armor carrying large spears, battle axes, and shields. And each one of them had a bow with a quiver of arrows tied to their horses' saddles. The horses also wore elaborate armor and seemed to share their riders' enthusiasm for expedition.

The column of armored cavalry took up the entire width of the road, and stretched back behind for nearly as far as the eye could see. There were easily a hundred thousand mounted soldiers, and behind them, from what I could tell, there was an infantry column as well. Great, giant siege engines followed. Catapults, trebuchets, enormous crossbows, three stories high, that fired projectile arrows the size of telephone poles.

One man from the command element at the front of the column stood out among the rest; a general, I surmised. He was in the middle, directly across from our Humvees, whose combined girth also took up the whole width of the road. The ANA trucks stood off to our left on the steppe, between ourselves and the molten lava river.

The man up front, the general, was able to demonstrate command through his presence alone.

He wore a metal helmet that formed a spike at the top, like a mosque's pointed minaret, with dark, shiny chain mail draped all around like a metallic mane, but he wore no visor.

His face was hard and cold, and he had a distinct mustache that curved down around his mouth like the whiskers of a catfish. His armor was plate and chain mail of a fine quality, and when I looked closely I could see thin grooves in the metal from strike marks around the ribs and on the right shoulder.

And though it was embroidered with fine jewels, especially on the helmet near the eyes, it was clear that his armor and uniform and the armor of his horse and of all the horses and all the men in the column were the uniforms of battle dress.

There was another man, hulking and fierce, who sat mounted on a tall horse just beside him. This second man wore a helmet with a visor that obscured his face completely. I understood that this large man was the general's second in command.

When we were within spitting distance of the great general and his aide-de-camp and the rest of the command element, the general let out a strong single-syllabled directive and stamped his spear butt end first into the sandy rock road, and the entire column commenced to halt. This took a little while, as the column stretched so long that the action had to work its way backward, and in the process, we heard the metal clanking and the hooves shuffling and myriad other sounds travel away from the men and horses in front of the column and eventually die out.

When the noise had subsided to a manageable level, the general locked eyes with the Sergeant Major and asked, "Do you know who I am?"

"No," the Sergeant Major answered smartly. "Tell me, who are you?"

"I am the Great Khan."

The entire column came alive with cheers and hollers and the rattling of weapons and armor. The Khan raised his right arm and the ruckus abruptly ended.

"This is my army," the Great Khan continued. "We ride west to Khwarezmia to address an insult."

"What insult?" I asked.

"I sent emissaries there, to Khwarezmia, to establish a trade agreement with the Shah. This road is very important to me; it connects the east with the rest of the world. It is vital to our economic interests. I sought to make the Shah a trading partner, but he murdered my emissaries. We ride to avenge their deaths and to bring them under the Mongol rule of law."

"I understand," I said.

"What does that have to do with us?" the Sergeant Major asked.

At this the Great Khan chuckled, and taking a cue from his master, the large man beside him also laughed. Then the laughter spread to the column, and before long, the laughter of men in battle dress became so loud it was impossible to communicate.

Then the Great Khan held up his right hand, and the laughter ceased.

"What are you doing on my road?" the Khan asked dispassionately.

"Who says it's *your* road?" the Sergeant Major gruffed, posturing behind the .50-cal, though not quite raising it in a threatening fashion.

"Two hundred thousand men and horses of the Mongol Army!"

The column erupted into furious roar. Swords clanked against shields, the butts of spears were pounded into the sand

and rock of the road, and voices called into the air at levels and intervals that shook the earth beneath our wheels.

"You think just because you have the power that you can invade and conquer any country you feel like?" the Sergeant Major questioned. "That's bullshit!" he shouted. "There are rules! You can't just ride out and murder people, you can't do that! People have rights, you know! Nations have rights!"

The men from the column broke out into laughter, and again the Khan raised his hand and they went silent.

"How does your country go about the task of expanding the empire? Do your leaders infantilize you with fantastical stories about your enemies? Do they convince you that you are at risk if you do not strike first? Or do they stage attacks so that you retaliate viciously against an identified target? All these are fine tactics, but we Mongols do not require such motivation in these matters. We march on our enemies simply because we can. It is more honorable that way."

The Sergeant Major remained silent, and a tense apprehension fell upon us as we did our best to prepare mentally for combat with the Mongol horde.

"And what about them?" The Khan pointed his great spear in the direction of the ANA trucks. The Afghans had up to this point kept themselves out of the discourse. "What are they to you?"

"They're our protégés," the Sergeant Major answered. "We train them."

"And yet you cannot rely on them not put their knives in your back when first they have the chance? Have they not already demonstrated their disloyalty? Do you know what I would do with men like that under my command?"

The Sergeant Major kept silent, and I kept silent as well. I thought about Mortin and my dad, and everyone else who had been killed in the whirling dervish of military force and civil unrest that had unfurled in the wake of the September 11 attacks. I thought about these things, but I kept silent.

"They will betray you, you know that," the Great Khan went on.

"That's the risk we take. We're their advisors. It's our job," the Sergeant Major answered matter-of-factly, as though he'd run through the same conversation in his own thoughts many times.

"Join me, join my men, and we may slaughter them like pigs together!"

The column lit up again with riotous energy, hooting and calling and clanking and clamoring all together in a collective drone. Then once more, the Great Khan raised his right hand and the men fell silent.

"No," the Sergeant Major replied.

"They will betray you, they will *all* betray you. You know this. Join me."

"No, I said," the Sergeant Major again answered, this time elevating his tone slightly to denote a small increase in hostility.

"I wasn't speaking to you," the Khan rasped as he turned his head to the right to face me directly.

"You know they will betray you, they will *all* betray you. Join me, and we may destroy them, then march onto Khwarezmia, then Persia, then Arabia and Europa. I know this is what you want."

He paused a moment. The air was dead and still.

"I know you want to kill them, to kill them all," he continued. "They will betray you." He made a sweeping gesture with his spear that encompassed both Humvees and the ANA trucks to our left. "They will *all* betray you."

"What's he saying, Doc?" Dr. Brydon asked curiously.

I put my hand up to my face and pinched the bridge of my nose so it looked like I was deep in contemplation, and the Great Khan would not see my lips move.

"He's trying to get me to defect to his side. He says the ANA will betray us, and that I should join him and ride west to Persia and Arabia and kill 'em all."

"Well?" Captain Harold inquired. "What are you gonna tell him?"

"Not bloody likely!" Dr. Brydon shouted. "Tell him, NOT BLOODY LIKELY!" he cried out a second time.

"Tell him to fuck off!" The Sergeant Major turned his head to face me and shouted, "Go on, Doc. Tell him to go fuck himself!"

I was in the unfamiliar position of having what felt like leverage over the Sergeant Major. And though I knew we could not live out our days here at this impasse with the Great Khan and his army waiting on his request for my allegiance, I still had a hard time letting go of that power.

"Well?" the Great Khan asked impatiently. "What will be your answer?"

"Not bloody likely," I said without shouting, but also not in a whisper.

The color of the Great Khan's face turned as red as the overcast sky, and I could see his eyes widen and his spear hand begin to raise into the air as though to give some unmistakable command to forward march. But, in an instant, the giant man to his left, his aide-de-camp, lifted his face mask, revealing himself to us, while at the same time leaning over to whisper something into the ear of the Great Khan.

It was Pat Tillman, once again, hard at work in the field on the top-secret mission he'd alluded to weeks earlier while we passed the football back and forth at Bagram. But what exactly was the mission's objective? It had to be something pretty high level to have him mixed up with the Mongols.

Whatever it was he said to the Great Khan, it must have cooled him down, because the Khan's face began to soften and his spear lowered slowly back down to his side.

Pat Tillman gave me a subtle nod, and I knew that we were on the same page still.

"Pull your trucks over to the side," he said, pointing at the ANA vehicles. "Where those idiots are."

I didn't have the nerve to look back at the Sergeant Major. I knew the humiliation over being backed down would have been painfully expressed on his face. Instead I instructed Captain Harold to reverse our Humvee onto the shoulder and park beside the ANA trucks, whose occupants sat frozen like scared statues for the duration of our encounter.

We stacked our vehicles side by side and watched the legions of Mongol cavalry move west along the Old Silk Road, like demons of retribution, in the direction of Khwarezmia and Persia and Arabia and Europa.

CHAPTER 18
ALEXANDER

As the final infantry battalions of the great Mongol column marched past our vehicles and the steady murmurous sound of boots stomping, men grunting, and weapons clanking softened to a dull roar and then faded out of earshot, the advisors of 4th Kandak, 1st Brigade and our Afghan counterparts sat silent and dumbfounded, allowing the gigantic cloud of dust kicked up by the men and beasts to eventually settle.

A moment passed. A minute, an hour, a day, a week, a month, a year. It was impossible to know for certain.

The sky remained a pomegranate red and the river of molten lava rushed continuously on behind us, with the occasional belch or tidal surge of white-hot liquid fire that we could feel displacing the air all around us.

"We'll lead, Sergeant Major," Captain Harold said finally. "We should be back at Mehtar Lam before dusk."

"Roger that," the Sergeant Major responded.

As we pulled off the shoulder onto the rocky dirt road, I shouted in the direction of the ANA soldiers and managed to compel them, through a series of beckoning gestures, to fall in behind us. The Sergeant Major came up behind them so our two Humvees bookended the formation with the three ANA trucks in the middle.

We pushed forward in silence, the intense heat bearing down on us, and in soft, meditative rhythms, I began to disappear into my breath. And though each great inhale burned with hot vapor, I was able to convince myself that everything was temporary. It could not last forever. This hell had to eventually end, one way or another.

I had given up trying to keep track of time. I knew only that we existed in this moment for no other reason than to continue east in the direction of FOB Mehtar Lam, the place from which we'd launched this failed expedition some weeks earlier.

And there was also the light to consider. I could see it from my position in the turret, beaming on through the red overcast sky like a lighthouse beacon, and I knew, if nothing else, we were at least headed in the right direction.

And so east we rode, until time and sound and thought all began to congeal into an indistinguishably singular misery. *What could be the source of that light?* I wondered.

I began to hear a loud thumping sound, not unlike the sound of the Sergeant Major's boot against the door to my quarters, and after a few more thumps, began to feel it in my chest. It was getting closer.

"Captain Harold, you feel that?"

"Yeah, it feels like mortars going off. But I don't see any."

It seemed to emanate from the brush to the right of the convoy.

I got on the radio. "Sergeant Major, I think they're trying to hit us with mortars, over."

"Look alive! Keep that fucking gun up! Fire on anything that doesn't look right!"

"None of this looks right, Sergeant Major!"

"Use your best judgment."

The thumping grew louder and I noticed some rustling in the undergrowth. Then I saw the giant hooves and ivory tusks of a great white elephant thrashing through the brush—trunk whirling side to side, trumpeting at full capacity. It moved directly into our convoy's path and halted.

"Sergeant Major, we got a problem up here!"

Captain Harold slammed on the brakes and the first ANA truck rear-ended us, knocking me forward into the receiver.

"What the fuck's going on up there?" the Sergeant Major hollered.

"Wait one, Sergeant Major," I answered.

Our vehicle stopped inches from the beast's enormous tusks. It was then that I noticed the rider. He was a young man—could not have been much older than me. But he held himself with an air of pride, such that I have never seen, before or since.

He wore a lion's head as a crown and a breastplate made of gold over his chest. He carried a long spear in his right hand and a large bronze circular shield in his left. There was no bridle around the elephant's mouth. How he maintained positive control of the beast was a mystery.

"Do you know who I am, boy?"

He stepped onto the animal's head, then walked down along its trunk and stood finally on the hood of the Humvee, an arm's length away from me, eyeing the .50-cal curiously.

"No, no idea," I replied.

"I am Alexander of Macedon, son of Zeus, king of Greece, pharaoh of Egypt, shah of Persia, lord of Asia!"

He stood there a moment, his face preserved in a look of anticipation.

"I am the greatest warrior the world has ever known—greater even then Achilles!"

I got the sense that he wanted me to respond in some way, but I had nothing to say.

"You do not know how to behave in the presence of royalty?"

"I'm an American. We have no use for royalty."

"You are an insolent young man!"

"I've been called that before."

He chuckled, and I laughed too.

"And, have *you* a title?" he asked.

"Yes."

"And, what is it?"

"Doc."

He laughed again.

"Very well, Doc. And why are you here?"

"My country is at war. We were attacked; this is our retaliation."

"Yes, of course. You must avenge those who were lost. How else could you call yourself a man?"

"What's he saying?" Captain Harold asked.

"Look, a bloody white elephant!" Dr. Brydon shouted.

I ignored them both and thought about Alexander's question.

"And is there someone *you* are avenging, Doc?"

"My father."

"Ah, yes. My father was also killed. In fact, his murder was the impetus for this campaign." He looked back at the brush from which he'd charged at us moments earlier. "The army is breaking camp. We'll be on the move shortly."

"I thought you said you were the son of Zeus?"

At this he laughed. "You are a troublesome boy. No good will come of it. It is unwise to question the official narrative. You must know this?"

"I'm just trying to figure out what's going on, Alexander."

He laughed again. It was the laugh of the informed.

"The men"—he looked back at the brush, which now bristled with cavalrymen and Greek hoplites moving in to take up position beside the white elephant—"they need to believe in something; something greater than themselves. How else could I demand of them to lay down their lives in the service of my cause?"

I wondered about my own service. *What cause did I serve that was greater than myself?*

"Wouldn't it be enough that they were patriots? That they would be proud to die for their country? Do they really have to believe you're descended from a god?"

"Patriotism is a fine motivator. Many men have proudly given their lives for their country, and many more will continue to do so. But God is the light, and a man does not live who will turn away from the light in favor of darkness. And so my men believe I am descended from Zeus."

He looked around to see if any of his soldiers were within earshot. They were not, so he continued.

"My father . . ." He paused. "My *true* father was a fine man, an excellent warrior and a wise general. But he lacked vision. For all his talk of a Persian campaign, he could scarcely keep the Greeks from cutting each others' throats."

"Doc, what's going on up there?" Captain Harold repeated.

"A bloody white elephant! Ha-ha!" yelped Dr. Brydon.

"Captain Harold, what the fuck is going on?" the Sergeant Major fumed.

"I'm trying to find out, Sergeant Major," Captain Harold said sheepishly.

"I know what they think," Alexander continued. "My nobles. They wouldn't dare speak it, not even in jest, but I know what they think. Who stood to benefit from my father's murder? Who but myself? It matters not; mine will be the history that is written. I loved my father. His sacrifice will serve the larger purpose."

"Why are you here, Alexander?"

He smiled for the first time genuinely, from ear to ear.

"We give chase to the coward Darius, third of his name. His Persians have abandoned him and he is without a state. I will follow him into the bowels of hell if I must."

A rider approached, a large man on a black stallion.

"Sire, we are ready."

"Very good, Strategos."

The large man gave a slow nod and I knew him to be Pat Tillman, as he pointed with his spear to the east, in the direction of the sweeping, pulsating light, indicating that we continue on after the army had broken camp.

"Doc," Alexander called out to me. "By this spear do I conquer Hades!"

He hurled the javelin over the river of molten lava, and when it struck the far bank, the ground beneath us began to quake. I held on to the sides of the turret to keep from being thrown around.

"Doc, what's happening?" Captain Harold screamed.

"I don't know!" I shouted back.

A wide stone bridge emerged from below the surface of the lava and rose to the level of the road, conjoining the two banks. Alexander mounted his great white elephant and set off over the bridge, his army of hoplites and cavalry close behind him.

"Stay the course!" Pat Tillman shouted as he galloped across the bridge.

The troop movement cut transversely across our path, so we were unable to advance until the last hoplite had brought up the rear and arrived safely on the far bank, at which point the stone bridge shifted and rumbled before submerging back below the surface of the lava.

"Doc, what the fuck is going on? Goddamn it, answer me!" the Sergeant Major roared.

"We're good to go, Sergeant Major," I replied as Captain Harold shifted the Humvee into drive and pushed further east in the direction of FOB Mehtar Lam, three ANA trucks behind us, and the Sergeant Major, Lieutenant Grey, and Raz Mohammed bringing up the rear.

CHAPTER 19
FIELDS

After what felt like several hours on the Road, Captain Harold began to slow our vehicle almost to a halt, as though he was searching for some clue off to the side, in the dense forest to the right of our convoy.

As we slowed our pace, the ANA trucks behind us also reduced their speed, and when this chain reaction finally reached the Sergeant Major's vehicle in the rear, he radioed up to us and said, "What the fuck are we slowing down for now?"

"Just making a pit stop up ahead," Captain Harold replied as he pulled off to the right down a small side road, barely visible to the untrained eye.

"What do you mean 'pit stop'?" the Sergeant Major thundered.

But it was too late. We had already turned and were forging ahead through the dense forest. The three ANA trucks followed closely, and the Sergeant Major, unable to regulate the situation, had no choice but to follow along.

"What the fuck are you doing, Captain Harold?" he objected.

"Just gotta make a quick pit stop up ahead. Won't take but a minute, Sergeant Major. Hold on tight, we're almost there."

Before the Sergeant Major could object we made a second turn, this time on the left-hand side of the road. Our convoy was halted in a J-shaped formation as our lead vehicle was held up at the entrance of what looked like a large farm or plantation. There were long rows of red maples on either side of the driveway into which we had pulled, and had I not peered closely into the entranceway, I might have missed the armed guard in plain clothes who waved us in.

There was something strangely familiar about him. He wore a grey unmarked ball cap and plain khaki pants and a plain grey T-shirt and sported one of those ridiculous black-and-white houndstooth-patterned kaffiyehs partially draped around his neck, perhaps as a show of solidarity with his Afghan brethren. A typical defense contractor getup.

Black ballistic sunglasses obscured his eyes, but I noticed nonetheless that he seemed to cast a recognizing glance at Captain Harold as we pulled up to the gate.

There was no steel-reinforced blast door like the one Lieutenant Grey busted down at Camp Phoenix. There was only a long cylindrical toll bar roughly twenty feet in length that opened and closed like a railroad crossing gate.

The bar went up and we rolled through the threshold, entering the farm. We moved slowly and with caution as the terrain dictated.

Up to that point I'd regarded myself as someone who understood things; someone in the know. At least to a greater degree than a large representation of my fellow brothers-in-arms—many of whom, at the time, believed the language of the Afghan people to be Arabic and the mastermind behind the attacks of September 11 to be Saddam Hussein.

Iraq was a joke, of that I was certain. But the mission in Afghanistan remained the *good* war, if only by comparison. What we were doing here had purpose, and was a direct proportional response to the attacks of September 11. All this I knew.

But as we came through the toll bar and followed the bumpy dirt road up a slight incline, I observed to the right of our vehicle miles upon miles of fresh poppies growing in a controlled, cultivated environment tended to by scores of peasant farmers. And I understood there were dimensions to this war I had not considered.

And I immediately remembered the face of the guard in plain clothes who'd moments earlier waved us in unassumingly to be the same man I'd seen entering Camp Scott at Bagram weeks earlier, though he was not the one who'd impressed me; not the one with the ancient look about him.

This was where the world came to buy dope, and here I was at ground zero. I felt blessed, in a way. I had nearly gone through my re-up stash from Camp Phoenix, thanks in part to the addition of Dr. Brydon to our team, but also to my own unquenchable need for opiates. It seemed as though the problem of supply had been resolutely solved, as there was enough opium fermenting in those flowers to pacify all the men on earth and more.

We cruised up the gentle grade of the dirt road and I noticed a row of B-huts on the left side. There were fifteen or twenty of them. I gathered that they housed the peasant farmers I'd seen tending the great field, procuring the milk of poppies from budded flowers and hauling it back in brown clay jars.

There were also more defense contractors in plain clothes standing a watch of sorts at the perimeter of the field. They seemed to be staring down the peasant farmers as they made their way back through the brush with their bounties in the large clay pots balanced on their heads or sometimes on one of their shoulders.

I imagined too that the guards were berthed in one or several of the B-huts, but I doubted seriously that they shared quarters with the peasants.

As we neared the end of the row, I noticed two figures standing outside the last B-hut, both of whom were familiar to me. The first was the plain-clothed defense contractor I'd seen outside Camp Scott at Bagram—the one that had impressed me. The other was our team leader, the bloated pig of a man, Major Peeve.

The contractor made me feel uneasy, but never in a way that caused me to fear for my safety. I had been in the presence of killers before, though it was different with him. There was something terrifying about his presence, as though he was privy to some unnatural truth about this war.

Peeve, on the other hand, I loathed. His rotund physique that bulged and protruded from every possible fold in his uniform had the effect of making the fabric appear taut against his skin.

As we approached the two men, Peeve began guiding us in with his hands, directing us to park beside the final B-hut in the row. As we did this, the ANA trucks parked along the perimeter of the poppy field.

Peeve made eye contact with the Sergeant Major in the rear and, through a series of hand gestures, beckoned him to drive up and park alongside our vehicle, which he did.

When we parked the Humvee, I noticed that Dr. Brydon lay motionless in the backseat, so I hovered over him a minute, determined that he was alive, though unconscious, and decided to let him be for the moment.

I popped back up through the hatch and climbed down onto the hood, then onto the dirt surface and waited for Captain Harold to exit the vehicle.

"What are we doing here, Captain Harold?"

"No big deal, Doc, just a pit stop. We'll be outta here in no time. What do you think of the foliage?" He nodded in the direction of the poppy field.

"It's beautiful," I said.

"I knew you'd like it."

Captain Harold and I and Lieutenant Grey and the Sergeant Major and Raz Mohammed approached the two men, Major Peeve and the defense contractor, and formed a semicircle around them.

"Fucking took you cocksuckers long enough!" snarled Major Peeve. As he spoke his many fat rolls gyrated and rippled beneath his uniform.

"Go see about their accommodations," the defense contractor ordered. His voice and intonation were without character or dialect.

"Yes, sir," Major Peeve snapped and turned and made for the final B-hut in the row. This puzzled me because Major Peeve was our ranking officer, and, as far as I knew, the man who'd given him a directive was not a military man; or if he was, it was not a military that I had ever known.

"Hello, Colonel," Captain Harold said with a great smile.

"Hello, Captain Harold," the man replied. "Glad you could make it. Sergeant Major, Lieutenant Grey, Raz, Doc." He did not take his bespectacled eyes off Captain Harold as he went through the process of greeting us one by one.

"Nice to see you all. Sorry to hear about Mortin. He was a good soldier."

We all let our heads roll forward slightly and kept our eyes on the ground a moment out of grief, or respect, or simply because we didn't know how else to respond.

Whether or not he, himself felt any great attachment to Mortin was impossible to know for certain. His face remained unmistakably expressionless. Tiny silver strands of hair haunted the perimeter of his high and tight, and a pair of black ballistic sunglasses with lenses like two horizontal teardrops obscured his eyes. Nowhere on his person did I recognize anything resembling an insignia denoting his rank. This was our Colonel; the man I'd seen walking into Camp Scott weeks earlier. I had misclassified him, it seemed. We all stood there with our heads down a moment before he addressed us again.

"What took you so long?" His tone stayed resoundingly even and flat, and when he spoke, the surrounding background noise—the wind rustling through the poppies and the thumping footsteps and shuffling of the peasant farmers moving in and out of the great field—would fall silent in the wake of his large but otherwise unremarkable voice until he'd finished his sentence, and the sounds would all come sharply back into focus.

"We had some trouble out on the road, sir," Captain Harold answered expediently.

"Nothing you couldn't handle, I imagine." The Colonel adjusted his head slightly so that his eyes fixed on the Sergeant Major.

"No, sir!" the Sergeant Major answered. It felt bizarre to hear him address a superior officer correctly.

"Sergeant Major, why don't you and the rest of your team get settled in."

"Yes, sir!" the Sergeant Major replied, shifting his weight and starting off in the direction of the last B-hut in the row.

I began to fall in behind him when I heard the voice of the Colonel address me personally.

"Not you, Doc."

The Sergeant Major turned his head slightly back and caught eyes with the Colonel and with me, but quickly remembered his place and turned back toward the B-hut and kept moving and did not turn around again.

Captain Harold hung back too, and before long it was just the three of us, myself, the Colonel and Captain Harold, standing between the B-hut and the great field of poppies with its several guards standing watch at the edge and its many farmhands moving in and out of the crop.

"Do you know who I am?" the Colonel asked me candidly.

"You're the Colonel," I replied.

"But you didn't know I was the Colonel until you heard Captain Harold address me, is that right?"

"Yes, sir," I answered matter-of-factly, as though our exchange was just another drill or part of some training evolution.

"Who did you think I was before you knew?"

I was puzzled by this question. I wasn't sure where he was headed, and I wanted to give the right answer, but it was impossible to know what that was, so I did the next best thing and told the truth.

"I wasn't sure."

"Oh, come on, Doc. You must have had some inkling?"

I was amazed at the Colonel's complete lack of dialect or affect even. It made me question whether or not he was speaking at all, or if I had just been reading his lips.

"I thought you were a defense contractor."

"Yes, but there are many different types of defense contractors," he injected. "For example, the men who scoop up the dirt with bulldozers and fill in the HESCOs—they're defense contractors." He paused and glanced at Captain Harold, who nodded his head in agreement, then back to me. "And the men who maintain the MWR facilities; they're defense contractors too."

I realized where he was going with all this, and I was beginning to feel the sickness come on, so I said what I believed he wanted to hear in the interest of expediting the whole process so that I could get some alone time and shoot some of that incredible looking dope the hadji farmers kept bringing in from the fields.

"I thought you were the other kind."

"The other kind?" He smiled. "Please explain."

"I thought you worked a personal security detail."

"A personal security detail?"

"I thought you were in the negative space; that you didn't exist. CIA maybe."

"Well, I'm not sure where you came up with this term 'negative space,' but I can tell you this: At a certain point, for people who do what I do, the lines all break down. The uniforms come off; the insignias disappear. And the mission changes. It changes constantly. I am not CIA, or NSA, or FBI, or DHS, or ICE. There is no acronym for what I do. I simply serve."

I nodded my head in agreement to keep things moving along, though I didn't understand a word of what he was saying.

"I thought you were stationed downrange at FOB Huey, sir. That's what they told me."

"I'm wherever my presence is needed."

A moment passed, and then he went on.

"You see what it is we're doing out here, don't you?" He swept his right arm out behind him in a semicircle and swiveled his head to indicate the poppy field and its workers.

"Now you're probably wondering why it is we're harvesting all that opium when you know very well, perhaps better than most, that opium and opiate derivatives are illegal in our country and in most civilized countries around the world."

He leaned in slightly, and I took this to mean that he expected me to answer him, though he had posed no actual question.

"The thought had crossed my mind, sir."

"Well, I'll tell you why, Doc. It's perhaps simpler than you might have guessed. We're doing it for the money."

He again pointed to the great field and for the first time ever I saw him smile.

"Ten grams of opium can be converted into one gram of pure heroin. Nowhere else on earth can we produce such a powerful product."

He glanced at Captain Harold, who nodded and smiled, then focused once more his attention onto me.

"This land is cursed, you know. You've heard this before, haven't you?"

"I have, sir."

"Do you know how?"

"Something about the blood of warriors," I answered, not really sure what all that meant.

"The blood of warriors is what causes the poppies to grow. That's what makes the opium so pure." He went into his pocket and pulled out a dried-up brown poppy flower. It was roughly the size of a golf ball and similar in shape.

"That is why soldiers continue to die here. Afghanistan is a country where armies come to die."

As he spoke I began to feel sick. At first I just chalked it up to withdrawals. I was due for a dose, that much was true, but I also felt like there was more going on. Something about the Colonel made me feel terrible, as though whatever pride I'd allowed myself to experience as the result of being a soldier and of going to war for my country had, in the presence of this officer, become the source of an overwhelming nausea.

"You thought perhaps there was more to it, but there is not. This is a place where warriors come to die, and their blood soaks into the soil and feeds the poppies."

"So you harvest the opium?"

"Exactly right, Doc."

"I told you he was sharp, sir," Captain Harold said.

"Yes, you did, Captain."

"For the money, sir?" I questioned.

"Yes, for the money, but not only for that reason. People addicted to drugs are quite easy to control."

"You don't need to lecture Doc on that point. I'm sure he's well aware," Captain Harold said.

The Colonel ignored the captain and continued. "Doc, the world is in a period of great transition. These next few years, decades even, are going to be difficult for us. But when we come out on the other end, it will all have been worth it. You'll see."

"I'm not sure I follow, sir."

"We're running out of resources."

"Sir?"

"Resources. Oil, food, water. We're running out. Or, depending on how you choose to approach the issue, we have too many mouths to feed."

"Forgive me, sir, I have no idea what you're getting at."

"Our options are clear," he continued. "We can either try to manage our resources . . . "

At this he and Captain Harold laughed wildly.

"Or we can adjust the population, which, as a practical matter, is something we're much better at."

Captain Harold continued to smile and nod and alternate his field of sight between myself and the Colonel.

"We know that you've suffered a personal loss, Doc. We know about your father, and I can't tell you how sorry I am about that. But that had to happen."

"What do you mean 'that *had* to happen,' sir?"

"All great progress requires great sacrifice. Try to look at things from the perspective of the larger purpose."

There was a still silence, then Captain Harold spoke.

"Doc, you're gonna want to be on our side when the change starts to really take shape. Back home, and everywhere else for that matter, it won't be pretty. We're already casting a wide net to catch just about every type of data or metadata that's transmitted, no matter who it is or what they're talking about. We look through e-mails, text messages, we examine phone records. But it's going to get worse. There's going to be some type of terrorist attack, or an outbreak of some virus, or a natural disaster even; we haven't yet worked out all the details. But when we really start to crack down, you'll see. There will be riots and unrest and martial law, and believe me, when that happens, you're going to want to be the one marshaling, not the one being marshaled."

It took all my strength to keep from vomiting there on the Colonel's boots. Sweat poured down my face in globs, and I could feel my eyelashes flutter.

"What do you say, Doc?" The Colonel placed his hands on his hips and stood tall. "Will you join us?"

I was too broken to even speak. I began to sway mildly from side to side, then forward and back, and it became obvious that I would not be able to stand for much longer.

"He's sick, sir," Captain Harold said.

"Of course he is. Who wouldn't be after a few months in this dump?"

The Colonel went into his pocket a second time and came out with a thick black ball wrapped tightly in Saran Wrap.

"You know, Doc, we don't typically perform the enrichment process at this location."

He thumbed the ball while he spoke as though it was a medal or some other object of great achievement. It appeared to be malleable as he left small impressions of his thumb on the spots where he pressed in.

"It's standard operating procedure to have the enrichment facility located within one kilometer of a major distribution center. Usually smaller air bases are used in this capacity. Makes it all easier. Simpler," he said almost in passing. "Things are a little more out in the open now. In the Vietnam days, we had to seal it up in the coffins of the returning war dead. What an insult to those who had made the ultimate sacrifice in defense of freedom and democracy. We don't do that anymore—ship the dope in the coffins. We don't need to, really. Nobody cares what we're doing out here."

Captain Harold smiled and nodded.

"We don't like to allow too many of the workers access to the final product. Of course we need them to do the labor, but we try to limit the number to a select few. Also, it's best not to let the product sit too long once it has been processed. We prefer to get it shipped out to the markets in Europe, Asia, and of course the US within twenty-four hours once it has been made pure."

Captain Harold continued to swivel his head back and forth, smiling and nodding at myself and the Colonel.

"In fact, that's what your team is here for."

He turned his head around and pointed to the ANA trucks parked at the perimeter of the field. The soldiers were collecting pots filled with the milk of poppies and loading them into their pickups.

"Moving the unrefined product to the enrichment facility is about all those useless cocksuckers are good for."

"Amen to that," Captain Harold said.

"Except sometimes they get lost along the way, and the product never arrives. So, we find it works best if they have an escort. That's why you're here, Doc; to help make sure the product makes its way to the enrichment facility intact."

I could feel sweat pouring down my face, into my eyes. I winced in discomfort and squinted as the salt began to sting. My eyesight blurred, but I managed to hold a visual of the Colonel's black tear-shaped ballistic sunglasses.

"As I said, we don't typically enrich the product here at this location." He rotated the black plastic-wrapped ball in his hand as though it were a marble.

"But Captain Harold here tells me that you're somewhat of a connoisseur, so we went ahead and made an exception."

He extended his hand out to me, palm flat, with the substance resting in the open space like a black pearl.

"Go on, take it," he said. "But be careful. That right there is the real deal. The purest stuff on earth. From the blood of warriors."

I vacantly opened my right hand and accepted the prize. The Colonel closed my hand for me and I dropped the ball of dope into my cargo pocket.

"Thank you, sir," I said.

"Of course, Doc. You earned it. There's a place for you here. When the change happens, you'll have a place with us."

The Colonel put his hand on Captain Harold's shoulder.

"Trust us, Doc," Captain Harold said. "It's for the best."

I nodded my head involuntarily. By this point I had secured the dope, which would help keep the sickness at bay. The subsequent banter was really just a formality. They would talk, and I would listen, and make them believe I cared about what they were saying or that I agreed with them. Whatever it took to bring the conversation to a close.

"And one more thing, Doc," the Colonel said as he once more pointed to the ANA soldiers at the field's perimeter. "The moment you reach the enrichment facility, that bunch right there will have outlived their usefulness. Once you've delivered the product, I need you to get rid of them." He leaned in slightly, then said, "All of them."

Captain Harold smiled and nodded and swiveled his head to and fro.

"Can you handle that, Doc?"

"Yes, sir," I answered.

"Good. Why don't you get cleaned up. You look like you could use a minute," the Colonel said.

"Yes, sir," I said again.

As I moved away from the two officers, I noticed Captain Harold was still smiling and nodding, still swiveling his head.

I encountered the Sergeant Major on my way into the barracks and he looked at me with that unique mixture of pity and disgust and said, "You alright, Doc?"

"I'm fine, Sergeant Major."

We both stood there a moment, neither man daring to move. A whole novel's worth of communication passed silently between us, and then I finally said, "Sergeant Major, would you take a picture of me?"

"Sure, Doc."

"Over there." I pointed to the poppy field. "No one back home will ever believe this shit."

I handed the Sergeant Major my 5.0 megapixel camera and moved into the field. When I felt as though I'd gone far enough in, I turned around and crouched down so that the poppies surrounded me at neck level.

"Ready, Sergeant Major."

"Say cheese."

He snapped off a series of shots, at least one of which, I imagined, captured the banality and the insanity of the image.

"Got it," he said.

"How's it look?"

"Like a million bucks."

"Thanks, Sergeant Major," I remarked as I climbed back through the thick of the field.

"Tell you what, Doc," he said as he placed the camera into my sweaty hand. "You ever write a book about this shit, you better put this picture on the cover."

"As I understand it, Sergeant Major, the publishers are pretty particular about what goes on the cover," I said. "Maybe I'll put it in the 'about the author' part, on the jacket."

"Sounds like a plan," he said.

We both headed back to the B-hut. It was very hot, and the sun beat down mercilessly. I felt very lucky to have a friend like the Sergeant Major.

CHAPTER 20
SPIRAL

Rather than heading straight to the B-hut to get lit, I checked on Dr. Brydon once more. He was still passed out in the back of the Humvee, so I gently woke him and gathered him up for the transfer to the hut. He was a patient, and I was a medic. This was, after all, my job.

"What . . . what are you doing there? Unhand me, you ruffian!" he snorted as I pulled him from the truck and put his arm around my shoulders.

"Relax, Dr. Brydon. I got ahold of some more anesthetics. Some really good stuff. You're going to be impressed, I promise."

His eyes illuminated and his posture improved on hearing the good news. "Oh, well, in that case let us not waste another moment!" he replied.

For the purpose of heating up the dope, a necessary step in the process of slamming true junk, I procured from the trunk of the Humvee a metal canteen case to serve as a surrogate spoon. The case was not ideal for cooking dope, but I knew similar cases had been used to brew coffee in World War II and Vietnam–era platoons, so I was certain the metal would at least stand up to the strength of the flame.

I also drew a full syringe's worth of normal saline from one of my IV bags because I knew I would have to lubricate the substance before putting the heat to it. Dr. Brydon leaned up against the Humvee and whimpered softly as I rounded up the necessary materials. He wasn't so hard, I thought.

The two of us staggered back to the B-hut, Dr. Brydon wailing out high British expletives every so often after a difficult step. I kicked open the door and darkness emerged from the space, and soon we were immersed in darkness, moving forward one hobble-step at a time. Two fiends, otherwise completely separate personalities, bound together by a common interest.

I managed to locate a corner rack and laid Dr. Brydon down on the bottom bunk. I then pulled my lighter from my trousers and twisted off a pinch from the ball. The lighter flickered, and it was difficult to see the small, sticky putty in the dark, but I was able to glob it into the metal canteen case, squirt a few cc of normal saline onto it, then put the flame underneath.

The case had small rings on either side, so I suspended it from a hook that stuck out of the bunk bed's support beams and cooked the dope and listened to it crackle like the campfires of my youth.

I decided unilaterally and without any debate that Dr. Brydon would be the first to try the dope because his injuries, by nature, were much more severe than mine, and also because the intensity of the junk had not yet been tested and was perhaps lethal.

I wrapped my CAT tourniquet around his noninjured arm, preparing him for the injection.

"Oh my!" he said enthusiastically. "This shall be quite something. Don't you agree, Doc?"

I drew up a small catch of the dope, which had coalesced with the water, boiled and bubbled and turned a thick, brown layer, like molasses, only not as thick.

"I hope so," I said as I grabbed his arm, stretched out the skin of his antecubital area with my left hand, and harpooned him square in the mainline with my right, hammering down on the plunger in one single fluid motion.

"Ohhh . . ." he gasped, then I heard his throat gurgle and I thought about Mortin for a moment, which frightened me, so I put my ear to his mouth to listen for respirations, which I eventually heard. They were shallow and far apart, and sounded like a leaky gas valve, but Dr. Brydon was still alive. The dose had not been fatal.

I took this as a great sign and quickly began preparing my own rig. There was at least enough for one more hit at the bottom of the metal canteen case, so I drew it up into my syringe and tied the tourniquet around my right arm.

And for good measure, I flushed the saline lock with the remaining normal saline solution after I had tied on the tourniquet. The water felt cool going into my vein, and did not hurt as I suspected it might have. I placed my Zippo lighter on the ground with the cap still open and the flame still dancing as it served as the only practical light source in the room, then put the spike up to my vein.

The floor beneath me opened up or collapsed, and I fell far and fast, as though I'd been dropped from a C-130. The knots in my back and shoulders which had formed from riding and humping and existing in this climate for so long at once released as my whole body went limp as a latex glove.

It felt as though the force of gravity had been multiplied exponentially and I was being pressed down through the floor of the B-hut by a pleasurable force which replaced every hint of discomfort from without and from within with a full-scale serotonin dump. A constant, prolonged orgasm.

The flame from my Zippo flickered and pitched, though there was no wind or movement of air to speak of. I fell deeper, and felt wonderfully warm and pleasantly cooled all at once. Lockjaw ensued. My knuckles tightened to form fists and I gasped for each new breath, sucking oxygen through my teeth.

Then I felt something lift me up and haul me into the air through the darkness; a giant. To steady myself, I threw my legs around its shoulders and wrapped my arms around its gigantic head.

It moved forward, one foot in front of the next, and I was thrown from side to side at first, until I gained my balance. The creature felt and even smelled familiar.

We thumped forward in total darkness for a while, when I saw a light from above, and before I could understand what was happening, we were moving upstairs, and I was bouncing up and down and side to side, holding on for dear life as we came closer and closer with each forward step to the light at the top of the dark stairwell.

As we emerged from the darkness, a flash of white light momentarily blinded me, but my senses quickly returned, and I came to recognize the surrounding area as the Financial District of New York City; specifically, the corner of Fulton and Broadway.

"Hang on, Norman!" the beast shouted. "Here we go. Wheee!!!"

I began to squeal and giggle uncontrollably as the giant thundered forward down Fulton Street toward the two towers which radiated and reflected a bright light like two giant rectangular mirrors.

"You wanna see where your daddy works, don't you?"

The giant stopped abruptly at the foot of the enormous glass and steel structures and pointed up to the very top of the building on the right.

"Up there, Norman. Look. On the one hundred and tenth floor. That's where your daddy works! Wanna go up and see?"

As I looked up at the obscenely tall buildings that seemed to stretch up infinitely to the sky like an elongated tuning fork, the light once more engulfed my sight and I could see nothing but the deep, white emptiness.

"Norman? Norman? Hello, is anybody home? Norman?"

I came to in full sweats laid out on the floor in total darkness, panting heavily like a dog that had been left out too long in the heat. I blinked furiously and licked my lips and ran the tips of my thumbs over the tips of my fingers and tried to allow my eyes to adjust to the absence of light.

I could hear Dr. Brydon shift his position every so often and let out the occasional coo, like an overgrown baby, indicating that his dose was still working wonders on him.

But for me, the sickness had again begun to take shape in my legs; in their autonomous inclination to kick violently, and in my intense urge to vomit, which I quickly subdued with the administration of a second dose.

I repeated the process several times throughout our tenure in the B-hut. And I could never determine if it was day *or* night, as the room remained dark at all times save for the occasional opening and shutting of the front door followed by snickers and jeers from the various advisors coming in and out of the space. I barricaded myself from these insults and judgments by remaining in the dark, and with subsequent doses of the pure for both myself and Dr. Brydon, who awoke eventually from his nod demanding more anesthetic for his injuries.

And the dope worked, and worked well. Until it didn't. And I found myself drenched in sweat on the floor in the dark, my limbs all firing involuntarily like those of a snared wolverine, and I conceded finally to myself what I had truly known all along: that I was a drug addict, and could not, for the life of me, put an end to this ritual abuse.

Under no known circumstance in the natural world was I able to part with my habit, and I knew what had to be done. Though this time, I would do it right. This time, there would be no Captain Harold to keep me from drawing my weapon.

I knew that I could not end this war or bring back my father or anyone else's father or brother or mother or son or sister or friend or lover. And as much as I both feared and loathed the ANA soldiers we had been tasked with training, I could not bring myself to execute them as the Colonel had ordered, because whatever I was, however great a failure or disappointment as a human being, I was no murderer. This much I knew. And I knew, too, what had to be done.

I collected my Zippo from the ground and pulled myself up using one of the bunk beds as support. I was shaky on my feet at first, like a newborn giraffe, but I got ahold of myself after a minute and felt my way through the dark to the front door of the B-hut.

"Where are you going, chap?" I heard Dr. Brydon mutter placidly as I moved through the dark room.

"Good-bye, Dr. Brydon."

I pushed through the door of the hut and into the red of the outside. There had been no movement of any kind to indicate an elapse of time. The field hands were still hard at work bringing in the product from the great field, and the contractors stood a docile watch near its perimeter.

I moved cavalierly to the back of our Humvee, pulled a gas can off the back, then waited for a break or a shift in the attention of the contractors before diving into the dense brush. When I had low-crawled several meters into the crop, I popped up and opened the can. The JP-8 fuel that we used to power our vehicles had a pungent gasoline smell that wafted up into the air and caused me to smile. This is it, I thought.

I raised the can over my head, dousing myself in the fluid, and as I did this, I wept. I cried for my family, my mother and brother who would survive me. And I cried for the boys and girls of America and Afghanistan who would grow up without fathers, brothers, uncles, mothers, sisters, sons, and daughters. And I cried out of relief that after a brief window of intense physical pain, this nightmare would finally be over.

I pulled my Zippo lighter from my cargo pocket and thumbed it over. This is it. This is finally it.

"Doc!!!" I heard Captain Harold's voice boom across the field like an air raid siren. "Doc, what the fuck are you doing?" he shouted as he ran toward me through the field.

"It's over!" I shouted. "I can't do this bullshit anymore! I can't fucking take it!"

"Just relax, Doc. Take it easy. You don't know what you're saying right now. You're all worked up." He went into his trouser pocket and came out with a ball of dope in shrink-wrap. "Go back in the B-hut and get yourself sorted out."

The rest of the crew, including Raz Mohammed, entered the field behind Captain Harold, and before long we were in standoff; them on one side, me on the other. The peasant farmers and contractors had all pulled back from the field.

"No!" I shouted. "No more of that shit! It ends now! Here and now!"

"Oh, cry me a river!" Captain Harold shouted at me. "Little boy blue is all butt hurt 'cause his daddy got burned up in the Twin Towers. Boo fuckin' hoo!"

"Fuck you, motherfucker!" I shouted.

"You ungrateful little maggot!" he shouted. "We offered you a place at the top, and this is how you repay us? I'm glad your dad is dead, you little bastard, and I'll tell you something else." His face was alive with vitriol. "He got off pretty easy compared to what's coming! You think things are bad now; just you wait! The world you know is history! Armed guards! Drones! Surveillance! That's what's in store for you and yours!"

"Sergeant Major, how can you let him get away with this?"

"I'm sorry, Doc." The Sergeant Major pulled a sullen, embarrassed face. Lieutenant Grey did as well. Raz Mohammed's face remained its model of neutrality. "We've got orders. We're just doing our jobs."

"The people won't stand for this!" I shouted. "There's no fucking way! Not in my country! My people won't stand for it!"

"Haaaaa!!!!" Captain Harold taunted me like a schoolyard bully. "This has been going on for years out in the open and your *people* haven't done shit to stop it!" He was now laughing at me as though I were an idiot child. "Between your Super Bowl and your *American Idol*, no one gives a shit about who's in power; who's *really* in power!" He laughed out loud, then said. "No one gives a shit about anything anymore!"

We were within an arm's length of each other when I flipped open my Zippo and thumbed the flint wheel, igniting the wick.

"You can't burn that dope," Captain Harold shouted. "That's property of the United States Army!"

"Watch me!" I yelled back.

Captain Harold lunged at me and the JP-8 that I had doused myself in caught fire and the field began to burn around us. Soon after Captain Harold caught fire, and the Sergeant Major tried to break us up, but then he too became engulfed in flames and then Lieutenant Grey and Raz Mohammed also began to burn.

We cried for our mothers, and we cried out to God, and we cursed the other soldiers for doing nothing, and they cursed themselves.

Smoke was everywhere. Smoke and red flames. Coughing and smoke and red flames and broken legs.

"Get us outta here! Cut us outta here!"

Hot and smoky and burning. This is it. This is finally it. It ends now. After all this, it ends here and now. Like this.

"Fuck these fucking doors!" We're trapped. We're burning alive and we're trapped. The doors are too heavy. Doors designed to keep from being blown off their hinges are too heavy and we're burning alive. I'm afraid. I must deserve this.

I don't deserve this. We're burning alive!

"Help, I'm alive! Help! I'm still alive! Help! Please!"

Broken legs and smoke and burning. This is the end. Never thought it would end like this.

"Hang tight, we're gonna get you outta there. Medic! Medic!"

"Trip the fire suppression system! The fire suppression system!"

"I can't, it must have been damaged in the blast!"

The best fire suppression system that money can buy, damaged in the blast. Flesh burning. A smell like moths that flew into the hot lamp and got stuck. Hair burning.

I must deserve this. I don't deserve this. Nobody deserves this.

CHAPTER 21
BOOM

I awoke suddenly with a startle to the sound of three great thumps that reverberated like the striking of a gong through my skull, then radiated down my appendages. I inhaled sharply and opened my eyes to a total blinding darkness.

The dream from which I'd awoken had been long and hot and haunted by feelings of impending doom. I ran my hands up and down my body, feeling for loose or liquid flesh, but soon realized that, in the physical sense, everything was in its right place.

The hair on my arms and legs and back all stood up a moment and my skin tingled all over. I spread my eyes wide open in the hopes that they'd adjust to the darkness, but it was hopeless.

"Doc, let's fucking go. We're rolling out in fifteen," the Sergeant Major hollered.

"Roger that, Sergeant Major."

I rolled off my rack and knocked my head against the cold cement floor. Blindly, I fumbled for the wall, then let my fingers crawl up and down, side to side like an alarmed camel spider until I located the light switch.

I flipped it on and had to hold my hands over my eyes a minute to keep the light from blinding me.

"Doc, let's fucking go!"

"Moving, Sergeant Major."

With my eyes closed, I reached for the door handle, turned it, leaned on the door as it opened, and fell into the dark of the hallway.

I moved toward the front of the hooch out of instinct, to where the foyer opened up to the front entrance, when I observed a glowing light emanating from the open doorway to the office. I recognized the floor plan. It was our hooch at FOB Mehtar Lam. We were back in Mehtar Lam.

Curious, I approached the room's opening and grabbed for the two opposite corners of the door frame and held myself up. My arms were both extended at forty-five degree angles and my body formed a Y shape. I was still very tired and out.

The Sergeant Major peered up at me from his perch on a beige metal foldout chair in the office underneath the blinding fluorescent overhead light.

"Doc, you filled out the Con-Op, right?"

"Yeah. I did it last night, Sergeant Major."

"Oh yah?" he replied in his stiff Minnesotan accent.

He rose to his feet and moved into my personal space all in one fluid motion. Slightly towering over me, and momentarily eclipsing the intense light of the fluorescent bulb, the Sergeant Major shoved a crumpled wad of paper into my chest, causing me to stumble backwards a half step. I was still managing a residual high.

"You wrote fucking Mongolian barbecue in the goddamned mission's objective field. What the fuck were you thinking?"

"Um, sorry Sergeant Major. It's Thursday, isn't it? Thursday's Mongolian barbecue day at Cobra. I just figured . . . "

"Well, you figured wrong. You're lucky your buddy Mortin here was around to correct your fuckup." The Sergeant Major pointed to the college-aged Anglo-Saxon male assisting the rotund Major Peeve with the radio.

"Mortin?" I gasped.

"Hey, man. Nice going with the Con-Op!" He cut up with laughter. "What the fuck were you thinking, dude?"

Major Peeve kept his focus on the radio. He and Mortin were loading crypto or doing comms checks, or just chatting with whomever was awake. Lieutenant Grey sat on the opposite wall of the office doing some administrative work.

"Mortin?" I repeated in disbelief.

"Yeah, dude?" he responded inquiringly.

"Go put the gun up," the Sergeant Major barked at me. "Both of you."

We went into the weapons locker and procured the enormous M2 .50-caliber machine gun. I carried the barrel, which weighed about twenty-five pounds and measured almost four feet in length, while Mortin shouldered the receiver group, which was about a foot and a half long and weighed roughly sixty pounds. I also grabbed an ammo can filled with .50-caliber BMG rounds. Without speaking, we climbed up onto the roof of the Humvee and began the mounting process.

The receiver went on first. Mortin had to drop into the turret to lock it down before I was able to screw in the barrel. When it was locked on and screwed in, Mortin moved the gun side to side, rotating the turret 360 degrees in both directions by cranking the winch forward, then backward. I had to stand toward the front of the hood so the barrel would not knock me over. Mortin laid the ammo can on the ledge inside of the turret's blast shield and pulled the belt of .50-cal BMG rounds across the carriage and locked it down with the latch. All in, the .50-cal weighed about 128 pounds and measured out to just over five feet. It was a cruel weapon.

"What the fuck, dude?" Mortin asked abruptly. "Why do you keep staring at me like that?"

"Sorry, I'm just a little tired," I muttered. "I've been a little out of it lately, but I'm alright."

It was still dark outside. The morning call to prayer had not yet gone out, and for that I was grateful. Though my gratitude was tenuous, tempered by a nervous anticipation. It was a matter of time, really. The call would go out; the call to prayer. The moment would come when the voice would call out to us, beckoning for our destruction and heralding our damnation. Of this, I was certain, though there was nothing I could do to stop it.

The Sergeant Major emerged from the hooch in full battle rattle.

"Get your shit, we're rolling now!" he shouted.

"Roger that," I said.

"Aye, Sergeant Major," Mortin said.

We both dashed into the hooch, Mortin to the transient quarters and me to my room. I threw on my blouse, then my flak jacket and grabbed my med bag, my M9 pistol, my M4 rifle, and my Kevlar helmet and shuffled outside to the Humvee. The sun had not yet risen and I was already beginning to sweat profusely.

I began to climb up onto the hood of the truck when Lieutenant Grey shouted, "Doc, what the fuck are you doing? I'm gunning, get in the front."

"Okay," I answered.

I wrenched open the impossibly heavy blast door, threw my medbag inside, and gently placed my rifle in the cab, then climbed into the shotgun position. I always found it silly to call the front seat "shotgun" when we had a turret with a mounted crew-served weapon in the center of our vehicle, but that was just me. I found many things to be silly in our great war.

Mortin came in through the rear passenger-side door and began firing up the radio and doing comms checks with Major Peeve, and with Brigade down in Jalalabad. He then passed headsets to Lieutenant Grey and me and we began talking on the comms.

It occurred to me that while Lieutenant Grey was in the turret and Mortin was behind me, the present would be the most opportune moment to shove off, but I didn't have my gear ready, so I leaned back into the seat and prepared myself for the sickness.

"Who's riding in the other vehicle?" I asked after a minute of comfortable silence.

"No one," Lieutenant Grey answered. "We're gonna be full up today for the ride to Cobra."

"Who's driving?" Mortin asked.

"Who do you think?" Lieutenant Grey answered.

The Sergeant Major and Captain Harold and our interpreter, Raz Mohammed, stormed out of the hooch and into the vehicle, and before I could make heads or tails of the situation, we were off and rolling, down the dirt road in the direction of the back gate, where the ANA soldiers who slung their AKs with the indifference of middle schoolers toting backpacks loaded into their beige LTVs and rode out in front of our vehicle to lead the convoy, as was protocol. Then we were out the gate, cruising down the winding road outside the FOB toward Route 1, the Old Silk Road, when I heard it; when I heard the call to prayer.

I knew immediately that something was wrong, but there was nothing I could do. There was nothing any of us could do. The voice grew louder and angrier and I put my hands up to my ears and gripped my headset to try and insulate myself from the sound, but it was useless.

I felt a tremendous force, like an earthquake in my bowels, then saw a great flash of blinding white light, and that's all I remember.

CHAPTER 22
VERONICA

Two metallic elevator doors open and a handsome middle-aged woman, olive skinned, steps out of the car onto the linoleum tiled hospital floor that gleams with the reflection of overhead fluorescent lights. She walks, one foot in front of the next, toward the Burn Unit on the fourth floor of Brooke Army Medical Center in San Antonio and is greeted at the nurse's station by a slightly younger black woman.

"Hello, Veronica," the older woman says.

"Hello, Mrs. Rogers."

"Please, call me Karen."

"I'm sorry, Karen. Of course."

"Besides, if anything, it would be *Ms.* Rogers."

"That's right, how foolish of me. I remember, you told me last time about your husband . . ."

"Ex-husband," the handsome woman replies smartly, but not curtly. "Norman's father and I were already divorced when that whole ordeal happened."

The two women eyeball each other a moment. Veronica's face softens. Her expression is empathetic. Her eyebrows raise slightly. These small changes indicate, without words, what has happened. Words are unnecessary, but Veronica is a professional, and the impossible task of forging simple words to convey news of the most devastating variety is a fundamental component of her job description.

"Karen, he's gone," she says in a straightforward tone that is sympathetic, but does not allow for disagreement of any kind. She has done this before, many times.

"I'm so sorry," she continues. "It happened last night. He went peacefully. He wasn't in any pain."

There is a long pause. Karen breathes in and out, fixing her gaze on the fire extinguisher at the far wall of the nurse's station behind Veronica. She is both prepared and unprepared for the news.

"I knew it," she responds, partially absent. "I could tell when I flew in last night, something was different. Something was wrong." She does not blink for several minutes.

"I'm just so confused," she continues, the first ripples of an impending breakdown apparent in her quivering voice. "He was doing so well before. He *talked* to me." She begins to sob.

"I could never understand what he was talking about, but he would talk to me. I could at least hear his sweet voice." Her footing becomes unstable, and she extends her arms out to either side to steady her balance.

Veronica rushes forward to catch her. She holds Karen in her firm embrace for several minutes as Karen sobs uncontrollably into her shoulder.

Veronica says nothing. She is familiar with the limitations of words in a moment like this. After a few minutes, she guides Karen to a waiting area with grey wool couches across from the nurse's station. Both women are grateful there is no one else on the floor.

"I know what you mean, Karen," Veronica speaks at last as the two women sit on the couches. "At first I couldn't understand what Norman was talking about. Ever."

Karen glances at Veronica, bewildered. She is dumbfounded a moment, unable to recall the remark she'd made minutes earlier.

"But I sat with him, night after night, for the entire five years that he's been here."

Karen's eyes, reddened still from her spell, widen at Veronica's words.

"Tell me more," she says innocently.

Veronica weighs her options carefully, but silently. She knows that any one anecdote about Norman could set Karen off. But she knows, too, that Karen's great sacrifice entitles her to every shred of information particular to her late son, and that that information is more valuable now than anything. She treads carefully.

"Sometimes he would call me Sergeant Major. Other times it would be Captain Harold, or Lieutenant Grey or Raz or Mortin, or sometimes it would simply be sir."

Karen holds onto Veronica's arm and leans in with eyes wide.

"But his condition was so unpredictable. It's a miracle he survived the IED. Everyone else in the Humvee was killed instantly."

Karen begins to tear up, and Veronica hesitates a moment. She considers ending the story right here and now. But she knows this is not an option. She has just begun; she cannot end now. Not yet.

"Some nights he would be lucid and talk for hours, others he would be comatose. I can't tell you how many times I've swiped this penlight over his retinas to see if his pupils were round and reactive to light."

Veronica pulls a small pen-shaped flashlight out of the breast pocket of her scrubs. Karen sees the object and is transfixed. She reaches for it.

"Can I have this?" she asks. Her hand is already wrapped around the light.

"Of course," Veronica concedes, releasing it into Karen's custody.

Karen stares incessantly at the light, turning it on and off with her thumb. She holds it in front of her eyeball and sweeps the light across, trying her best not to blink as the bright light flashes in her pupil.

"Like this?" she asks.

"Yes," Veronica says. "Just like that."

Karen loses interest in the light after a moment and returns her focus to Veronica.

"What else?" Karen asks genuinely. "What else can you tell me about my son?"

At this, Veronica is reticent. She's not sure what to do.

"Tell me the truth." Karen begins to cry. "Tell me the truth about my son!"

She collapses into Veronica's shoulder once more. Veronica caresses and consoles the distraught woman. She is very strong. She has done this many times before.

"When we got here, he was already heavily addicted to opiates."

Karen nods her head.

"I've never seen anything like it. Every time we tried to lower his dosage, he would go into violent withdrawals."

"I can't say I'm surprised. After his dad died, Norman really went to pieces. He loved his daddy so much, it tore him up to lose him like that." She sighs. "He went into the Army to try and get straightened out, God knows what he went through out there. And now, this. I was so proud of him—*am* so proud of him."

Karen takes a deep breath and adjusts her posture. She is also very strong. She wipes a few tears away with a handkerchief pulled from her beige purse.

"Do you think he was getting high out there?" Karen asks candidly.

Veronica is cautious. She has, herself, spent much time deliberating on this very topic. She waits a moment.

Finally she says, "It's possible, Karen." She takes the mournful woman's hand and holds it firmly. "But there's no way of knowing for certain."

Karen nods benignly. The two women remain silent. Veronica is a pillar of strength. She has done this many times before, and will repeat the process many times over before the wars have ended.

CHAPTER 23
THE END

I came to just beyond the edge of the dirt road that connected FOB Mehtar Lam to the Old Silk Road. I recognized the area immediately, as I had ridden through so many times on convoys to Jalalabad or Dola Cha or into Kunar Province. It was the stretch of road that lay just beyond the back gate.

There was some type of commotion going on; I heard screaming, and there were weapons firing, but it didn't seem as though the convoy was under attack. Just a bunch of chaotic outgoing fire.

I moved forward in the hopes that I could be of some use, as I could hear the chorus of men and their distress call: "Medic! Medic!"

But when I got close enough to really see what was going on, I realized there was nothing I could do. The situation was beyond my control.

Soldiers of the 82nd had spread out in a horseshoe pattern around a great fire of what I imagined had been a Humvee. There was so much black smoke billowing up from the wreck that I couldn't make out the shape of the vehicle.

I looked around for the advisors of 4th Kandak, 1st Brigade, particularly the Sergeant Major or Lieutenant Grey, because I knew that of our modest crew of technical and operational experts, they were far and away the most battle ready. Only, I couldn't find them. I scanned with my eyes, but they were nowhere near the wreck. I ran to the front of the convoy, but there was still no sign of them.

Nor was there any sign of the ANA trucks that had been up front when we'd left post, as was protocol. They must have hightailed it out of there conveniently before the strike occurred. In the absence of the ANA, there were Humvees from the 82nd at the front of the convoy.

I happened upon of group of soldiers bound together in what looked like a football huddle up front. I tried to get in close to see what they were looking at, but they wouldn't create an opening for me in their scrum. In fact, they didn't acknowledge my presence whatsoever. I called out to them more than once, and I'm certain they must have heard me, but they all acted as if I wasn't there at all; as though I did not exist. But I could hear them when I got close enough.

"That's what you get, you hadji fuck!"

"Look at him squirm!"

"How's that feel, motherfucker?!"

Puzzled and exasperated, I turned around and moved back down toward the fire, past the other Humvees in the convoy that were all parked on the road beside the ledge that rose up on the left shoulder.

When I got back to the site, I realized that the vehicle had been flipped onto its side. Smoke hemorrhaged from the site of the blast, and I stepped back so I wouldn't inhale any of it.

I felt very far away from the whole scene. I went into my cargo pocket to pull out a syringe of morphine sulfate, but I came up empty. Shocked, I checked my other pockets, but there was nothing. I began to panic a moment, but soon realized I wasn't sick at all. In fact, I felt great. For the first time in a long while, it felt great to be alive.

"It's time," I heard a familiar voice call out from behind me.

I turned around, and sure enough, it was Pat Tillman, this time in woodland cammies with his sleeves rolled up and his green beret pulled over his enormous head.

"It's time, Norman."

"What do you mean?" I asked, confused.

"You know what I mean." His tone was no nonsense. "It's time to go."

I noticed then he was not alone. Behind him in a row, standing at parade rest, were the advisors of 4th Kandak, 1st Brigade, including our interpreter, Raz Mohammed. There was another figure as well at the end of the row. A local hadji kid. He could not have been much older than fourteen. Tiny black whiskers dotted his upper lip. He too stood at parade rest. His face remained expressionless. His eyes did not betray his thoughts.

"What's he doing here?" I asked, pointing to our new ward.

"He's here for the same reason that you are," Pat Tillman answered. "That we all are."

"What's going on, Sergeant Major?" I asked.

The Sergeant Major did not respond. In fact, there was no evidence at all that my question had even registered. He kept his focus on the space directly to his front. Thousand-yard stare. They all did, except for Pat Tillman, who remained in a neutral stance.

"Lieutenant Grey!" I shouted. "Captain Harold! Mortin! Raz!" I shouted to each of the men in formation and each time got the same response: no response at all.

"What the fuck?" I shouted at Pat Tillman. "Why won't they fucking answer me?"

"They're at parade rest," Pat Tillman laughed. "You can't speak at parade rest, you know that Norman."

The soldiers of the 82nd continued to scream and shuffle and attempt to rectify the situation that had unfurled on the road behind me. But their voices felt very far away. It was as though I was hearing them underwater.

"It's time, Norman," Pat Tillman said in a kind but stern tone of voice.

"You keep saying that!" I shouted. "Time for what?"

"It's time," he said again, and turned his head to the east, indicating with his movements that I do the same.

The bright, sweeping, pulsating light was closer than it had ever been, and I understood suddenly that we were extremely close to the source.

As I peered in the direction of the great white light, I noticed there were two gigantic rectangular shimmering structures that rose up into the sky with such power and majesty, it was all I could do to stop and stare a moment. I raised my arm involuntarily and pointed to the twin buildings of glass and steel that radiated with silver and white light.

"There?" I uttered, dumbfounded.

"Yes, Norman," Pat Tillman answered. "There."

Taking it all in at once, and realizing for the first time there was no going back, I began to sob and shake with fear. It all made sense. I stared at the advisors of 4th Kandak, 1st Brigade, and they, like iron statues, stared back at me.

"I'm not ready to go," I pouted. The fear and anger and sadness and sorrow and loss that I'd gathered up over a short lifetime had now reached critical mass, and I was coming apart.

"It's not fair!" I shouted. "I'm not ready! It's not fucking fair!"

"Don't I know it!" Pat Tillman chuckled. "You're preaching to the choir with that one. My whole fucking life, I did the right thing. And when this bullshit started, I sacrificed a lot to serve, more than most. And this is the fucking thanks I get?"

He pulled a sour face.

"So, I understand where you're coming from, Doc, I really do." He went on: "Only thing is, it doesn't matter what you think or how you feel. That's all she wrote. It's time to go. Now."

"I'm not going!" I shouted. "I won't go! What are they gonna do, huh? Kill me?"

I laughed and cried and laughed more.

"Most of your friends—the people you grew up with—did not have the heart to fight in this war. But you did. You showed up, Doc. You put in the time, and you treated the injured and helped evacuate the wounded. And for that America is grateful."

"Are you with God, Pat Tillman?"

"I don't believe in that nonsense."

"And what about him?" I pointed to the hadji at the end of the row. "Did he even set the IED?"

"Does it really matter?"

"I guess it doesn't," I answered. "I'm still not going," I said calmly.

"There's someone I want you to talk to," Pat Tillman said.

"Who?"

"I think you'll recognize him."

A large figure approached from behind Pat Tillman, waddling side to side somewhat as he moved forward. He was a giant."

"Hello, Norman," the giant said in a gentle voice.

"Hello."

"Norman, it's time to go." He pointed to the large, imposing twin buildings to the east, and the light that seemed to radiate from them both.

"Don't you want to go to the top with me, Norman? Don't you want to see where your daddy works?"

"Yes," I said.

"Okay, let's go. Give me your hand. Let's go, Norman."

The giant took my hand and I noticed that I had shrunk. A good deal, I had shrunk. I was a child again, no more than six years old, and the giant hoisted me up onto his shoulders, and I wrapped my arms around his mammoth head, and he began to run, and I held on and smiled.

"Wheeeeeeeeee!!!!!!" he shouted.

And I shouted, "Wheeeeeeeeeeeeee!!!"

We moved toward the two buildings. The giant put one foot in front of the next, and we moved forward toward the great white light that seemed to grow larger and more brilliant with each step.

Before long we were at the foot of the great towers, in the space between them, and I looked up into the light. The towers, to either side of myself and the giant, closed in around us, creating a great tunnel, with a blinding white light at the end. We moved forward together, one consciousness, through the tunnel toward the end; toward the light.

And if things truly happened the way that I remember them, or if my memories have been corrupted by the unreliable distillation of time, if our worlds are built and broken in the hands of monsters and men, if there really is a God, complicit in our failures, or if we, ourselves, are the architects of our damnation, there will forever be no way of knowing.

ABOUT THE AUTHOR

Brandon Caro is a prior US Navy corpsman (combat medic) and former advisor to the Afghan National Army. He deployed in 2006-2007 to Afghanistan in support of Operation Enduring Freedom. His work has appeared in the *New York Times*, *The Daily Beast* and *WhiteHot Magazine*, among others. He resides in Austin, TX.

59069

21 542 3323

Joanne
moves

philip Bus-
chester fields
4 30
hill
Canine Stye

Arch